I0656477

VOYAGEUR CLASSICS

BOOKS THAT EXPLORE CANADA

Michael Gnarowski — Series Editor

Dundurn presents the Voyageur Classics series, building on the tradition of exploration and rediscovery and bringing forward time-tested writing about the Canadian experience in all its varieties.

This series of original or translated works in the fields of literature, history, politics, and biography has been gathered to enrich and illuminate our understanding of a multi-faceted Canada. Through straightforward, knowledgeable, and reader-friendly introductions, the Voyageur Classics series provides context and accessibility while breathing new life into these timeless Canadian masterpieces.

The Voyageur Classics series was designed with the widest possible readership in mind and sees a place for itself with the interested reader as well as in the classroom. Physically attractive and reset in a contemporary format, these books aim at an enlivened and updated sense of Canada's written heritage.

VOYAGEUR CLASSICS

BOOKS THAT EXPLORE CANADA

FLYING A RED KITE

STORIES BY HUGH HOOD

INTRODUCTORY NOTE BY MICHAEL GNAROWSKI

DUNDURN
TORONTO

Cover image: istock.com/diane39
Printer: Webcom

Library and Archives Canada Cataloguing in Publication

Hood, Hugh, 1928-2000, author
    Flying a red kite / Hugh Hood ; introduction by Michael Gnarowski.

(Voyageur classics)
Previously published: Erin, Ontario: Porcupine's Quill, 1987.
Short stories.
Issued in print and electronic formats.
ISBN 978-1-4597-3855-3 (softcover).--ISBN 978-1-4597-3856-0 (PDF).--
ISBN 978-1-4597-3857-7 (EPUB)

    I. Gnarowski, Michael, 1934-, writer of introduction II. Title.
III. Series: Voyageur classics

PS8515.O49A159 2017   C813'.54   C2017-902149-4
                                               C2017-902150-8

1   2   3   4   5   21   20   19   18   17

We acknowledge the support of the **Canada Council for the Arts**, which last year invested $153 million to bring the arts to Canadians throughout the country, and the **Ontario Arts Council** for our publishing program. We also acknowledge the financial support of the **Government of Ontario**, through the Ontario Book Publishing Tax Credit and the **Ontario Media Development Corporation**, and the **Government of Canada**.

Nous remercions le **Conseil des arts du Canada** de son soutien. L'an dernier, le Conseil a investi 153 millions de dollars pour mettre de l'art dans la vie des Canadiennes et des Canadiens de tout le pays.

Care has been taken to trace the ownership of copyright material used in this book. The author and the publisher welcome any information enabling them to rectify any references or credits in subsequent editions.

— *J. Kirk Howard, President*

The publisher is not responsible for websites or their content unless they are owned by the publisher.

VISIT US AT

Dundurn
3 Church Street, Suite 500
Toronto, Ontario, Canada
M5E 1M2

CONTENTS

HUGH HOOD:
AN INTRODUCTORY NOTE

MICHAEL GNAROWSKI

*F*lying a Red Kite, Hugh Hood's first book, was published by
Ryerson Press in 1962.

Ryerson, which had been established as the publishing arm
of the Methodist Church in Canada, had a curious existence.
Under the guidance and management of a sensitive editor in
Lorne Pierce, it had one foot in the area of Church publications
while the other did "missionary" work in the fields of Canadian
literature. Established in 1829, Ryerson Press was a significant
literary publisher in its own right, having brought out the work

*Hugh Hood as he
appeared on the back panel
of the dust jacket of the
first edition of* Flying a
Red Kite *(1962).*

of major Canadian writers, from Charles G.D. Roberts in the nineteenth century to Earle Birney, Louis Dudek, and Dorothy Livesay in the twentieth.

For Hugh Hood, publication by Ryerson meant that he had stepped out of the world of occasional appearance with short stories in literary periodicals such as the *Tamarack Review* into the challenging environment inhabited by well-established and admired practitioners of the art of storytelling such as Mavis Gallant and Alice Munro — the latter, as is well-known, destined to win the Nobel Prize for Literature — and the older Morley Callaghan. Callaghan, it may be noted was an early presence if not a readily provable early influence in Hood's life, since Hood had been a friend of Callaghan's son Michael from their university days, and had spent much time in the Callaghan household.

Hood, who was born in 1928, came from a middle-class Toronto family with strong Roman Catholic convictions, something that lingered as a sort of moral compass in his fiction. In a tell-tale conclusion to an interview with Victoria Hale recorded in 1974 and published in *Le Chien d'Or/The Golden Dog*, he concluded his remarks with "… I'm in favour of tradition, and the seat of Christianity and Judaeo-Christian mythology." He attended Catholic schools and went on to study at St. Michael's College in the University of Toronto, from which he graduated with a Ph.D. in literature.

In 1957, he married Noreen Mallory, a professional graphic artist and set designer, with whom he would have a family of four children. The newly married Hood accepted a teaching position at St. Joseph College in Hartford, Connecticut, where he stayed for four years, and where he began to write with serious purpose. When a story was accepted and published by *Esquire* magazine in 1960, Hood was also tentatively offered a position with the magazine in New York but, tempting as that was, the Hood family preferred to take up an offer of an academic appointment in the English Department of the University of Montreal* where they arrived in 1961.

The Hood family lived first near the University of Montreal at 2541 Maplewod Avenue, now renamed Boulevard Édouard Montpetit, moving later to the comfortable, middle-class neighbourhood of Notre-Dâme-de-Grâce. On Maplewood Avenue, one could cross the street and climb the lightly forested (now crowded with buildings) slope of the mountain behind the main building of the university and through a stand of young saplings find one's way to open spaces where one could fly a red kite.**

In many ways this must have been a curious situation. The University of Montreal was, largely, a francophone institution, and its English department, small and anomalous, with mainly graduate students, was chaired by an unusual individual with a wide range of non-literary interests. Thomas Greenwood (he also has a literary identity as Alain Verval, who published poetry in French), a man of undetermined European background, had studied at the universities of Liège, Paris, and London, was interested in philosophy and mathematics, and had corresponded with some of the twentieth-century's leading thinkers (reportedly the likes of Bertrand Russell, the British philosopher, and Pierre Teilhard de Chardin, the

---

★   In Hood's own words "… I got a letter from the secretary of the Faculté des Lettres of the Université de Montréal, asking if I would be interested in accepting a position there…." The letter would have been instigated by Thomas Greenwood, Hood's chairman-to-be, and would have been signed by Jean Houpert, an irascible Frenchman who was secretary, but, in effect, dean of the Faculty of Letters. The University of Montreal had been in a state of some intellectual "turbulence" in those two post–Second World War decades, partly because of strong currents of French-Canadian nationalism, and partly because it harboured individuals, both political refugees from France and Quebeckers, who were known for having sympathised with fascist thinking. (See Esther Delisle, *Myths, Memory & Lies: Quebec's Intelligentsia and the Fascist Temptation 1939–1960*, Montreal, 1998.)

★★   The University of Montreal is built on the northern slope of Mount Royal. For a sense of locale, see Hugh Hood's *Around the Mountain: Scenes from Montreal Life* (Toronto: Peter Martin Associates, 1967).

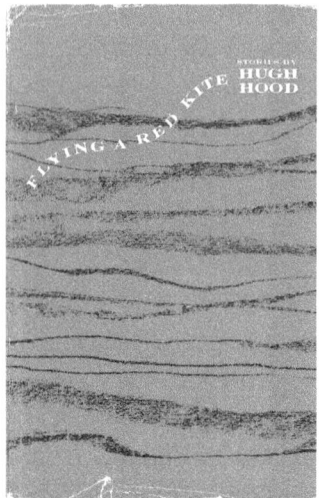

Left: *Unattributed front cover design for the dust jacket of the first edition of* Flying a Red Kite: Stories by Hugh Hood *(1962).*

Right: *Unattributed design for the front cover of the first paperback edition of* Flying a Red Kite *(1967).*

French paleontologist), and was invited frequently to lecture on the geopolitics of the Cold War at American institutions from the State Department in Washington to the United States Air Force Academy in Colorado Springs. His English department was eclectic and free-ranging in its approach to the study of literature (Greenwood himself was keen on the *Mabinogion* and the bardic trouvères), and Hood found both Montreal and the English department a comfortable fit. He was given interesting core courses to teach and had enough time to devote himself to his own development as a writer of serious fiction.

As he recollected a quarter of a century later in a chatty and detailed autobiographical essay which prefaced the 1987 reissue of *Flying a Red Kite*, misleadingly subtitled "Collected Stories: I,"

Hood went about the business of turning himself into a professional writer by a very disciplined and deliberate process. Starting out early in 1957, shortly before he got married, Hood took aim at the short story markets available in the pages of major American magazines such as *Esquire* and the *New Yorker*. He wrote with great diligence, some might say furiously, so that in the span of five years, between 1957 and 1962, he had written something like thirty-eight stories from which he would cull the dozen or so that would go into his first book, *Flying a Red Kite*.

As he worked on his stories, Hood was developing certain fundamental principles that would become defining elements in his writing. As he recalls it, "Throughout those six years I was trying to learn to write fiction, by the method of trial and error …" although, and almost in the same breath, he harkens back to his university days and the influence of Marshall McLuhan, who had pointed Hood towards James Joyce and the stories in *Dubliners* as key examples of the modern method of blending symbolism with a calm-eyed naturalism. As important an example as that work might have been for Hood, he also says (as a Canadian) that he knew the work of Morley Callaghan, Stephen Leacock, and Ernest Thompson Seton, whom he saw as "not a bad sample."

Among other things, the 1960s, when Hugh Hood was embarking on what would be a remarkably prolific career, were also the harbinger of significant new developments in Canadian writing. With the appearance of Margaret Atwood, there was a coming into their own of a cohort of women writers who quickly displaced the major male figures of Canadian fiction. Mavis Gallant had led the way for some time, but she was now joined by the previously mentioned Alice Munro and the impressive Margaret Laurence. In addition, the names of Adele Wiseman, Ethel Wilson, and Marian Engel would lend their weight to what can be seen as a substantial claim on the reader's imagination. Hugh Hood was entering a new world in which the women writers' revolution had firmly established the female point of view in Canadian fiction. Post-modernism was just over the horizon.

Having established himself and his family in Montreal, Hood embarked on an ambitious programme in which long fiction, which is to say the writing of novels, would claim most of his time and efforts. Living in Montreal, he was at a certain disadvantage. A seismic shift had taken place in writing in English in Canada in that English-language publishing was now firmly centred on Toronto, and the literary scene, meaning visibility, connections, and all that matters in literary life, was now removed from the setting in Montreal.

Hood appears to have been undeterred by these developments. A glance at a bibliography of his work shows a steady output of published work in the years following the appearance of *Flying a Red Kite*. He connected successfully with several major publishers – E.P. Dutton and Harcourt Brace in New York and Longman in Toronto – gradually edging towards a long-term relationship with a smaller but more literary Oberon Press of Ottawa, which, in 1975, would take on his ambitious life's work: a multi-volume sequence of novels which he called *The New Age / Le nouveau siècle*.

What is particularly interesting about Hood is his intense delving into his art. The essay that opens this collection is an example of Hood examining the nature of his own writing. Testing, as it were, his own devotion to his art. He was interested in what can be described as the great flow of literature, in which he saw himself as a willing and happy participant. One notes his not infrequent reference to towering figures such as Tolstoy and Proust, who were clearly totemic presences in his imagination, but then there is also mention of Somerset Maugham, Graham Greene, James Thurber (hugely important), and (of all people) Walter de le Mare as models of practical approaches in addressing the problems inherent in a writer's efforts.

Upon its release, *Flying a Red Kite* was well-received by critics and reviewers. There was general recognition that an important new voice had emerged in Canadian fiction, a voice that had its own timbre, and one which would have to coexist with the new sounds of an imminent post-modernism, a development in literature that would leave Hood happily distant. *Canadian Literature*, the pre-eminent journal devoted to Canadian writing, published a short but positive review piece in its Spring 1963 issue in which the reviewer noted that Hood's stories were about "life, death and eternity," and that the collection as a whole was a "subtle and generous book." In the popular press, Arnold Edinborough, then an influential newspaper columnist, devoted a two-column spread to *Flying a Red Kite*, in which he said of the stories, "All have a professional polish and every page is a joy to read."

Hood's determined and self-imposed apprenticeship to his art would now begin to reap its rewards. Greatly encouraged by the reception of his book, Hood would continue to write and publish his stories in literary magazines such as the *Tamarack Review* and scholarly journals like *Queen's Quarterly* and publications intended for a general readership such as the *Montrealer*. Hood had entered on the most important and productive stage of his life. Creatively, he was endowed with prodigious energy which resulted, ultimately, with an *œuvre* of some thirty-plus books, which included an impressive range of collections of short stories, the twelve-volume novel sequence *The New Age/Le nouveau siècle*, as well as essays and other writing of a more general interest, such as sketches about Montreal and a popular book about Jean Beliveau, the great centre of the Montreal Canadiens hockey team. He also found time to do public readings from his work as a member of the Montreal Story Tellers.

Hood died in Montreal in 2000.

RELATED READING

A very useful annotated bibliography of published material by and about Hugh Hood was assembled by J.R. (Tim) Struthers and published in Volume Five of *The Annotated Bibliography of Canada's Major Authors* by ECW Press in 1984 under the general editorship of Robert Lecker and Jack David.

In the course of his lifetime Hood managed to write on a variety of topics, some of which could be described as fugitive pieces. He remained current on the literary scene, appearing in long and short-lived little mags, magazines and periodicals such as *Yes*, *Prism*, *Parallel*, *Canadian Forum*, *Intercourse*, *Quarry*, and others.

Various critical responses and assessments of Hood's work have been gathered in a single volume entitled *Before the Flood: Hugh Hood's Word in Progress*, edited by J.R. (Tim) Struthers and published in 1979 by ECW Press. For a study of Hood's major opus, *The New Age/Le nouveau siècle*, the reader is referred to W.J. Keith's *Canadian Odyssey: A Reading of Hugh Hood's The New Age/Le nouveau siècle* published by McGill-Queen's University Press in 2002.

SOBER COLOURING: THE ONTOLOGY OF SUPER-REALISM*

Super-realism, yes, because that is how I think of my fiction, quite deliberately and very likely unconsciously too. When I started to write novels and stories about the year 1956, I had no clear idea of what I was doing. I had had a literary education and knew something about critical theory and method as applied to the work of other writers, the classics especially, and some moderns. I got a Ph.D. in English in late 1955. After that I did more or less what I wanted. I began to write independently, feeling liberated from the need to defer to what other people might think. I was glad to get out of the graduate school.

---

*   Hugh Hood published his essay on super realism on several occasions with some "tailoring" to suit the material being prefaced. In this instance he chose to focus on the example of two stories, "Socks" and "Boots," which were being included together with his essay in *The Narrative Voice*.

I had no theory of my own writing, and belonged to no school, so I wrote most of a novel which was never published, and a dozen stories, in 1956 and 1957, instinctively, making all the important artistic decisions as I went along, with no theoretical bias for one kind of writing as against all the others. Instinctively, then, I turned out to be a moral realist, not a naturalist nor a surrealist nor a magic realist nor in any way an experimental or advance guard writer. That was in effect where I began.

All my early writing dealt with the affairs of credible characters in more or less credible situations. As I look back, I see that this instinctive moral realism was tempered by an inclination to show these credible characters, in perfectly ordinary situations, nevertheless doing violent and unpredictable, and even melodramatic, things. A brother and sister go visit their mother's grave and are unable to find it in a cemetery of nightmarish proportions; a man kills his newly baptized girlfriend thinking that she will go straight to Heaven; a young priest molests a child sexually; a young boy goes mad under great strain. A yachtsman runs a boat on a rock and sinks it, drowning his wife and her lover, who are trapped below deck. I would never choose actions like these nowadays, not because of their violence but because of their improbability. I still write about intense feelings which lead to impulsive and sometimes violent acts, but I am better able to locate these feelings in credible occasions.

In those days, and for several years afterwards, I tried to control these melodramatic tendencies — murder, suicide, hanging about in cemeteries, drowning in burst boats — by a strong sense of the physical form of stories. I arranged my pieces according to complex numerologies. A novel might have seven main sections, one for each of a specific week in a given year, so that the reader could tell exactly what time it was when something happened. Or the book might be divided in three main parts, each with a specific number of subdivisions. I once wrote the rough draft of a book in two main sections and when I had finished, each half of the manuscript was precisely a hundred and forty-four pages long: twelve twelves doubled. This play with numbers is a recurrent feature of my work. *Around the Mountain* follows the calendar very precisely, with one story for each month from one Christmas to the next. I have always had a fondness for the cycle of the Christian liturgical year. My first, unpublished, novel was called *God Rest You Merry*, and covered the seven days from Christmas Night to New Year's Eve, in a most elaborate arrangement.

I still do this. My new novel, which will appear in the fall of 1972, *You Can't Get There from Here*, is in three parts. The first and third sections have ten chapters each; the middle part has twenty, which gives us: 10/20/10. The Christian numerological symbolism implied is very extensive. It makes a kind of scaffolding for the imagination.

I had then, and still have, an acute sense of the possibilities of close formal organization of the sentence, syntactically and grammatically, in its phonemic sequences. I paid much attention to the difficulties of writing long sentences because I knew that simple-minded naturalists wrote short sentences, using lots of "ands." I did not want to be a simpleminded naturalist. I hoped to write syntactically various and graceful prose. I took care to vary the number of sentences in succeeding paragraphs. I rarely used the one-sentence paragraph; when I did so I felt mighty daring. I kept a careful eye upon the clause-structure of each sentence. I wouldn't use the ellipsis mark (…) because Arthur Mizener wrote to me that he considered it a weak, cop-out sort of punctuation.

I sometimes use the ellipsis now … and feel guilty.

My interest in the sound of sentences, in the use of colour words and of the names of places, in practical stylistics, showed me that prose fiction might have an abstract element, a purely formal element, even though it continued to be strictly, morally, realistic. It might be possible to think of prose fiction the way one thinks of abstract elements in representational painting, or of highly formal music. I now began to see affinities between the art I was willy-nilly practising and the other arts, first poetry, then painting and music. I have always been passionately attached to music and painting — I have gone so far as to marry a painter on mixed grounds — and have written many stories about the arts: filmmaking, painting, music less often because it is on the surface such a non-narrative art. I find that it is hard to speak about music.

I have also written some stories about a kind of experience close to that of the artist: metaphysical thought. My stories "A Season of Calm Weather" (with its consciously Wordsworthian title) and "The Hole" are about metaphysicians. The second of the two tries to show a philosopher's intelligence actually at work, a hard thing to do. Like musical thought, metaphysical thought seems to take place in a nonverbal region of consciousness, if there is such a thing, and it is therefore hard to write about, but to me an irresistible challenge.

My novels *White Figure*, *White Ground*, and *The Camera Always Lies* dealt respectively with the problems of a painter and a group of filmmakers. It is the seeing-into-things, the capacity for meditative abstraction, that interests me about philosophy, the arts, and religious practise. I love most in painting an art which exhibits the transcendental element dwelling in living things. I think of this as true *super-realism*. And I think of Vermeer, or among American artists of Edward Hopper, whose painting of ordinary places, seaside cottages, a roadside snack bar and gasoline station, have touched some level of my own imagination which I can only express in fictional images. In my story "Getting to Williamstown" there is a description of a roadside refreshment stand beside an abandoned gas pump, which is pretty directly imitated from a painting of Hopper's. I see this now, though I didn't when I wrote the story. That is what I mean by the unconscious elements in my work which co-operate with my deliberate intentions.

I have to admit at this point that my Ph.D. thesis discussed the theory of the imagination of the Romantic poets and its background. The argument of the thesis was that Romantic imagination-theory was fundamentally a revision of the theory of abstraction as it was taught by Aristotle and the mediaeval philosophers. The kind of knowing which Wordsworth called "reason in its most exalted mood" and which Coleridge exalted as creative artistic imagination, *does the same thing* as that power which Saint Thomas Aquinas thought of as the active intellect. I do not think of the imagination and the active intellect as separate and opposed to one another. No more are emotion and thought *lived* distinct and apart. The power of abstraction, in the terms of traditional psychology, is not a murderous dissection of living beings; on the contrary it is an intimate penetration into their physical reality. "No ideas but in things," said William Carlos Williams. I believe that Aquinas would concur in that — the idea lives in the singular real being. The intellect is not set over against emotion, feelings, instincts, memory, and the imagination, but intimately united to them. The artist and the metaphysician are equally contemplatives; so are the saints.

Like Vermeer or Hopper or that great creator of musical form, Joseph Haydn, I am trying to concentrate on knowable form as it lives in the physical world. These forms are abstract, not in the sense of being inhumanly non-physical, but in the sense of communicating the perfection of the essences of things — the formal realities which create things as they are in themselves. A transcendentalist must first study the things of this world and get as far inside them as possible. My story "The Hole" tries to show a philosopher working out this idea in his own experience. Here, as everywhere in my writing, I have studied as closely and intensely as I can the *insides* of things which are not me. The great metaphor in human experience for truly apprehending another being is sexual practise. Here, perhaps only here, do we get inside another being. Alas, the entrance is only metaphorical. In plain fact no true penetration happens in lovemaking. It is not possible for one physical being to merge into another, as D.H. Lawrence finally realized. Bodies occupy different places; there is nothing to be done about this. Sex is a metaphor for union, not itself achieved union.

What we are united to in this world is not the physical insides of persons or things, but the knowable principle in them. Inside everything that exists is essence, not in physical space and time, but as forming space and time and the perceptions possible within them. What I know, love, and desire in another person isn't inside him like a nut in its shell, but it is everywhere that he is, forming him. My identity isn't inside me — it is *how I am*. It is hard to express the way we know the forms of things, but this is the knowing that art exercises.

Art after all, like every other human act, implies a philosophical stance: either you think that there is nothing to things that is not delivered in their appearances, or you think that immaterial forms exist in these things, conferring identity on them. These are not the ontological alternatives, but they are extreme ones, and they state a classical ontological opposition. The bias of most contemporary thought has been towards the first alternative, until the very recent past. But perhaps we are again beginning to be able to think about the noumenal element in things, their essential and intelligible principles, what Newman called the "illative" aspect of being. The danger of this sort of noumenalism is that you may dissolve the hard, substantial shapes of things, as they can be seen to be, into an idealistic mish-mash — something I'm not inclined to do. I'm not a Platonist or a dualist of any kind. I think with Aristotle that the body and the soul are one; the form of a thing is totally united to its matter. The soul is the body. No ideas but in things.

That is where I come out: the spirit is totally *in* the flesh. If you pay close enough attention to things, stare at them, concentrate on them as hard as you can, not just with your intelligence, but with your feelings and instincts — with your prick too — you will begin to apprehend the forms in them. Knowing is not a matter of sitting in an armchair while engaged in some abstruse conceptual calculus of weights and measures and geometrical spaces. Knowing includes making love, and making pieces of art, and wanting and worshipping *and* calculating (because calculation is also part of knowing) and in fact knowing is what Wordsworth called it, a "spousal union" of the knower and the known, a marriage full of flesh.

I want to propose the Wordsworthian account of the marriage of the mind and the thing as a model of artistic activity. I don't think that the Romantic movement failed. I think we are still in the middle of it. Of the Romantic masters, Wordsworth seems to me to have understood best how things move in themselves, how they exist as they are when they are possessing themselves, having their identities, living. Wordsworth has an extraordinary grasp of the movement, the running motion, of the physical, the roll of water or sweep of wind, changing textures of fog or mist, all that is impalpable and yet material. In this fleeting, running movement of physical existence, for Wordsworth there is always the threat of an illumination, "splendor in the grass, glory in the flower." Things are full of the visionary gleam.

The illuminations in things are there, really and truly *there*, in those things. They are not run over them by projective intelligence, and yet there is a sense in which the mind, in uniting itself to things, creates illumination in them.

> *The clouds that gather round the setting sun*
> *Do take a sober coloring from an eye*
> *That hath kept watch o'er man's mortality;*

This is a triple eye, that of the setting sun which colors the clouds, and that of the sober human moral imagination, and finally that of God as brooding, creative Father of all. The colouring of the clouds is given to them by the Deity in the original act of creation. Every evening the sun re-enacts the illumination. The moral imagination operates in the same way, though it is not originally creative; it projects colouring into things, true, but the colouring has already been put there by the divine creation. The act of the human knower is an act of reciprocity. It half creates, and half perceives "the mighty world of eye and ear."

The poetry of Wordsworth supplies us again and again with examples of this colouring of imagination spread over incidents and situations from common life. The figure of the old Leech-Gatherer in "Resolution and Independence" is perhaps the most overwhelming example of this capacity of very ordinary persons and scenes to yield, on close inspection, an almost intolerable significance.

In my mind's eye I seemed to see him pace
About the weary moors continually,
Wandering about alone and silently.

The concentrating eye, interior/exterior, giving to things their sober hues, is constant in Wordsworth. I have imitated it from him in my work. In the deliberately paired stories "Socks" and "Boots" I have chosen incidents from ordinary life and characters such as may be met with everywhere, and I have attempted to look steadily at these persons in the hope that something of the noumenal will emerge.

These stories are, to begin with, political; they are about the ways in which living in society modifies our personal desires, a very Wordsworthian theme. Domenico Lercaro in "Socks" does not want to work so hard. Nobody wants to work that hard. He doesn't want to work on a garbage truck or do snow removal, but he is driven to it by the need to survive. The fictional "my wife" in the story "Boots" wants to buy a certain specific kind of winter footwear, but the stores simply don't stock the boots she wants.

We can buy only what we are offered, and our range of choice is surprisingly limited.

I have tried to move beyond the fiction of social circumstance by taking a very attentive look at my two main characters. In "Socks" poor Domenico sees the enormous, noisy, snow-removal machine turn before his eyes into a divine beast or Leviathan. Everyone who has seen these machines at work recognizes their intimations of violence, in their noise and in the sharpness of their rotary blades. They have actually killed and eaten people. Modern life is full of these mechanical beasts.

"My wife" in "Boots" feels trivialized by fashion; most women in middle-class circumstances do, I think. To wear high heels and a girdle is to enslave yourself — to adopt the badges of humiliating subservience. This story tries to make its readers sense the galling limits on their activities felt by intelligent women in the face of the clothes which fashion and *chic* propose for them: the necessary sexual exhibitionism, the silly posturing, the faked little-girlishness.

The two stories insinuate larger issues than their subjects would suggest; they are following Wordsworth's prescription. I have at all times endeavoured to look steadily at my subjects. I hope that my gaze has helped to light them up.

Hugh Hood
The Narrative Voice
Edited by John Metcalf
Toronto, McGraw-Hill Ryerson, 1972

FALLINGS FROM US, VANISHINGS

Brandishing a cornucopia of daffodils, flowers for Gloria, in his right hand, Arthur Merlin crossed the dusky oak-panelled foyer of his apartment building and came into the welcoming sunlit avenue. Grey-green poplars and shining maples leaned encouragingly over him like counselling elder sisters, whispering messages, bough song, bird song, in his responsive ears, in an evening of courtship. He sang softly in stop time:

> *There'll be no one unless that*
> *Someone is you.*
> *I intend to be*
> *Independently*
> *Blue oo oo oo*
> *Da da da dee dum.*

Volkswagens are period pieces, he thought, circa 1954–1958, the sense of period. Thirty years from now *Volkswagens* will look quaint, fixing a colour page or an old movie as exactly in time as an *Apperson Jack Rabbit* does now. If I conserve my *Volkswagen* and drive it ten more years, I'll begin to be a period piece. He slid back the sunroof and rolled away into the sound of cicadas, the little engine grinding like a coffee mill, energetic, valiant.

Up the avenue and around the corner he surprised his favourite antique, a 1929 *Oakland Landaulette*, all rich brown body and stiff black leather upperworks, owned by a doctor's widow, ghosting home from the drugstore, its timeless driver erect on the mohair cushions. She preserved the car in exquisite running order as a memorial; Arthur had often discussed it with her. Tonight, as every time he saw the car, his fancies and recollections merged in a Gestalt that shot him back there when the 1929 *Oakland* was modish and new. He could be there in imagination in his body, his present age, in 1929, in 1829. My grandmother was born in 1870, he thought, amazed, and could have spoken to men who knew Mozart, it's possible. You can be there. 1929.

My father had a 1929 *Essex Challenger*, dark blue, with chased imitation silver handles on the inside of the doors, with little window blinds that rolled zipping up and down, with creamy-fringed tassels. It could take Roxborough Road hill in high gear from a standing start. Then he was three-dimensionally in the car, his thirty-four-year-old self, the day they started for the cottage at Rouge Hills in the early summer of 1931. The upholstery, a deep-piled dark blue, exhaled puffs of linty smoke when you bounced on it, motes dancing in the shafts of sunlight. If you drew the blinds, a darkness loomed in the back seat.

His mother said: "Stop for gas, Alex!"

His father said to the garage attendant: "*Castrol*, please, and put the cap on good and tight."

They didn't see him there, thirty-four-year-old ghost from 1961, in the little boy squirming on the back seat. He shrank into the little boy and swelled into himself in his coffee-mill *Volkswagen*, and there were two of him, four years old and thirty-four.

"Put the cap on good and tight." Alex turned to Margaret. "Did I ever tell you about the man who drank all the liquor?" They nodded their heads and gazed lovingly at each other and (thirty-) four year old Arthur looked on, feeling safe and happy.

Five years later they changed the name and called them *Essex Terraplanes* and then just *Terraplanes* and at last they stopped making them. They don't even make *Hudsons* anymore but we were able to keep that car until the war was halfway over. The two of him expanded into three — as multiple as he ever became, even with his sense of period. I was learning to drive our old *Essex* the day I first saw Mrs. Vere in Westport. It must have been 1942 because I got my driver's licence the next year, in the other car. I might have had the *Essex* for my own; but it died with sixty thousand miles on the clock the second time around, a bare grey spot that always hurt my eyes on the upholstery in the driver's seat.

We were by the slips when she came along in the Saturday morning sun. The codgers stared behind her and gossiped as she passed, mourning Lieutenant Vere, hero of Pearl Harbor, and commending his widow's fair beauty. Her four-year-old trailed behind her and, Heavens, thought Arthur seeing it, relishing it, the ghost of twenty-three-year-old Gloria was in that toddler, and I couldn't see her. I saw Mrs. Vere, how I saw her in white tennis shorts, mourning behind her, fine gold fuzz on her legs catching the sun. I saw the glint, cowering in my rickety *Essex*. How she strode, how she put forward her perfect ankles, coming to look at the sunlight on the water. She looked, oh, she looked like a girl, like an attainable girl to me at fifteen, and how I loved her as she sauntered along I feel still, all three of us feel, four, fifteen, and thirty-four, comfortably here in my little period piece.

On the other bucket seat the paper cone of flowers moves lazily with the car's motion, wetness from the leaves shining on the leather, tiny rustle of green leaves, flip of the yellow blossoms catching Arthur's eye as he rolls along in June, coming for Gloria, thinking of her marvellous mother at twenty-six. She looked like a co-ed, with that funny authority one's older sister has, that sway compounded of a trifling difference in age and a cloud of otherness, mystery of being a woman. How I adored Mrs. Adam Vere, that golden widow as she said, looking into my *Essex*: "Where

do we swim around here, that's safe for children?" She listened
attentively to my knowledgeable counsel.

> *Love me or leave me*
> *And let me be lonely.*
> *You won't believe me*
> *But I love you only.*

I gaped, I croaked, I blushed:

"At the Boating Club," I told her, "afternoons I'm on duty
as a lifeguard and I'll look after your little girl." I scarcely looked
at the toddler out of the corner of my eye, using her as a comic
prop, an introduction-arranger, something out of a comic-strip
or the opening paragraphs of a *Ladies Home Journal* story. There
are ghosts out of the future, the unborn, as well as the dead from
the past. How could I fathom marriageable Gloria, twenty-three,
inside a pouting four year old? I looked instead at her unmar-
riageable mother and yearned and Gloria has her revenge.

She turned away and the back of her knees dimpled at me, her
thighs like butterscotch, to the edge of her shorts. Fifteen is hell! I
shook all the way home and the knob of the gearshift loosened in
my hand. And all that summer I bounced baby Gloria through the
wavelets at the water's edge, on her stomach, on her back, rolled
her yellow red blue white beachball along the sand and chased it
when the wind caught it and she cried, and Mrs. Vere laughed.

"Get it, Arthur, get it!" they commanded together, their
voices blending. That ball took off, sailed, spinning along the tops
of the ripples, nothing inside to hold it down. I often chased it
a quarter of a mile, coming back digging my toes into the beige
sand to lie panting beside Mrs. Vere, while Gloria jumped up and
down on my sacroiliac.

"Don't jump on Arthur, sweetie, he's winded!" I peeked, pulse
racing, through a screen of sand at an expanse of butterscotch flank,
and pressed my aching adolescent length flat on the sand's heat.

★ ★ ★

Pulse, he thought, that's funny. He was Assistant Circulation Director of *Pulse Magazine*, man of a thousand details, and had spent this long June day checking the results of a sample mailing piece which he'd tested in Philadelphia and Boise. They drew a three-percent response in Boise, so he took the figures to the files, digging out the results from a campaign of thirty-second TV spots which he had tried on Cheyenne, the year before. No one in the world knew as much about the circulation of *Pulse* as Arthur Merlin, historian, builder of archives, ranker of green filing cabinets. He loved Gloria best; but next to her he loved documents on circulation figures broken down by region, and third he loved the files of *Pulse*.

Twenty-five years of *Pulse* — it came out first in 1936 with a famous picture of Boulder Dam on the cover, a picture which he had a hundred times affixed to his mailing pieces. His adolescence and young manhood slumbered in the files. Often on a working day, on the excuse that he was seeking promotional material, he spent an afternoon at *Pulse Index* where Gloria worked, or with a swash of twenty-six issues from 1938 on his desk, admiring the page layout, studying the changing typefaces, loving the unlined face of Brenda Diana Duff Frazier, the Jimmy Lunceford piece, the *Studebaker Champion $537 F.O.B. Detroit*, all the stories in those old issues landmarks of his trip to adulthood, documents as familiar to him as MS. C. (Cotton, Otho A. 6) to some brother scholar.

He stopped for a red light and hoped that they would arrive at the beach before the sunshine died. He wanted to see Gloria illuminated by the sunset on this, nearly the longest, day of the year. Lately she had been petulant and pouty, which made him think of her behaviour at the age of four. The child is mother to the woman, he reflected as he crossed the intersection, I suppose she'll always be a pouty one. When she had come to him looking for work she'd pouted.

"School's out forever," she said dolefully, "nothing will be the same."

"You can't go to school indefinitely, Gloria," he told her. "I'll help you find a nice job, and you can have some fun in New York. Most girls like to live in New York for a while before they get married."

"I'm not 'most girls.'"

"You're certainly not average," he said, laughing beyond hilarity, "no, definitely not average." He had never really seen her before; he had this troublesome treble vision; but he saw her now and she was very good. "How old are you now, Gloria?" he asked her, avuncular, disinterested, beginning to tremble.

"I'm twenty-two, I guess."

"I guess?"

"I never think of it. Are you going to give me a job?"

"I don't give jobs but the company certainly will." On his recommendation they put her to work on the *Index* and he saw her all the time. All day she read stories from the files, and examined yellowing pictures, and prepared case histories; the pictures puzzled her.

"You mean *that's* Frank Sinatra? But he looks young?"

Arthur started at her in amusement. "Frank Sinatra *is* young."

"He's a foolish bald old man."

"Whom do you consider young, for goodness' sake?"

"Any girl whose bust hasn't developed."

"How do you tell about boys?"

"There isn't any decent way," she said, laughing.

So he was afraid to ask her how old she thought him. He hadn't had his real life yet, none of it, he told himself. All his college classmates were settled into the beginnings of middle age, with wives and a plethora of children. Of all his generation, he thought, only a few like himself could sometimes feel like children. I'm young, he swore earnestly, I'm a baby. He picked up the picture of Sinatra and studied it, the floppy necktie, the luxuriant curls, the hollow cheeks, the swaying back and forth with the microphone clutched in both hands. It must be from the story on Frank's first date at the Paramount, 1942 perhaps, certainly no earlier than 1941. Gloria would have been three years old, and should remember the excitement.

"He was a swoon-crooner, Gloria," he said kindly, "surely you remember the phrase."

"A swoon-crooner?" He might as well have said a dough-boy, a wise-guy, a tough egg, she didn't understand the language. "Your crowd must have the equivalent, Paul Anka perhaps or Fabian," he hazarded.

"I don't have a crowd," she said positively.

He wanted to shake her but said instead: "Come to the beach with me tonight?" He imagined beachballs yellow red blue white rolling along far stretches of beige sand.

"I love the beach," she said simply, and he took it for assent.

As he handed her the daffodils and watched her bury her face in the petals, he checked his watch and guessed that there were almost two hours of sunlight left. It was a dying sunlight though, a seven-thirty slant of the beams which traced the flowers on the beachrobe she wore, and the ties on her sandals. At least she's ready to leave, he realized, we may not get into the water but we can stretch out together on the sand for maybe an hour. The daffodil girl, the primavera.

"Where did you get these, so late in the season?"

"I had them refrigerated months ago, just for you," he claimed extravagantly but truthfully. He had said to the florist: "I want an assured supply of daffodils, I don't care what it costs. Keep them in cold storage for me and I'll pay extra." He thought he stood to win or lose on daffodils, her favourite flower. If he kept her like spring, she might never think of the eleven years' difference in their ages. I'm a child, I'm young, young, he reflected, watching her put them carefully in water, afraid to hurry her. Don't make her think of time, he advised himself, and other voices in his mind supported the strategy, never nudge her out of the glorious present. Don't give her time to think about time. So he waited patiently until she pulled her beachrobe modestly around her and started for the door. He opened it quickly, rang for the elevator with sharp precision, started the car with unobtrusive speed, and hastened across the graceful old town towards the Boating Club, zipped into the parking area, plucked a beach-basket from the back seat, and felt an urgent joy. It would not be dark until nine-thirty, lots of time, hours, hours.

"Start down the beach and find a place to sit," he commanded, feeling his excitement stir, "I'll get out of my clothes and catch up to you." He trotted towards the clubhouse and paused at the door to watch her make her lovely way along the beach, no longer beige, the sand, but a darker shadowy hue spreading as the light changed and the shadows lengthened. At every second stride she dug her toes in the sand and kicked out like a colt. The onshore breeze took her robe and filled it like a pregnant sail as she shook out her hair, and then it cradled every yellow lock and made them dance. He broke all records for changing into swimming trunks and chased her down the strip of sand.

A dozen yards from where she halted at their favourite spot, he stood still and watched. Her back was to him as she bent and loosened her sandals, kicking them off. Then she straightened and slipped off her flowery robe, stood erect on her bare toes, scrunching them into the sand for balance, stretching her arms above her head, looking for a bizarre instant like a piece of radiator sculpture. Then her form seemed to zoom in on him, taking his sight, and she was so perfectly *there*, so *present*, that his heart paused and his throat constricted with his press of feelings.

Gazing, he recognized her power and her everlasting triumph, and how it was that the aureole, the haze of recollection in which he wrapped her appearance when he imagined her, was not around her now — the glory was in her. She pressed outwards against the air, filling out her lines.

"She's only a pretty girl in a bathing suit," he told himself, to make his head stop spinning. As he came up to her he made a commonplace remark about the sea. "The moving waters at their priest-like task of pure ablution," he said.

"It's a lot of water," she said, inhaling.

"Do you know," he said, a little desperately, "that water connects everything? It's the only element that goes everywhere. This same water washes the shores of the Ganges, the floes in Franklin's Land."

"It's Long Island Sound," she said, looking away, "it comes out of the tap in my bathtub."

"Why do you come to the beach at all?"

"To get out into the air. The beach makes me feel good, I like to get my clothes off. I wish they allowed Bikinis at the club."

"They don't forbid them."

"They don't allow them. I know what they think."

He pounced on it. "How do you know?" The trivial question suddenly assumed importance in his eyes. How could she know? How could she ever grasp a tradition or a moral convention? How do these people manage to live, he wondered, how do they make their calculations?

"I don't see anybody else wearing one," she said defensively.

"Why let that stop you?"

"Don't quiz me," she said impatiently, "I'll wear one when I see somebody else wear one."

"Give me the ocular proof," he said, "unless I put my hand in the wound, unless I see the nails, I will not believe." He looked at her but she wouldn't look back. "Blessed are they," he said gently, "who have not seen and yet believe."

"Why can't you be content with me as I am?" she complained. "Instead of puzzling yourself with all that stuff. I came with you, didn't I?"

"I'm glad you did," he said, "and thank you." He returned to the charge. "Don't you feel anything about the ocean, about the water? Think of all the fish in the sea, of all the ships, the treasure. There's supposed to be a galleon lying somewhere off Montauk, blown a thousand miles off its course by freakish gales. And over there," he gestured widely, "lies the *Andrea Doria* with millions of dollars worth of stuff inside, just out of reach, just too far down."

"Hundreds of people in her," she said, "floating at the portholes, knocking at the glass trying to get out, their hair washing behind them. Do you know where my father is?"

He ought to have remembered, he had remembered, and perhaps that was why they were where they were.

"He's still in the *Arizona*," she said in a shaking voice, "he's down there with hundreds of other men who didn't get out. I've been to Pearl Harbor, you know, and I've seen it. The masts are sticking out of the water and the men are still inside; they've been there twenty years. My father was younger than you are when he drowned. To hell with the moving waters at their priest-like task. They've melted my father's flesh — what do you suppose he looks like now?"

"Forget what I said!"

"How did you hear the news about my mother, Arthur, did you hear it the way I heard it? They called me at the dormitory, I was asleep, and told me that I wasn't going to see her again. She was all smashed to pieces, you know. There were bits of the car along the Parkway for half a mile. They didn't open the coffin, and I hadn't seen her for a month before the accident. She just disappeared; there was nothing left for me. I wasn't born without a memory, Arthur, I just don't want to remember."

"Let me tell you something," he said, "we all become orphans in time. My father died late last year but before that my world was just what you make yours now, static. Things went along and never changed from year to year. Everybody was always there when I went home, the same books and pictures, and the litter of papers maybe a little thicker every spring. Then my father died, and I thought it would all change, that the house would be empty and my mother all at once shrivelled and old."

"And it was!" she positively guessed.

"Not in the least," he denied, "not at all. My mother looks younger every day and my father advises me constantly. He's closer to me than ever. I'm not a superstitious man, Gloria." She laughed. "I'm not superstitious but I can hear him talking to me, telling me how to handle things. It isn't like a voice, it's a ... I don't know what it is ... it's a tendency, a feeling. I know what to do, because that's what he would have done. It's as though his intelligence were in my own, like a habit."

"That's a hangover from childhood."

"No. It's as if there were another mind in mine."

"You're simply highly suggestible."

"Cut it out," he said, "you have these flashes too, admit it."

"I'll never have them," she said, "I only see what's there."

He saw her mother over again. He had seen her closer to death than Gloria had, the weekend she died, and she had looked as though neither time nor death could ever touch her. At thirty-five she looked exactly as she had looked twenty years ago on this same beach, fresh, unlined, immortal. And over a Saturday to Monday she had disintegrated, to be redistributed along the universe like the moving waters. He shivered. Twilight is coming, he thought. They were sitting with their backs to a ledge of rock four or five feet high, which ran the length of the beach and some days acted as a windbreak. If you lay down near the ledge, the air was completely still, all its currents diverted and passing over you. You could bake under the ledge in unadulterated sunlight on days when it was downright cool in less sheltered spots. Tonight, in the declination of the sun, the ledge threw a shadow towards them which lengthened as they lay there. Already their bodies lay in it to the waist, and in a few minutes it would cover them up. It was cold in the shadow and soon they both shivered.

"It's too cold to go in," said Gloria, musing.

The sun sat on the edge of the world and to the east the moon was an unimportant shred of cotton batting. Way way out on the Sound a single sail hovered, almost seemed to disappear, was there again. Underneath them the sand grew black and lost its daylight warmth.

I never had any father, thought Gloria, it's useless to have a father who dies before you're three years old. I can't remember him. I don't know what he looked like. There was, of course, that formal black and white photograph which Mother carried around for years, that stranger with an enormous officer's cap. He must have had a huge head, to wear such a cap. Black tie, black shoulders, white shirt, white teeth. The picture was too mat; there were no glosses, no highlights. When you looked at it closely, it stopped being a face and became a flat arrangement of masses in black and white, and that was Father. *Arrangement in black and white.* Like Whistler's Mother, and I can see what Whistler meant. Nothing human was in that picture. Mother, with her mind's inventive eye, could see Adam Vere whom she loved, round and fleshed out, in the harmonies of black and white. All I could see were masses and edges. She looked at the water and the sky and observed the same techniques Nature imitates Matisse, she thought. He was her favourite painter and almost the only one she knew of.

What I see are flat patches of colour. Three dimensions are a binocular trick of the eye, the chance result of having two eyes instead of one or three. If I had a single eye, the world would be a huge Matisse, flat patches of unrelated colour lying next one another. She began to feel cold and to reassure herself she looked down, pressing her chin down almost against her collarbone, and stared at the length of her body stretched in an unfamiliar perspective in front of her. Her body looked flat but she knew that it wasn't. I'm not flat, she felt happily, I'm round but I can't see it. I see planes and shadows. I *feel* round.

She put her hands on either side of her in the cold sand and rocked gently from side to side in a movement of dazzlingly innocent sensuality. I *feel* that my hips are soft and round, she realized. I've never seen them. If I shake out my hair my scalp feels good, but I've never seen the top of my head. I only feel that it's here along with the rest of me.

She closed the useless eyes and inhaled, feeling herself from the ends of her hair to her toes. She sensed herself being here. She was simply here with a full dark warm heaviness in her middle that grew cooler towards fingers and toes and scalp. She filled her lungs with cool twilight air and felt it grow warm inside her. She could hear Arthur scratching in the sand for pebbles; he picked them up one at a time and launched them towards the water. Some must have fallen in the sand; they made no sound; others fell with a plopping noise into wet sand and water at the very edge; a few plinked into deep water. Her weight on her hands made the sand beneath grow harder and harder like a soft pillow beneath an insomniac's head. If she leaned on her hands much longer, she would be able to feel each individual resistant speck of sand pressing upwards against her palms.

The sun had gone down while her eyes were shut. The sea breezes began to flag, grew gentler, licked at her toes with weakening tongues and finally were still.

After the sun goes down on the beach, as the earth loses its daytime heat, the water for a little while retaining some warmth, the air currents begin to shift. The onshore breeze flags and stops; in a few moments the offshore breeze begins. But there is always a moment of calm at the point of reversal. The sand stops moving; the water flattens and is silent; nothing and nobody moves the few grasses and weeds that grow in the sand. The soul of the world turns in on itself and is quiet, just before the dark.

In this moment of temporary stillness, in herself, Gloria felt more a woman than she ever had before. I feel what I am, she realized, with an intense joy. I can taste myself being me. I'm this woman, No, that's wrong. I'm me. No. I. I. I. I. There isn't any way to say it. She fell silent in her thoughts, content to exist.

When the offshore breeze began she found herself wondering what it was like to be a man, though she knew she didn't care for the idea. She looked slyly at Arthur, lying disappointedly beside her, and wondered how it felt to be inside his mind, as he said his father was.

> *I want your love,*
> *I don't want to borrow,*
> *To have it today,*
> *To give back tomorrow.*

He had been whistling that song when he came to fetch her, a song that suited him. If there were two people, and possibly a great many more, congregated in his head, how could she possibly single out one of them, the nominal real he, to love? If she were to love him, as he wanted her to, and as she longed to, it would have to be the only genuine Arthur Merlin in captivity whom she loved. She didn't want that crowd of others along for the ride no matter who they were, his father, her mother. She couldn't compete for his attentions with a host of spirits, and least of all with the spirit of her mother.

He stood up and walked to the edge of the water, putting a toe forward to test the temperature. Then he recoiled.

"When the sun goes down," he exclaimed, "it's impossible. Do you want me to take you home?"

"We've only just come!"

"We've been here over an hour," he said, "it's nearly nine-thirty." She wished he weren't so acutely conscious of the passage of time. It hadn't touched him. She scrutinized his legs and arms and waist as he walked awkwardly back across the sand. He might be any age, she thought. Except for an almost invisible accretion of fat over his kidneys, he looked like a boy her own age. He's young, she realized with surprise. He was part of her present; he had always been around, but then so had she. She wished that he would stop mumbling and stumbling and tell her that he loved her. She was sure that he did. What else could all the fussing be about? And he was as good a man as she'd ever known, and part of her scene, her life. Of course she would love him, if only he would come out towards her instead of manufacturing these smokescreens.

"Do you remember how you used to bounce up and down on my back?"

A crazy notion. "On your back? When?"

"When you were small."

"Oh, for God's sake, Arthur, I'm not small now. Do you take me around because, once upon a time, I was small? I'm a grown woman. Why don't you treat me as one?"

He was gathering up towels and sandals and stuffing them in the basket. He knelt on his knees beside her and his kneecap touched her thigh. It felt cold. Put your arms around me, she thought, there's nobody here to see, give me a kiss and then we'll have something to go on. But he lingered and did nothing, kneeling and looking at her. What could she do, she wasn't a man.

"It isn't right," she said, "to love a girl because of what she was when she was small." But he was gone again, gone back inside, she could tell from his eyes. They glazed and grew opaque as they always did when he was thinking of something else. She wanted to slap him to bring him out of it.

"Look," he said, "I'm not just a hundred and seventy-five pounds of flesh and bone dropped out of nowhere into the twentieth of June. I've a whole life behind me that I love and that I wouldn't want to lose. I'm everything that I've ever been, I'm what's happened to me, not what's happening this instant, not just that."

"If I prick you with a pin, you'll bleed."

"That's not me, that's not me. You think that anything that happened more than a year ago simply doesn't exist."

"Well, it doesn't," she said deliberately.

It made him groan. "You can't live like that," he declared, "have you no respect for the past? What about your parents?"

Very patiently she began to explain things to him. "I loved them when they were here. But they aren't here anymore. They're dead, Arthur, they're gone. I don't believe in ghosts." It was quite dark on the beach; it was time to go.

"Gloria, Gloria," he moaned.

"Oh, God," she ejaculated, "didn't you bring me here tonight to tell me that you love me and that you want me to love you? Wasn't that what you meant to do?"

He said nothing.

"I know it was," she said, "I'm certain of it, and I'm proud. It means something to a woman, when a man tells her he loves her and wants her. And, don't you see, here I am. I'm all right here! Oh, you poor dear idiot, can't you see how much I'm here? I'm what they call a beautiful girl, a hundred and twenty pounds of flesh and bone dropped from Heaven, not from nowhere. I bloom, can't you see? Damn you, Arthur, I'm packed full of sensation, I ache with it, you … you exorcist! Just come and get me!"

"It's wonderful," he said, stuttering slightly, "it's unbelievable!"

"What's unbelievable?" She had a horrid presentiment of what it might be.

"You're the heiress of every past beauty," he said exultantly. "I've never seen anything like it. You're your mother over again perfectly, to the last detail, but more than that, you're surrounded by the past. The way you cock your head, your gestures, your words, everything that you do is fixed by the tradition, and that's what makes you a beauty. Your inheritance."

"Damn it," she swore, meaning it, "are you in love with me or with my mother?"

"With all of you, with the whole great gang!"

"They're dead," she shouted, "they're underground. You!" She felt a physical revulsion. "You're haunted! You're a ghost-ridden man, you're a horror!" She wanted to run. "I don't know where you get to, when you disappear inside yourself, but you won't come out, oh, you'll never come out." She turned and strode along the beach towards the car.

He watched her go; and as she began to merge with the twilight and the firm outline of her figure wavered, she seemed to him to be one, only one, of a long file of daffodil girls marching out of the past and into the future, girls he'd read about in story books, girls he'd known, girls he hoped still to meet some day. Multitudes forever young, beautiful golden girls long dead and others unborn, the descending heirs of Eve, all going out of the light through the twilight and into the dark. Away up the beach her form quivered in his sight, and then his eyes lost her and he was standing alone in a sandy place. I'd rather be lonely, he thought.

> *I'd rather be lonely*
> *Than happy with somebody new.*

O HAPPY MELODIST!

Yet sport they on in Spring's attire,
Each with his tiny fire
Blown to a core of ardour …
— Walter de la Mare,
"The Children of Stare"

A few days after her thirty-sixth birthday, it struck Alexandra Ellicott that nobody had given her anything lately; she exempted her birthday presents from this dismal inventory, for there had, in fact, been the customary observances, an enormous black stiff leather purse from her brother-in-law, with her initials on it. It had been advertised in the Sunday *Times* and the initials were included in the price.

And there had been those three books from Jim Savitt whom she could visualize on a shopping trip in Accra or New Haven, vainly trying to empathize with her, and at last settling for books, which he knew something about.

She was honestly not disturbed about birthdays, how they came and went, but brooded instead about the absence of the casual presents which she was accustomed to receive. Looking around her apartment she counted dozens of tributes to her attractiveness, gifts from men who made no claim to the status of lover, pillows that elderly lonely ladies in neighbouring apartments had urgently pressed her to accept (for she attracted all kinds). That armchair in the corner. She had simply bought a piece of batik and pinned it on, and she had used the chair for three years. It looked perfectly fine in its corner and a married couple two floors down, whom she hardly knew, had given it to her on the pretext that they were replacing it, and they hadn't replaced it but she had their chair and used it with vague compunction and small regret. They had so much wanted her to take it, had wanted her to have something of theirs, but she hadn't seen them lately.

She had that damned inconvenient floor-lamp shaped like a spear, the kind of thing that you might see in a production of *Macbeth* in Central Park. Wrought-iron, last-century, right out of a bachelor apartment beside a moosehead and a set of Owen Johnson — Alexandra had a perverse sense of parody — and a pipe-rack and a humidor and panelling and *Fellowes On Torts* — and here she began to let her imagination sport and play, furnishing the room in which the lamp belonged.

It had been a gift from a boy's admiring uncle; she used it to read by as she loyally used her extensive catalogue of presents. She had bought no furniture in the twelve years she had been living in the city, but her apartment had filled and overflowed repeatedly. She had had to make a personal signature of eclecticism and nobody could say that her place looked like a page layout in *Signorina*.

Which was what it ought to look like! She was Assistant Fiction Editor at *Signorina* but she avoided all designers and decorators and concentrated on people who could read. Her friends across the hall in layout, in the magazine's offices, were a flossy crew who couldn't read. They could peer and stare and look but they obviously didn't know how to read, else why was the fiction locked in that crowded bunched-up unreadable type face? Her place should not aggressively take the eye, as decorators' contrivances did. It should simply look like her, should have her charm, the aggregate of the things other people had offered her. Armchair, floor lamp, the small but important Hopper, qualities her friends' imaginings had bestowed on her.

Those who knew her casually and thought they knew her well called her "Sandy." There were degrees. She smiled, looking around her apartment, thinking of the steep gradient of familiarity. Those who didn't know her and wished they did spoke of her as "Alexandra Ellicott" in tones which certified that Alexandra Ellicott was a person whom it must be simply sheer Heaven to know, to be *in* with. This Alexandra Ellicott was a pure mere fiction, a holy of holies or Castle Perilous, a test for the uninitiate.

It certainly is odd, isn't it, how one is able to sense how other people speak one's name when one is out of hearing. Something like the way one's peripheral vision assures one that one is being looked at when, dear me, one gives not the slightest sign that one is aware that one is even seen. How lucky to be one! Then there would regularly come those days when some of the uninitiate succeeded in forcing themselves around the peripheral curve of one's hooded vision, managing to make themselves known. These people would begin to call her "Sandy" and oh, the bliss of it.

"*Sandy* wants to see the dummy before it goes across the hall."

At this, a freckled girl from Sarah Lawrence stares angrily at the speaker. "So now it's *Sandy*, is it?" She is the last new girl in the office and painfully aware of it.

"Shut up, Betsy," orders the department head cheerlessly. Then to the exultant girl on the first-name basis: "I'll get it in to her in ten minutes. I'll slide along with it myself. Will you tell her that?"

The first-namer scuttles the length of six cubicles and whispers the message as disappointed Sarah Lawrence cranes her neck.

"Knock it off, Betsy!"

The fun of the thing is that her twenty intimates call her "Alix." It's the difference between the *doctorat de l'Université* and the *doctorat d'Etat*. The Fiction Editor, poor chic brainless thing, calls her "Sandy" and Audrey Wood calls her "Alix." And it always comes as such a shock to the Sandy's to meet the Alix's. One has worked and worked to establish terms of intimacy, only to discover like a traveller in the Himalayas that there is a further higher range of unsuspected intimacy beyond. Do the Alix's ever wonder what she calls herself to herself? But to herself she is nameless.

What is charm, anyway, she wonders to herself, looking around the room, forgetful that she is thirty-six and worrying slightly about the stemmed flow of tribute, not permanently damned really, somebody will be along with a parcel in a minute. In its roots it must have something to do with magic or at least the fundamentally irrational, the thing as well as the word. For all of her life, without the least exertion, like an instinctive artist — a natural — she has been able to watch the other person and smile and be perfectly true to herself, never flattering, never lying, never putting herself to the least trouble, never saying what she doesn't think, with her adorable candour, and like a cat lazily stretching sleepy legs, wind herself into the other person's heart, not wanting love or affection or respect, asking nothing, but charming, charming, and in the end *having* him or her, that suppliant other.

But she doesn't want to *have* anybody, doesn't care to use anyone, the notion is repellent. And yet a look, a smile, an undulation of tone in her unquestionably beautiful voice, any of these things brings people on the dead run.

So here she is just past thirty-six and not precisely a promising young woman any longer, at the point where her adolescent promises must be redeemed. But she can't write, she knows, though she can tell good writing from bad, and she will never enter the theatre now, as her admirers have been advising her for two decades. Alix, Alix, Alix, with your talents! What talents? Only the gift of pleasing uncontrollably with her person: but not sexually. She feels her clothes on her skin, like the expression of herself, tight around her and beautifully fitted, assuring her that she will be the sought-after Sandy Ellicott for a long time yet.

She can look down upon Gracie Mansion and Carl Schurz Park from her windows, so now she stares the length and breadth of the charming little park, noting the clumps of trees, the children's swings and slides, the rivers on the other side and a red and black Moran tug hauling a bargeload of boxcars up towards the bridge. Up from La Guardia swims a DC-6, a silver sliver in the sunny haze, the river is a network of ripples and currents and the shouts of the children float to the tenth floor and swim in her ears, the frail frolic limbs of the children tiny ten floors down, tender and new in the haze. She remembers last weekend in Fairfield, can you imagine, Fairfield, not the county, the town itself, where her brother-in-law is General Counsel for a manufacturer of heat controls for gas stoves. One needn't be ashamed about Fairfield, and she and her sister Helen and Helen's husband Bob are all Waterbury kids anyway and it is quite a display of upward mobility from the side of the hill in Waterbury to Fairfield, the town, not the county. In her poor way, Helen has managed as big a jump as she.

Oh, who wants to be somebody's glamorous relative in New York? What a stupid stereotype, and yet they force her into the mould, Mr. and Mrs. Robert Pyle and their charming children, seen at their barbecue pit behind their lovely home at 146 Leafy Hill Lane, Fairfield.

Bob had grinned at her knowingly all weekend. He knows her age because he knows Helen's, and he never refers to it. But he so plainly thinks that she, with her friends in the agencies and all those writers she knows, is something straight out of *La Dolce Vita*, and he has such mixed feelings about the sweet good life, that she can meet him on no ground but that of charm. He knows he prefers his own life but feels that hers is the only one. And then they have those children, and she thinks of the poem:

Their small and heightened faces
Like wine-red winter buds;
Their frolic bodies gentle as
Flakes in the air that pass,
Frail as the twirling petal
From the briar of the woods.

Last weekend had been late in the season, late for the pool, but they had sat around and sunned themselves, she and Helen and Bob and Jenny and Michael. She couldn't take her eyes off the children, those soft round brown tender limbs, the air of terrible innocence and fragility, the trust, the ignorance of charm and strategy. Watching Jenny stretch out a plump leg, touching her toe to the cold water, the movement so supple and so calm, Alexandra had forgotten what she never forgot, that she was Alexandra Ellicott of *Signorina*, and had surrendered herself to the sweetness of the perception, the unawareness, the piteous drift and sleep of the affections, of the little girl.

Oh God, she had thought angrily, she'll be going to college in two minutes, a year has become a minute in my scheme of life. Then she forgot about that for a minute (a year) and watched the child play, unaccustomed to the love that flooded her senses, the fierce protective urge that made her leg twitch with the felt physical wish to get up and go and put her arms around the little girl.

Banal situations, chances missed? Not in the least, she has what she has and is, and who speaks of Bob Pyle with bated breath? No transient movement of the affections is worth a lifetime's work, she concludes, but the disquieting voices rising from the charming park ten floors below blend with her recollections of the late summer Saturday beside the pool, and won't stay put.

She has never quite heard Bob say anything like this but she can perfectly imagine the puzzled dialogue:

"Why don't you get married Alix, a nice girl like you? It's a shame." Bob admires her, not dishonourably, but really. Helen is younger and almost out of the things between them, things like this at least. And besides, look at all those copies of *Signorina* they leave lying around on coffee tables, and look at the Gore Vidal manuscript she gave them.

They've framed the manuscript with a printed page from *Signorina* beside it. Nobody else on Leafy Hill Lane has anything like that to display.

"I'm so fond of you Alix, I wish you were settled."

"Why, Bob, I am settled."

"You could keep on at *Signorina* after you were married."

She is obliged to stifle a giggle. "But I have no intention of getting married."

"No," he says gloomily, "I suppose not." Can he perhaps be thinking forward thirty years? No, that wouldn't be like Bob, a year limits his foresight, a new coat of paint for the house, a new line of heat controls. And all at once, imagining herself in the midst of this debate, she can feel her drink begin to sweat in her hands, as she sees herself at sixty-five. Get married, get married, the cry clangs in her ears and she reacts courageously. Why should I not have a good long life and a happy retirement though unmarried? Lots of men do.

Or do they or do they?

There is of course terrible Jim Savitt, and she tries to remember whether Helen and Bob know anything about dreadful Jim. Connecticut is full of gossipy playrooms and patios and if you're seen in one, you're the prey of all. She remembers Helen making a school-mistressy joke about the Alsop house, the Pantheon, and Greek Revival, a joke nobody saw, but it shows that the Pyles have heard of Middletown. They've doubtless married her off to him already, got her up to here in autumn leaves on her matronly patio. A patio of one's own. *Why do you sit on your patio?* Patios have become the main arena of the folklore of the upper-middle class, where the assignation begins, where the agon twines around itself. Scene One: ON THE PATIO. Why it's as confined as A ROOM IN THE PALACE, and much much duller.

She had been sitting mousily on the edge of a flagged patio in West Cornwall, Conn., saying nothing and looking like a receptionist in an inconspicuous dark blue wool, feeling like a veiled searchlight. The trouble with being a celebrities' celebrity is the impossibility of modesty, you begin to feel as important as they make you out, but no one could possibly be as important as Alexandra Ellicott, that monolith of insideness.

But there she was with one leg of her lawn chair off the stone flags, digging into the soft turf, the chair canting sidewise and threatening at any second to dump her on her side, rolling her down the grassy slope like a ninepin. She kept hitching round in her chair, not wanting to stand and so intrude on the conversation. If she stood up, five men would come over and ask what she wanted, and that was what she did not want. On the other hand, if she fell on her head in the grass she'd draw attention anyway. They were all for some reason talking about Chet Bowles. It appeared to the generous liberal spirit of the group that Chet was a shoo-in for the senatorial nomination. Bill couldn't command serious support, and the other fellow was a laughable hack.

She laughed, remembering, because the laughable hack has been the sitting senator for three years.

But they had all felt very cheery about Chet, so Alexandra sat on, still as a mouse, while before her and to her right a slender lane, really two narrow parallel dirt tracks, ran down along a line of white-washed rocks over the edge of the valley into a sea of riotous greens and yellows, a puff of foliage that seemed as though you might dive over the edge of the hill to swim in it. Up above and in front of her, as she lifted her half-closed eyes, an enormous hill swelled and rounded in a fecund green curve, all stippled and dotted with subtle accents in green and black, and across this hill slantwise shot the yellow beams, refracted and reunited by hundreds of thousands of softly moving green and yellow leaves and their shadows. In the warm late afternoon summer sun she might almost have drowsed behind her hot eyelids, when a gentle friendly hand took hers, or at least took the glass from her palm as she floated upwards through a wave of threatening sleep.

"Can't I get you something else, Miss Ellicott?" said this light tenor, slightly husky, voice, and she opened her eyes to a stranger, and then she did IT, damn damn damn wouldn't she *ever be able to stop herself from doing it* and she saw instantly that she'd done it again. For she opened her eyes lazily and wide, unveiling eye-whites she knew to be of an astonishing clear shining brightness — they simply were and it wasn't her fault — and she focussed her splendid lucid gaze on this strange man and gave him all innocently the warmest and friendliest of looks, a look without appeal or enticement, a full shining regard that would seem to understand him and sympathize with him, and take him on his own most hopeful terms, never expecting too much, never making demands, this sheerly *fine* candid look, and as she did it she heard herself speak, and down to her boots she was familiar with the tone, harmonizing it with the sleepy beauty of the day. All this she did perfectly gratuitously. Her voice wasn't brittle, nor suggestive of wit, nor of politics and great affairs. It wasn't a lover's voice, nor quite an older sister's, nor a friend of thirty years' standing, but all these things without any suggestion of commitment or repulsion and she could feel her old familiar sinewy winding movement of attraction winding into the stranger, could feel its pull and thrust, and all this she did involuntarily. Then to save the situation, to cut a little the richness of her gift of self, she comically angled her chair to one side and whispered her request for help.

"Prop me up on that side, will you?" He seized the back of her chair as she half-stood, and swung it under her, flat and secure on the stone.

She could hear Mel Allen doing the Yankee game inside the house, Mel's voice snatched out of the swarming air by an aerial sixty feet high, and perhaps she should have been in New York today instead of in Cornwall helping to elect Abe Ribicoff. This stranger in front of her had something to do with all the talk but like herself seemed to want to stand slightly to one side. So she gave him her glass and let him get her another ginger ale, and when he came back they introduced themselves.

"I'm only here because of my expertise," he said, "I'm a professor of Government at Wesleyan, and my name's Jim Savitt."

"Mine is Alexandra Ellicott," she said with unfeigned simplicity, a quality she'd forced herself to acquire, "people call me 'Sandy.'"

"Oh I know," he said eagerly, and she winced. "When I heard *you* would be here, it made all the difference, because I've heard a lot about you." He waited for her to ask what he'd heard, and then went on. "In my position," and she winced again more inwardly, "in my position right now, I have to be in the city quite a lot, and Washington sometimes, and I wonder if you might have dinner with me one night? Could you?"

It made her think of Waterbury and it was on the end of her tongue to ask him which of the small grimy Connecticut factory towns he came from, Bristol, East Hartford, Bridgeport, but she let it go. Nobody had offered her entertainment in just this way for a decade and the novelty at once tickled and repelled her.

"Well I'm on East 87th Street," she said, "and of course I'm in the book."

How can one be so far IN IN IN that nobody else can appreciate such holiness, or is everybody in the whole status-seeking stinking country forever outside? The Taste Makers, the people who, this very afternoon, are playing the parlour game that in a hundred days television announcers and vulgar bouncing weather girls in Cleveland will be excitedly introducing at their smart parties. *In and out*. Everybody's out but me and I'm so far in that I'm invisible.

I don't know, she thinks, I don't really really know that I want to be this way.

This bumbling schoolboy Jim Savitt called her three or four weeks after the superb weekend in West Cornwall, and to do his image justice she forever after associated him with long sleepy golden summer afternoons — a thing which can tell powerfully during a courtship — and she sighed, THE COURTSHIP OF ALEXANDRA ELLICOTT. It sounds like VILLETTE or SANDRA BELLONI but to be utterly non-self-deceptive, she has always fancied herself vulgarly as a Meredith heroine, as Sandra or Clara or Diana. What a disgusting way to see oneself as a Meredith heroine, all lightly springing peeping breasts and buttocks seen through too-sheer silk, and always with a fresh spring breeze blowing.

Jim on the other hand sees her as a Roger Angell heroine or as a Vance Packard, and she shivers, sitting there and waiting for him, remembering that first time. It had taken him three or four weeks to get his courage up, and at length he had called in a flourish, a welter, of gaucherie, of which she wouldn't have supposed a man of his age capable.

"Tonight, goodness me, no, I can't manage tonight. Isn't that a shame?"

"It is indeed because, you see, I don't get in all that often." Then with innocent manly pride: "I've been at the U.N. all afternoon. Maybe we can have lunch in the delegates' dining room someday."

"Perhaps we can. Are you going back tonight?"

"No. I'm going on to Chicago for foundation money. I wrote the prospectus and it looks like it might go."

What kind of writing can terrible old Jim Savitt do? "I'd like to see a copy."

"Good. I'll send you one. Can I see you when I get back?"

"Don't college professors ever do any teaching, I mean, why aren't you in Middletown most of the time?"

"Oh, I am, I am. Quite a lot of the time anyway, but right now we're trying to get the Institute rolling."

She thinks of a song learned in childhood and starts to percolate with mirth:

> *Rooty-toot-toot, rooty-toot-toot,*
> *We're the boys from the Institute.*
> *We don't smoke and we don't chew*
> *And we don't go with girls who do.*

"I neither smoke nor chew," she says defensively, but he doesn't catch the allusion, there are only fifty men in America who would, and *damn them anyway, they're all writers.*

"Maybe when I get back?"

"Why not make the appointment now?" she says kindly, and he springs back to lively attention. "Say the fifteenth October?"

"Fine."

"Seven-thirty?"

"Fine."

"I know this terrific steakhouse in the Village," he concludes, and before the shock has worn off the conversation is over and he is on his way to Chicago. A steakhouse in the Village, Hmmmmmm!

Damn it, his geography had been all wrong, it hadn't really been in the Village at all; there is something pathetic about these people from out of town who try so hard to get their street-names straight. It had been awfully close to Eighth Avenue and 14th Street, with a dismal homosexual bar diagonally opposite, and that's not the Village.

What a place! A menu with six hundred illustrated items on facing pages, with a lot of little cards clipped to each leaf, with a special Jumbo-sized cocktail, and Chianti bottles hanging here and there. They drank some weird South African wine that tasted like mouthwash, nobody had known her, the headwaiter called her "lady." The walls had been a curious blond pine — it wasn't an Italian place nor a Jewish place nor any kind of a place. It was a labyrinthine, brightly lit, superlatively noisy, hole in the wall, that reminded you of a shooting gallery. She never said a word. But after that there was a natural hiatus in the relationship. She could fancy him exclaiming to himself, all the way up the Parkway, that wasn't you, Sandy, it just wasn't you. I'll find a better place, a place that's YOU.

It took him eighteen months to do it, because he had made up his mind that lady editors his own age were a bit out of his league. "You just took me into camp, Sandy," he said adoringly, like some kind of a Boy Scout, "took me into camp" indeed, where could he pick up phrases like that? "All the time we were in Jerry's place, I could see that it didn't suit you. Funny thing was, it cost like hell."

"It has to, it's the only thing that makes the place seem any good, you figure if the cheque is sixty dollars the place must be all right, but that doesn't prove a thing. All the same, I don't mean to get involved with the myth about the little restaurant where they chalk *l'addition* on a slate, it comes to three dollars for two and it's one of the great restaurants of France. This doesn't happen here or in France. I remember one night a nice lad took me to one of those places, the cheque was three dollars and that's what we got, three dollars worth of food. That was when I was first in New York."

"It will be all right tonight," he said magnificently, "because we're going to '21' courtesy of the Governor."

"What Governor?"

"Ribicoff."

"I thought you might mean Stevenson."

"No."

But the Governor's name was not quite as magical as it was shortly to become, or else Jim didn't know a good table from a bad, or else he simply didn't care, and if their location were the result of the third alternative she might be able to admire him slightly. Only visiting firemen fight over tables.

He must have made some notes from a wine-and-food text — she suspected him of consulting them covertly, perhaps shielding them in his coat sleeve or under the tablecloth, because the meal turned out to be all right. She nodded desultorily now and then to an acquaintance or two, in a way that discouraged visitors. Then she set herself to discover what Jim did, besides being a professor. He must have some mark of distinction — she had met him in West Cornwall after all, and while West Cornwall was no great catch it was something, something, and one usually found few professors there, only, once in a great while, MacLeish, and lately somebody called McGeorge Bundy, a name out of the comic strips. Two professors, could she think of a third, besides the oldest inhabitant, and besides Jim? Everyone knew everyone else, it was awful, and they had all at one time or another been panelists on "What's My Line."

If you got involved with Connecticut you would sooner or later find yourself sitting in a corner with Arlene Francis, and there was no way of getting around it.

"What happened that time you went to Chicago, it must be nearly two years ago? Did they ever give you any money?"

"Chicago," he said thoughtfully, "when did I ever say anything about Chicago?"

She giggled inanely at what she was about to say. "Just before our first date." What a phrase in the mouth of a woman her age. And forty years later there would be old Darby and Joan comfortably in front of their fire, exchanging reminiscences of the titanic days. A magazine has a lifespan of thirty years, after that it's change your format or go back to the woods. *Signorina* was reaching its grand climacteric, the zenith of its power and influence, and soon the decline would begin.

What use would an ex-editor of *Signorina* be to anyone after the magazine had stopped making money, wasn't even a sound tax write-off, had lost most of its colour pages and didn't attract writers? But she would be on another magazine, that's where she'd be, not toasting her toes in front of a cozy fire. If you're any good, you attract jobs, there would always be jobs for *Alexandra Ellicott*, and anyway there was a lot of life in *Signorina* yet, and still would be for ten years.

Ten years.

For the fowl reposing, or more accurately, floating on it, her plate was too small. Little waves of a questionable wine sauce rippled dangerously close to the edge, nobody is perfect. So she bent her eyes to her food, raising them carefully only now and then. If people *would* react that way when she looked at them, she would shut her eyes.

"They gave us a lot of money, and since then we've got more," he said pridefully, "a great deal more, and we've got a building."

She had no idea of the symbolic value of real estate properties, actually in being, to academic promoters. "What sort of a building?"

"An archive with three seminar rooms and an auditorium. Very good sound equipment. We were really clairvoyant, you know. When we projected the Institute back in 1957, the first man we interviewed in depth — I wrote the questions — was Jack."

"Institute of what?"

He looked at her blankly. "Ethics and Politics, didn't you really know? The Institute of Ethics and Politics."

"Sweetie, it isn't exactly my field." One of the least charming things she'd ever said, and she knew it very well. His eyes begin to range around the room and in a minute, she was certain, he would begin to tell her who were there, she could feel his eyes growing rounder and rounder as he stared. It was very quiet. In a corner somebody was bouncing a pair of dice off a glass.

"You're a celebrity too, don't forget that," she said, looking at her drowned duckling.

"I'm simply old Jim Savitt."

"McGeorge is simply old McGeorge, and you're very close to Jack."

He beamed. "But I can sit here and nobody knows me."

"Ah," she gave him, feeling her kind regard move around him and warm him, "ah, now you're getting the idea!"

"I'd sooner everybody knew."

"No you don't, no you don't."

"And this isn't your *métier* either," he said, in bewilderment. "I'd have thought this was you, absolutely to the *teeth*."

"Nobody knows me."

"Oh, that's not so," he said, wounded, "everybody knows you."

"Everybody has heard of me. But I keep pretty well to myself."

The heavy silence which ensued lasted all the way uptown. There had been some question of listening to music in a club way downtown but they gave it up. When he got her home, he left abruptly and she concluded, with imperfect satisfaction, that she'd scared him off for good. And she must have been right because he didn't show again for a long time, and when he did, he'd learned some new tricks.

The red and black tug on the river had just about made it through the bridge. The children were beginning to leave the park. In half an hour the twilight would begin to rise, all purple, from east of Idlewild, and she sat on in the shadowy room waiting for old Jim Savitt, just in from Accra, to come and fix dinner for her. He'd told her his troubles at length on the telephone only yesterday, off the plane forty-five minutes and through customs as a diplomat.

"I figured two strikes was enough," he'd said angrily, "after that silly business at '21' because I'm too old to learn new modish habits, I'm forty."

"Jack is forty-three," she'd said gaily, "and the papers treat him like a baby."

"What's young in politics is old in love or baseball. Forty-year-old lovers, good heavens," he'd exclaimed helplessly and then paused.

"What made you decide to call me?"

"Just before I took the plane I was standing on the corner of 49th Street, just before noon, looking up Madison, innocence itself. I'd intended never to bother you again, imagine *you* in Middletown! You know how sunny that long street can be at noon. Well, I just looked up and down, standing there minding my own affairs, and folding and refolding my ticket in my hands — I'd just picked it up and I'd been reading the fine print on the back."

"You know where *Signorina* is."

"But I hadn't remembered, so I couldn't help but see you leave the building for lunch and that little blond boy with you."

"Him," she said, grimacing, "I remember that day but I didn't see you. Honestly, Jim, I'd have preferred you to him, oh, say eleven thousand times."

"Alix," he said tentatively, beseechingly, "what do you want to fool around with those types for?"

"It goes with the job."

"Anyway you came along in a camel-hair coat...."

"*Not* camel-hair!"

"… and my vision blurred like a Steichen photograph, all full of sun and haze. I don't know about *chic* but I thought your hair looked marvellous. The new anchovy hairdo."

"Anchovy?"

"Isn't it anchovy?"

"You mean artichoke," she said, howling with laughter. She began to think what an anchovy cut would look like, spiky and nipped off at the ears, and at that there were fool women who'd wear it if you ordered them to.

"Anybody can make a mistake," he said a bit sulkily, "and it's artichoke if you say so, although one sounds as ridiculous as the other. But you looked like something out of that darned old magazine, and I guess that's what I want."

"Not for export."

"No, you're indigenous to the island, you wouldn't bloom in Middletown, but I might just survive here. I survived in Ghana and I was thinking about you all the time. I decided never to take you to a restaurant again."

"That limits things."

"Not at all, because if you'll let me I'll come up and fix dinner for both of us, and I won't have to worry about forks."

"Come ahead then, Thursday, and I'll stay home."

She had been afraid that he might proffer a Ghanaian meal, which dismayed her because among the profoundest of her few political notions was the conviction that Mr. Nkrumah was a jerk who needed a kick in the pants. She was uninterested in the menus of Ghana. So when Jim appeared in the doorway with his face pink from the last of the sun and breeze, with his two bulging paper sacks of obviously gourmet foods from the delicatessen, she was much relieved.

He was the kind of man who is attracted, even sold, by a connoisseur label in a fake Baskerville font. He would buy "Callard and Bowser's" butterscotch instead of "Fanny Farmer" because he liked the execution of the thistle on the wrapper, and the butterscotch was tasteless and not so good as the native line. The words "Crosse and Blackwell" were a kind of incantation to Jim. Around Thanksgiving he always went through the little announcements in the back of *Esquire* and *Sports Illustrated* and sent by mail-order canned smoked turkeys and hams, pheasant, and frozen porterhouse, to people in Departments of Government all over the continent.

Tonight his paper sacks bulged with enough overpriced food for three meals — he had succumbed to the rigours of the delicatessen. There were several bottles of wine, none of them labels she knew; but as she knew nothing about wine anyway she wasn't discomfited. He absolutely bounced into the kitchen area, opening the refrigerator possessively and staring in transfixed.

"For once I've been right. There's nothing in here."

"There's some cottage cheese in the crisper," she said, feeling proud that she knew the word "crisper." She never used the kitchen.

"Where do you eat? How do you live?"

"Here and there," she said evasively, "sometimes I eat in Nedicks."

"What do you weigh?"

She was in her turn transfixed; she had never been asked that before. "A hundred and six," she said automatically, "and I ought to take off about three pounds." She didn't know what had gotten into him; it couldn't have been the Accra trip and she was certain that he hadn't been offered a Washington appointment.

"You ought to put on about thirty-three pounds," he said positively, handing her a glass of sherry and a dry biscuit, and at the same time pulling a handful of endive out of one of the bags. She had an exact horrid intuition of the menu and all at once she couldn't bear it or prolong it any further.

"Look," she said, "now look Jim, this is foolish. You don't want to hang around me."

He bumped his head on the refrigerator as he straightened up. "Yes I do."

"There isn't even any ground for discussion," she said candidly, "none whatsoever and I won't let you try. You can't make it."

"The salad?"

"The scene, the time, the rhythm, making it in the media world, look at me, for heaven's sake, would you willingly be like me?"

"As close as I can get."

"You're very foolish."

"Oh, you don't know what you are," he said fondly, "don't you know that all the way from here, through Westport, to Middletown, *you're it?*"

"*It?*"

"To be alone in this apartment with you, over a private supper, is as far as I can go, I've made it, I'm in."

She was looking at the label on a bottle of Margaux; there was a vineyard scene in three off-register colours, very badly executed, on the paper. "Tell me all about it," she said quietly.

"To begin with, you're entrancing. Nobody talks like you, nobody else has a voice like yours or jokes as you do or dresses as you do, or is so much admired. If I were married to you Alix, even for six months, I'd have everything I've ever wanted."

"Even for six months" is so deeply naively corrupt that she shudders. "I want to try to tell you something that's hard to express, an abstract idea, and I'm not used to them. You're the one who deals in abstractions, so you can piece the thing out."

"Say it then!"

"Jim, I've gotten to the point where I no longer care, *I do not care, I don't have to care.* I don't have to look onwards and upwards because I'm up where one arrives. Jack and Jackie aren't here yet, they're still trying to arrive."

"That's right," he says, his face glowing.

"I think that on this continent there may be a hundred people like me, hidden away here and there, people who don't have to care, who are really *really* free who don't have to have a car or a telephone or a new dress. There was once an old Duke of Norfolk, oh, eighty years ago, who wore smelly old clothes and when his friends remonstrated with him he said: 'On my estates everybody knows me and in town no one does.' And he did as he pleased, as I do."

"The Duchess of Gracie?"

"Exactly, the Duchess of Gracie, because I can be simply purely unaffectedly independent."

"You could lose your job, you could lose your looks, you could starve."

"As to my job: the whole tone of American life would have to change for me to lose my job, or the certainty of always having such a job. Jim, I'm further left than Nikita, I say things that no one can say, and I say them publicly, and I'll never want for jobs. To destroy me would be to destroy what everybody wants. Therefore I won't starve. As to my looks: I'm thirty-six, Jim, and I was never a beauty, I carry no charge of sex, thank the good

God, no one desires me for bed. That's not what you've wanted from me. I please you, I charm the hell out of you, but you don't want to get my dress off. I don't mean that I haven't been loved, because I have, I've been adored by everybody and I've had what's better than sex and I've never had to take my dress off. Men don't treat me like a comfortable divan for lounging, they respect me and I please them, they talk to me and listen. When he's with me, that poor little blond boy isn't afraid of girls and isn't, for the time being, homosexual, for a while I make him whole and able. The men who are true men can talk to me without my sex getting in the way, and so they come to respect a woman for once in their lives, instead of wanting to parade me before them nude, or spank me indecently, like one of those poor girls in *Playboy*. I can even make somebody who reads *Playboy* feel like a man, and that's extremely hard."

"This is all true, but it's hard on you."

"Yes, it's taking everything I have, it's making me invisible. Nobody knows me, everybody aspires to me, because I'm the untouchable Sandy Ellicott."

"Who could have you, Picasso?"

"No, he's too old and not pure enough."

"Sidney Hook?"

"Sidney Hook is a salesman and you know it."

"General De Gaulle?"

"Married already, but you're close."

"Me?"

"Uh-uh."

"Then I suppose that's that."

"I think that it is, Jim. You can't make it, Jim, you don't have the kind of mind."

"Shall I leave the wine?"

"Leave it on the counter. I'll drink some of it sometime."

"Goodbye, then."

"Goodbye, Jim."

She hears the door close softly behind her but she doesn't pay much attention because she's watching the spectacle that pleases her more than anything in the world. Now it's just past eight o'clock and from over in the east past Idlewild the twilight has moved up along the whole horizon, purple mostly, with softening patches of black; the vault of the sky is full of daylight and she can see the purple move and flood up into the pink sky, *Signorina* colours, purple and pink, how about a pink logotype on purple, the stars come out and the lights go on, the crowded river darkening below her window, the shouting children leaving the park with their nurses early in the late summer evening. Their last shouts rise faintly and a helium-filled balloon floats on somebody's balcony railing two floors below.

The purple comes roundly on, coming to meet her, and the light is changing so fast now that she can see the values altering second by second, dying pink merging to green to purple to black, and for an instant she is at the poolside watching Jenny and Michael flicking the water with their toes, and once more the roundness of their limbs makes her heart move lightly.

Now at length the sky is full purple, all the city lights are on, and she forgets about the children and thinks hard about jumping a story from page 113 to page 64 in the January issue, deciding that she will almost certainly have to do it though she hates to do it, and wondering if anybody will understand.

SILVER BUGLES, CYMBALS, GOLDEN SILKS

When I was a child of six, in the summer of 1934, my parents sent me to a camp on the south shore of Lake Simcoe, at the upper end of the Trent Canal system, wonderful trolling and cruising waters in those days, and nowadays just about fished-out. The camp was run by a religious community of men, teaching Brothers who also conducted several Toronto schools, and I remember seeing their brochure around-the house for several days before my agonized and unwilling departure. It quoted Whittier, as I recall:

> *Health that mocks the doctor's rules,*
> *Knowledge never learned of schools.*

There was a certain amount of truth in the second line. There were little line drawings in a green ink, in this brochure, of boys fishing, diving, running races, gashing their knees on rocks, the whole myth, overnight hikes, nature lore. I was still practically an infant. I hadn't gone to nursery school — it wasn't the fashion in those days — or to kindergarten, as the Catholic School System in the city didn't provide them. So I was still an inhabitant of the warm intimate world of post-babyhood, denned by the length of one's block. I was allowed to cross streets, but I wasn't venturesome about it. I suppose that my parents wanted to get me out of the house for a summer, a motive I would have questioned then, with the fierce possessiveness of the young child, but which I can fully appreciate now that I've two of my own.

The camp seemed enormous to me that first season. Last summer I drove past it, and you wouldn't believe how small and shrunken it seemed. In 1934 it seemed limitless and wild, the woods growing right up behind the straggling line of tents inhabited by the older campers — the littlest kids slept in neat wooden cabins and were very grateful for the added touch of civilization; it meant something to graduate into a row of tents.

In front of the Administration Building stood a tall flagpole, where a flag-raising ceremony was enacted each morning, and where two buglers blew *retreat* at sundown. I had never heard the *retreat* call before, and I haven't heard it blown for fifteen years, but I can still whistle it note for note.

Two different boys served as duty-buglers each week. I didn't understand how it was, having learned nothing of the great world as yet, that so many of the older boys at the camp could play this beguiling instrument, on which I longed to be able to execute myself. After I had been there two weeks my parents drove up for the weekend to see how I was getting along, and I can see now that they had been as affected by my absence as I had been by theirs. I had missed them unutterably, though in different ways, my slim pretty mother with her comfortable big French-Canadian nose, her "proboscis" she called it, a funny word which always made me gurgle when she said it, and my handsome excitable father whom I adored and whom I longed to understand. He made a lot of remarks which I knew must be very funny because my mother laughed and laughed at them, and I wished I knew what was funny in what he said. I found out later on: he had a desperate streak of defensive irony. He was a man of position but no education, and it strained him dreadfully to hide this.

I asked them about all these buglers. "Why can Paul and Harold Phelan, and all the Juniors and Seniors, play the bugle? Do you think I could play the bugle sometime?"

It happened unluckily that the Phelan boys were the sons of a dentist in our parish whom my father particularly despised for his jumped-up ways. He raised an expressive eyebrow at my mother, as one who regrets an ill-considered action.

"Bog-Irish!" he exclaimed. It was a favourite phrase for he was a man of many prejudices, none of them violent but all irritating to him. He also disliked French-Canadians, which made things difficult with his in-laws, who all had names like Esdras, Telesphore, Onesime, Eugenie, and the like. My mother smiled at him shushingly.

"They're all in the Band," she said, and it was the first time I ever heard about the Band, the famous Oakdale Boys Band, an organization whose structure was to preoccupy me for a dozen years. The Brothers conducted parish schools in Toronto but also, and pre-eminently, a private high school, Oakdale, "in a park in the center of the city" as their advertisements had it. It was an institution that one paid to attend which in those Depression years meant that it was exclusive, if only in the sense that you had to be employed to send your sons there. The chief ornament of Oakdale was its famous hundred-piece drum and bugle Band which took part in all the major Toronto parades, the Garrison Parade in June, the Armistice Day Parade, the Argonauts' half-time shows, and ever so many more. The Band travelled all over the province making paid appearances at religious and civil functions. I had never heard of it before and at six years had no suspicion that such marvellous institutions even existed.

"Perhaps you'll go to Oakdale and be in the band," said my mother, off the end of her tongue, making my father glance at her in some perturbation. He didn't say it in front of me but he was likely thinking "yes, and perhaps you won't."

But my fate was sealed, and the sealing was confirmed on Dominion Day weekend when, to my intense gratification, the dozen or more boys at camp who were buglers, and another dozen who were drummers, suddenly blossomed forth early in the morning in gorgeous uniforms, a dress of an absolutely inconceivable splendor. They wore navy blue officers' caps with gold metal cap-badges and white naval cap covers, white gloves, navy blue high-necked tunics with brass buttons, and red, white, and green trimmings at the wrist, and gold-trimmed collars, a golden rope-lanyard across the chest and around the left shoulder, navy blue trousers with a rich gold stripe at the seam and, most bewitching of all, long navy blue capes fastened around the neck and depending in soft folds below the waist.

These capes were lined with golden silk, and the most distinctive mark of the Band uniform was the bright glitter of the silk. It was regimental to make three precise folds in the cape, so that two broad bands of gold hung from the shoulders to the waist. I had never been so captivated in my life and at this revelation would willingly have exchanged my home, my cozy family life, my brother and sister, for the chance to live with these marvellous boys and dress like that. We soon heard that the rest of the Band would appear in the early afternoon for the patriotic ceremonies.

A few of the biggest boys wore *medals.*

At one-thirty three fat old busses appeared at the gates with seventy other bandsmen, the two bandmasters, Mr. James and Mr. Thompson, the bass drums and tenor drums, and wonder of wonders the mascot, a boy smaller than myself though older, named Jimmy Phillips, who marched in front of the bandmasters and swung a small baton. I have never since seen anything to compare with it for glitter.

Jimmy Phillips was the son of a man who owned a house on the lowest corner of the Oakdale property in Toronto. He had in some way been a benefactor of the school and still lived in the house on the grounds with his family, and his boy was the Band mascot until he outgrew the job. I don't know just what Mr. Phillips' connection with the Brothers was, but it was certainly a matter of money and/or property. And because of it, Jimmy Phillips marched in front of the Band and carried a silver baton … it was my first faint intimation of the uses of influence and wealth.

When he grew out of the job, he was succeeded by Fred Crawley, the son of a wealthy Catholic stockbroker whose bene-factions to the school must have been indeed munificent because Fred wore a special white and gold uniform (which the Phillips' boy hadn't) and held the post of mascot long after he had ceased to be as wonderfully small (isn't he *darling*!) as a mascot should be. At last he was succeeded by the Bandmaster's son, little Billy Thompson, who lasted out my tenure with the Band. This time, the Brothers had to pay for the white and gold mascot's uniform.

That first wonderful day I saw the Band, wheeling and counter-marching in intricate patterns in front of the Administration Building, I noticed many things. For example, the two Bandmasters were of slightly unequal rank. Mr. James was Drum-Major, and Mr. Thompson was merely Sergeant-Major, and the former's gold was shinier and less brassy. There didn't seem to be any animosity or competition between them.

I noticed as well that there were some strutting little boys, scarcely bigger than myself, marching in the cymbal section. I call it the cymbal section, but the line of eight included three awfully small boys who played triangles. As far as I could tell, playing the triangle demanded no musical skill beyond the ability to keep time with a striker, loud enough to be heard in the uproar. I decided right then and there that as soon as I should be sent to Oakdale I would try out for the triangle.

It's singular how sharply the child's mind will calculate. I could foretell at six a course of action I would follow exactly over four years later; and in the interval I forgot not one detail of my plan.

At ten years, having completed the sixth grade, I was finally allowed to quit parochial school and begin at Oakdale. This was a considerable step for my parents to take, because it implied seven years of fees for me, and the like for my brother later on. In 1938 Toronto was by no means fully recovered from the Depression.

The parish schools and the public high schools were free whereas my father had to pay for me to go to Oakdale. The fee wasn't outrageous but it was something, and as my father's affairs were at this time not uninvolved, it was a damned decent thing for him to do. To tell the truth, he couldn't afford it, then or long after, but he tried his best to manage the thing gracefully.

So I went, and on one of the first of a series of tender sleepy fall days, hardly fall at all, the soft gold end of September, a meeting for Band recruits was announced for after school in the Cafeteria. I was there with bells on, already clutching my triangle in rapt anticipation. The senior NCO in regular school attendance, a full-grown man of nineteen, spoke briefly. That was Sergeant-Drummer Johnny Delancey, killed two years afterwards in a burning Wellington bomber, over the railway yards at Hamburg. He spoke of the Band's traditions and its reputation.

"You won't see any of us with ten medals on our tunics," he said, with a certain heat. He had a posthumous DFC later on, the only medal he ever won. He was making a dig at the Saint Ursula's Boys Band, also conducted by the Brothers at a parish school way downtown in a slum district. Saint Ursula's school went through the tenth grade, so they were able to maintain a band almost as big as ours, and there was a sharp rivalry between us. Saint Ursula's went each year to the Band Competition at Waterloo, Ontario; and every year they won their class competition, so that everyone in their outfit had a medal for every year he'd been in the competition.

The Oakdale Band disdained the competition as a rather plebeian thing. Only those very senior NCOs who had been awarded an Efficiency Medal at the annual inspection of the Band and Cadet Corps wore anything on their chests. We Oakdale bandsmen gave out that we were above competition, and we regarded the Saint Ursula's medals as an unseemly display, or at least we were tacitly encouraged so to regard them. A medal in our Band meant something. Johnny Delancey never won one.

"You'll find me conducting practices after school," said Johnny Delancey, "but 'Tommy' Thompson runs the Band, and don't ever forget it. He's the best Drum-Major in Canada, he used to play with a British Army Band, and everybody at the Armouries — even the Queen's Own and the Army Service Corps — wants him. But he's staying right here and we want you to appreciate him."

I pondered this. There had been *two* Bandmasters up at camp. Where was the other one?

"Now we'll take your names and the instruments you mean to learn. We need some tall fellows for the Tenor-Drums. You there, you're big enough." He pointed at a gangling boy near me, named George Rait.

"I was going to try out for the bugles."

"Tenor-drums," said Johnny Delancey peremptorily, determining forever the shape of George Rait's Band career. "Corporal McGarry will take that side of the room and I'll take this." They began to move along the lines of recruits. I was way down at the end, and I grew more and more overawed as big Ted McGarry came nearer. A Corporal! Finally he looked down at me and smiled.

"What would you like to be, sonny, mascot?"

"No," I said indignantly. After all, I was ten, and going into Junior Fourth (Grade Seven as it is now) and I couldn't quite allow "sonny."

"I want to try out for the triangles," I said, abashed but outspoken, the way I've always been.

Ted McGarry was very decent. "Triangles it is!" he said, writing down my name. "One of the most important sections in the Band." He passed on to the end of the line. Afterwards they announced the hours of the recruit practices, telling us that we would have to learn our instruments, how to march, the meaning of the various commands, and how to care for a uniform, before we were accepted. Those who didn't co-operate with their instructors, and those who couldn't maintain a decent standard of drill, would be rejected and would have to join the Cadet Corps. Then they let us go and I ran all the way home to tell my mother.

Toronto is not a beautifully-built city by and large, though you can find good-looking buildings if you know where to look. But the natural situation of the city is attractive, the long gentle slope of the hill rising off the lake. And the light can be superb, especially in the spring and fall, a clear but oddly smoky light softening and enriching the raw green of spring and especially grateful to the mellow browns and yellows of early fall. All through late September and early October of that year the weather held on beautifully, the air soft and clear, and the lovely Toronto light — something nobody in the city ever talks about, as though they hadn't noticed it or took it for granted or were afraid to praise lest it should disappear — the faintly smoky hazy yellow light ran on and on as we little kids drilled and practised our rhythmic noises on the campus, under the direction of the junior NCOs.

Just before Armistice Day we were told whether or not we would be accepted, so that the successful candidates might march in the big memorial parade to the Cenotaph. One Friday after-noon we were admitted to the Bandroom, a cubby-hole on the ground floor of the Cafeteria, where the sixty-four bugles could be racked up line on line in a glass case, to draw our uniform issue. Brother Willibald was there, the teacher in charge of Band activities, and he presided as chief outfitter as one by one we were herded in and matched to tunics and trousers and, best of all, our capes. None of the uniforms was quite new and the gold on some of the capes was a little greenish when you saw it close to; but if anybody noticed it, nobody said anything, we were all too excited.

They had a little trouble fitting me, I was small for my age and for a moment I was terrified that I might be turned down. But kind Brother Willibald, seeing my desperation, rummaged at the very back of the closet and came out with an old discarded uniform of Jimmy Phillips, the ex-mascot.

"Have your mother adjust the cuffs," he advised, "and be sure you have the whole uniform cleaned and pressed before Armistice Day." I nodded mutely, frozen with excitement. "Are you sure you know how to clean your buttons?" I nodded again, afraid that at the last minute he might change his mind and not give me the uniform. But then he smiled and handed it to me, and told me to pick a triangle and striker off the rack. I did as he said and left the Band-room as quickly as I could for fear somebody might take it into his head to shout after me, "You're too small!" I was always hearing that.

But no one did, and in common with the other recruits I appeared at Band Practice the following Wednesday night for our first formal practice with the Band. When the weather was clement we practised outdoors on the lower campus, and the sound of the music could be heard rolling across the city a good three miles and more. After I left the Band years later, when I was living down on Sussex Avenue, over two miles from the school, I used to hear the music of the evening practices as clearly as if it were coming from the next room. God only knows what the apartment dwellers next to the parade ground thought of these practices, for the music was indeed cacophonous; they made constant efforts to have them stopped, or at least muted in some degree, but nothing ever came of it.

As it was now early November and the yellow light had gone blandly grey, the late fall rains setting in, we practised that night upstairs in the Cafeteria, the tables and chairs shoved to the wall, and you can imagine the impression made upon the nerves of the recruits by the noise of thirty-two snare drums, eight tenor drums, two bass drums, sixty-four bugles, and eight cymbals and triangles. It was Homeric in scope, at least as far as volume was concerned; musically it was constricted. We were then using the conventional British Army brass bugle on which an ordinary bugler could produce five notes, or if he were better than average, six. To these bugles could be fitted a "crook" which changed the key of the instrument by lengthening the air column. Another four to six notes could be produced with the crook, in the key of the dominant, and these ten to twelve notes constituted the whole musical range of the Band, the drums and percussion being tuned to no key. And yet we had a repertoire at that time of over sixty marches from the simplest, "Cry Baby," to a pretty jazzy number called "Susan Jane," which Mr. Thompson had just put into the book, and which we supposed him to have composed himself. As a matter of fact he hadn't for he got his new material out of British Army manuals, or by attending other band practices at the Armouries, but we didn't know this and we regarded him as an accomplished musician and composer. He used to teach us new marches by humming them to us, first the open and then the crook parts:

> *Dee-dickety-dee, dee-dee, dee-dee,*
> *Dee-dickety-dickety-dee, dee-dee.*

If there were any special effects for the drums he would illustrate them until the NCOs caught on; then they taught them to the other drummers in the afternoon. Our repertoire seemed almost illimitable to us, but to the un-instructed listener it must have seemed as though we were always playing the same tune, just as Corelli, Torelli, Boyce, Vivaldi, and Handel sound alike to the ignorant.

"Tommy" Thompson — the very senior NCOs called him "Tommy" but to the rest of us he was always "Mr. Thompson" — was a remarkable man in his way, though not a musician. He had formerly been second-in-command with the rank of Sergeant-Major, and people sometimes forgot and referred to him as "Sergeant-Major Thompson." The Brothers sometimes did this, whether accidentally or to keep him in his place I'm not certain. But his former superior, Drum-Major James, had quarreled with the Brothers of "Oakdale" in some obscure way, and had left the Oakdale Band and gone over to Saint Ursula's where he now fed the flames of his resentment by attempting to bring the Saint Ursula's Band to the same pitch of reputation and excellence as that of his former command. When I found out about this it explained much of the attitude towards Saint Ursula's of the older boys and men (there were some grown men) in our outfit. It was a romantic feud and conflict of loyalties which impressed me powerfully.

Mr. Thompson was at this time securely in the saddle at Oakdale. In fact he was one of the most universally liked and respected men I've ever known. I guess he was then about thirty-eight, he must have been the same age as the century or thereabouts, because he had been a bandsman with the rank of Boy at the outbreak of the first war. He had served right through it, three years as a drummer and the last year-and-a-half as an infantryman. He was very, very short, not more than five feet one or two, but he didn't seem small because he had a solid square head and a big chest and a perfect, very striking, military carriage, shoulders well back, chest up and out. One never thought of him as small; I considered him enormous during my first years in the Band. He had a firm tanned red impassive face, and neatly clipped brown hair beginning to grizzle. Looking back, I would guess that he was not a highly intelligent man but he was purposeful and disciplined and so got by, which is all anybody can hope for.

In his other, less romantic, daytime life he was a salesman for Canada Packers, a moderate to good one but not the best or most productive. Away from the Band he had a pleasing natural diffidence that would have held down his sales. He was economical; the year I joined the Band he bought a new car, a compact Willys sedan, and he maintained this car superbly and was still driving it a decade later. Once a year without fee the Band put on a demonstration at the main Canada Packers warehouse out past St. Clair and Keele Street, in a sort of plaza bounded by loading platforms and railway sidings and dominated by a monumental stench. All the employees and, I suppose, some of the managers, maybe even J.S. McLean himself, used to watch leaning out of windows. It must have proved annually to his superiors that there were places where Mr. Thompson too was admired and obeyed without question. His uniform was always particularly regimental on these occasions.

He was buying a home in one of those Toronto districts where lower middle-class English people used to congregate. It might have been in lower Parkdale, or a few blocks west of Dufferin north of Bloor. But in fact, as I remember, his house was on Belsize Drive or one of the shorter streets parallel to it between Mount Pleasant and Yonge. Could it have been Davisville? No. Too much traffic, and he would have lived on a quiet street and a modest one. It was one of those five-room brick houses with a veranda and a wooden railing painted white, with Gothic cut-outs in it, the veranda floor painted a sturdy battleship grey. There were shrubs and geraniums in front of the veranda and a big maple tree and a neat cement walk. We used to ride past his house on our bikes on Saturdays; it made us oddly confident to know that he lived there.

Mr. Thompson had at this time a great and overmastering ambition. He wanted to obtain new instruments for the Band and had been after the Brothers to buy them. Our old bugles, dating from before the war, were full of dents which impaired their tone. And the drums, though impressive in appearance, were the type which you tighten by adjusting ropes around the side of the shell. They were old and the ropes would not stay taut, which caused a lot of broken drumheads.

The Brothers were most reluctant to spend the several thousand dollars needful for the new equipment, and were looking around quietly for somebody to donate it to them. The high spot of my first few months with the Band was the evening at practice just before Christmas when Brother Willibald made a great announcement. The well-known public figure Senator Frank J.

Mulhearne had agreed to donate half the purchase price if the Band itself would contribute the remainder from the earnings of its engagements. There was much cheering and noise and Mr. Thompson's face was a picture of joy and delight. Band outfitters' catalogues were passed around for us to stare at and of course the proposition was accepted by unanimous vote and the Senator's generous offer taken up.

The new instruments were months and months coming from England. One of the major department stores jobbed the order. I don't remember whether it was Eaton's or Simpson's, but I have the feeling that it was the latter. During January and February of 1939, an individual picture was taken of each bandsman in his uniform with his instrument, and then these pictures were hand tinted and cut out and mounted on little stands, providing an entire miniature band. When the instruments were at last delivered, the department store set up an enormous window display, with a dummy bugler in full Sergeant's uniform, pyramids of the new drums, great sweeping files of the silver bugles, their bells plated with fine gold, the regimental colours of the Oakdale Cadet Corps and Band, and in the centre the cutout miniature Band in the act of executing a right wheel, so that each bandsman was plainly visible. The display was featured repeatedly in newspaper advertisements and was instrumental in obtaining the publicity which decided the Brothers to accept an engagement at the New York World's Fair, just about to open for its first season in Flushing Meadows.

The New York trip, which we actually took with huge success, was the second great event of my first year. My father used to go to New York two or three times a year, spending a great deal more than he could afford while there. It made him laugh, he said, to think that I was getting a free trip to the Fair by playing the triangle; by then I was almost old enough to catch the full inner sense of his joke.

"Wait until they hear you play 'The Star-Spangled Banner,'" said my father jovially. He had heard us practising and knew whereof he spoke. You couldn't really play a tune on our bugles, even the marvellous new ones — there just weren't enough notes to go round. We could eke out "God Save the King" because its intervals are easy; anything more recondite taxed our musicality excessively. But Mr. Thompson was determined that we should play the American anthem at the Fair, so he pieced out an arrangement using what notes we could command, and where we couldn't get the required tone he settled for a loud, positive, self-assertive BLAAATTT from all buglers together, thus:

> *Da-da-da, da, da, dee,*
> *Dee-dee-dee, da, da,* BLAAATTT.

It was a direful strain, and when we executed the number, bang in the middle of the Plaza of Nations at the Fair, there were shocked stares of horror and surprise from our hearers. Next day in two of the New York papers there were heated remonstrances; nobody seemed quite sure whether a joke or slight had been intended — the Americans are notoriously touchy about such things. Anyway wiser heads prevailed. Brother Willibald persuaded Mr. Thompson to drop the offending piece. He did so with reluctance, substituting "There'll Always Be An England," a tune just out and by no means as famous as it was shortly to become — for we were in the summer of 1939. We couldn't play "There'll Always Be An England" either, without disfiguring it with weird atonal — almost Schoenbergian — effects:

> *Da, da, da, da, da, da-da,*
> *Da, dee-dee, dee-dee,* BLAAATTT.

But this song had no political, national, or warlike overtones as yet, and nobody at the World's Fair was offended by our rendering, so that the excursion went unmarred by further incident.

If we'd been so foolhardy as to use the same arrangement at the Canadian National Exhibition, say, next summer or any time in the next five years, we'd have been execrated and consigned to obloquy by our hearers, for the war was coming on, came on, engulfed us, and the Gracie Fields recording of the tune, unmistakable in its clear, true, unmusical clang, became the anthem of Toronto patriotism and remained so until the advent of the Bomb.

We had to give up playing it.

Mr. Thompson was not, you must understand, a man given to the frivolous adoption of novelties for their own sake:

> *Be not the first by whom the new are tried,*
> *Nor yet the last to lay the old aside,*

as Mr. Pope so beautifully says. If anything he erred in the direction of conservatism, and in the end it undid him. He would now and then introduce an outlandish and unplayable tune but he would never consider transforming the group into a brass band, for two reasons. One: he couldn't so far as I'm aware read music. Two: the Band had always been a drum and bugle corps; it was the best of its kind; he could see no reason for change.

Once or twice in the years at the end, and just after, the second war, he did make certain concessions to modernity. He got the notion somewhere, I believe from an American newsmagazine, that the Band should acquire what he called "bugle bells." I think he made up that term himself. I've never heard anybody else refer to them as "bugle bells." They're often called glockenspiels and sometimes bell lyres, but they remained "bugle bells" to Mr. Thompson.

It must have been late in 1944 when he began to talk about them at our post-practice NCO councils. I was by then a lance-corporal in the bugles, having outgrown (or rather outlived, I hadn't grown more than an inch, I was under five feet until my last year with the Band) the triangle and cymbal section.

"We've got to move with the times," he would say anxiously, casting an uneasy glance upon Brother Linus, who had succeeded Brother Willibald at the latter's death, "we can't get them from England on account of the war, but I believe I can get them made up locally." Ten years before, he had introduced leopard skins for the bass and tenor drummers and still thought of this as a greatly novel *coup.* He had the reverence for history that I admire, and no itch for the sensational.

He did get the new instruments made up in Toronto, and when we finally introduced them they looked lovely. If you think of a glockenspiel you'll know what I'm describing, a lyre-shaped, xylophone-type of instrument with a dozen metal bars which the player struck with a knobbed wooden hammer. Ours had a fatal flaw when we first got them. The bars were made of the wrong sort of metal; they gave the correct sequence of notes, but only very softly, having neither ring nor resonance. You couldn't hear them even when they played solo, and it was over two years before they were finally re-worked into playable condition. Meanwhile they were carried on parade, the way band-singers in the thirties used to hold guitars with rubber strings, for the look of the thing. By the time the bugs were out of our glockenspiels everybody else had them, the war was over, we had failed to move with the times quite fast enough.

I grew through adolescence to young manhood during the last years of the war, being seventeen when it ended, too young to have served and probably just old enough to miss the next one on grounds of age, which won't make much difference, I'm afraid. While I was growing up, the complexion of the Band altered drastically, somewhat undermining it as an institution. In the late thirties there had been several young men in their twenties in the Band as senior NCOs. During the war they all disappeared, many of them were killed, like Johnny Delancey and Morgan Phelan, and the rest were almost middle-aged when they came back and wanted nothing to do with bugles and drums.

A whole new generation of bandsmen grew up, boys my age and younger, during the first half of the forties. None of us had any close touch with British Army traditions; we leaned if anything closer to the style of the University of Michigan Marching Band; there was a movement afoot to step up our marching pace from the conservative British step, but Mr. Thompson wouldn't hear of it, and he had two powerful supporters, Perce McIlwraith the Bugle-Major, a man almost his own age, and George Delvecchio the Quartermaster-Sergeant, only slightly younger and a family man who had not gone to war. These two chaps were the last of the veterans who had been in on the Band's first years and who had stayed with it out of loyalty to "Tommy" long after they had grown up. Perce McIlwraith in particular retained the enthusiasm of a child right into his forties. I can see him still — as Bugle-Major he marched at the right of the first rank of buglers — raising his arm at the end of a long drum section to signal us to put our bugles to our lips as one man. He was a tirelessly energetic second-in-command and a man of perfect, admirable, unquestioning loyalty. He used to lecture us at NCO Council when the Drum Major was out of the room.

"I don't know if you realize how much 'Tommy' Thompson has done for you fellows. Who got us the Lindsay parade, the trip to New York, the new bugles? By God, there isn't a better man alive than 'Tommy,' and see you remember it." I think that even then poor Perce had an inkling that an older order was passing away. He must have been close to fifty when he left the Band. His company transferred Perce to Windsor, and it nearly broke his heart.

As second-in-command, Perce McIlwraith was senior NCO and presided, ex officio, over our NCO Council, the strategic and disciplinary assembly of the Band. Before I became an NCO I often came before this body on various minor charges. I fell in with a crowd of older boys who congregated in the last rank of the bugles and horsed around during practice. Evil communications corrupt good manners. Mr. Thompson never appeared to notice our carryings-on but he knew perfectly how to squelch them; he gave us responsibility and finally gave most of us a stripe, that first treasured stripe, the lance-corporal's.

After I became an NCO I grew sober and mature at practice — we all did — we were all hoping for another promotion and then a third, if you made corporal you would likely make Sergeant before you left the Band. A Sergeant had the right to wear a broad red sash over his right shoulder and down across the chest, it was the ultimate accolade, only one or two men in the Band's history had risen higher. I finally obtained the long-coveted Sergeancy in my last year in high school, in January 1945. I remember it vividly because the promotion came through suddenly and unexpectedly just before the annual Battalion Ball, the major dance of the year at Oakdale. As it happened, there wasn't an extra sash in the stores at the time, and I had to travel halfway across the city to bor-row one from an unfortunate Sergeant-Drummer who was down with mumps and would therefore not appear at the dance. I had had mumps and wasn't worried about the communicability of the disease. My date caught them instead, most likely off the sash.

That was my last Battalion Ball and my penultimate stage with the Band. I graduated from high school in June 1945, in that uneasy period between VE and VJ Day, just before they dropped the first bomb, and at the annual Cadet Inspection of that year I was awarded the Most Efficient Band NCO Medal, which I wore on my chest for the first time on our VE Day parade, a riot-ous occasion.

The end of the war punctuated my love affair with the Band because I had to go to work. I meant to go to college of course, and eventually did so two years later; but I was short of money and there could be no question of my father's sending me as he was then at the absolute nadir of his financial career. Like a good many of those who achieved a Sergeancy, I decided to stay on, partly in the desperate ambition of earning an even higher grade,

Quartermaster-Sergeant perhaps or even, if anything untoward should happen to Perce McIlwraith, Bugle-Major. It was an unrealistic and adolescent ambition because nothing was going to happen to Perce; several years elapsed before his company transferred him out of town, and by then the Band had so evolved that my love affair with it was long long gone.

I tried to keep up to practices even though I had a full-time job in the Civil Service; but there was a lot of reorganization going on at Oakdale and little by little I fell out of touch. For the first time, in the winter of 1945–46, Mr. Thompson introduced a wholly new kind of march, a complicated species developed during the second war, featuring rudimentary harmonics. The bugle section was split into four, two sections of open bugles, and two of crook. Each section had — and this was genuinely revolutionary and a great credit to Mr. Thompson — an independent musical line to play which required much greater prowess on the bugle than we had been accustomed to display. We regularly had to produce the sixth note on the instrument, and sometimes even the seventh, a thing extremely difficult to do. And we had to learn not to listen to what the other sections were playing and stick to our own line.

Our first march of this type was called "Field of Glory." It took us all winter to master it — it was like a symphony to us — and we meant to create a sensation with it, but there were two defects in the production. Everybody else in town, even Boy Scout bands, had the same number. And no matter what band played it, not matter how carefully rehearsed, it sounded crazily incoherent as though we had our signals crossed and were playing two quite different marches at the same time. For some reason, the harmonics simply wouldn't blend into a meaningful whole.

In vain did Mr. Thompson introduce variations on the idea; in vain did we practise and practise. It was a question of a search for a new musical form that didn't exist. I didn't understand then, but I do now, that Mr. Thompson was in the position of Haydn in 1792, confronted with the Opus 1 of the young Beethoven, those revolutionary trios. He knew blindly and obscurely that there were new forms to be created and explored, that the old forms had been worked up to their zenith by himself and Mozart (I mean Haydn, not Mr. Thompson) but he had grown too old to discover the new forms. Mr. Thompson might, with the aging Haydn, have written *hin ist alle meine kraft* at the last page of his latest efforts.

I left the Band in the spring of 1947, having decided that it was time to put away childish things, and having saved a certain amount of money, I started to college that fall. From first to last my love affair with the Band had lasted thirteen years, and I guess that was time enough.

I moved away from the immediate neighbourhood of Oakdale, and became involved with the usual collegiate misadventures. I took a flat on Sussex Avenue near the corner of Huron, so as to be near the centres of undergraduate activity. I began to drink beer and get around to the pubs with the boys, and I thought my twenty-first birthday the happiest day of my life. I acquired a card-sized birth certificate and started to tell the waiters in beverage rooms not to bug me about my age. I looked sixteen then but in the interval I've aged. Nobody asks me to prove my age nowadays, and I wish to God they would, such is the perversity of man.

Sometimes on a fine night in the spring or fall, I'd be sitting by the kitchen window in our flat on Sussex, drinking an ale with my roommates, and way, way off across town, softly at first as they marked down from the upper campus, and then with perfect clarity, I would hear the Band practising, and if I had had enough to drink, and sometimes even if I hadn't, I'd feel a wave of longing and nostalgia. I would want to sober up, hustle uptown on the Avenue Road bus, and take my old place in the last rank of the bugles. But I couldn't have done it; my lip had gone soft and I wouldn't be able to hit the sixth note.

I couldn't escape the Band though. Now and then I'd see them on the street during a parade, or in a newsreel of a Royal visit, or at a football game. Around the University there were always people from Oakdale with a similar sentimental attachment. Through one of them who'd been in a later class than mine I heard about the later stages of the Band's history, sometime around the summer of 1951. There had been at lot of palace rivalry within the group, between the Brothers and Mr. Thompson. The out of town engagements with the large fees had stopped coming, the Band wasn't the draw or the novelty that it had been fifteen years before. Perhaps attachment to the Crown and the British connection had generally been enfeebled, I don't know, but there was feeling among the Brothers that the Band ought to break new ground, that it should somehow look different.

Then around 1953 I heard that Mr. Thompson was out. I wish I could narrate that final interview. But maybe there wasn't any such scene, maybe he quit. But I don't see how he could have quit, it wasn't in him to do it. He couldn't have done it.

They replaced him by Warren Haggerty, an Oakdale grad, a former Sergeant-Drummer and ex-Air Force officer, a real punk. He lasted two years. After that they appointed a boy younger than I, who'd been in first year high school when I was doing Senior Matric, and was therefore five years my junior. I couldn't see then, and I don't now, how little Norm Hutchings could have the effrontery to stand up there in Mr. Thompson's place, but he was too young to have appreciated "Tommy" Thompson, he was a creature of the Haggerty regime and can't have known what he was doing.

They did a lot of things to the Band, to revive it as a Toronto institution. They discarded the bugles and drums that Senator Mulhearne had donated, and, my God, they'd only seen ten years' service, they might as well have been brand-new. Nowadays they have a slew of bastard trumpets; "valve bugles" they're called, soprano, tenor and, baritone, and they try to play things like "The

Tennessee Waltz" and "Tzena, Tzena, Tzena," and even "Rock Around the Clock" and they violate the integrity of the organization, the way Andre Previn plays jazz piano. I hope that Mr. Thompson can't hear the practices but I'm afraid that he can.

Last summer I met a group of Oakdale bandsmen on a Toronto streetcar; they were wearing what they call their summer uniform, a shoddy sweatshirt, a $2.98 item, and sleazy cotton trousers of a vile light blue, the colour of faded blue jeans. They don't wear gold capes anymore, winter or summer, and they have some sort of plumed shako, and they look like ushers in a second-run movie palace. Nothing endures.

So I imagine Mr. Thompson, as old as the century, which would put him in his early sixties, sitting in the summer twilight on the veranda of his house, which must be paid for by now. He'll be getting on to retirement age, if he hasn't already reached it. But perhaps he left Canada Packers when he left the Band; I don't know and I haven't any decent way of finding out. It would have been hard for him to carry on at the office, don't you see, because in a way he loved that goddamn Band.

I think of him sitting upright in a porch chair somewhere on Belsize Drive or one of the little residential streets in through there, between Yonge and Mount Pleasant, impassive in the changing light, hearing the dreadful new sound rolling across the city, miles and miles, to remind him, sitting innocently there, of past glories, things that are utterly vanished, that will never come back again, his face firm, his chest out even though he's seated, his face sunburnt an even red, eyes unblinking in the growing darkness, listening to the young in action.

And as the summer darkness comes on, the children riding their bicycles noiselessly along the quiet street, going home, shadows in the dark, I almost feel myself sitting on the veranda steps beside him, and I want to tell him what we thought of him, Perce

McIlwraith, Johnny Delancey, Morgan Phelan, Ted McGarry, all of us who loved him in return. It's almost time to go inside now, but in the darkness, oh, in this last time, I can almost reach out and take him by the hand.

RECOLLECTIONS OF THE WORKS DEPARTMENT

In the spring of 1952, six weeks after I finished my M.A. courses and involved myself in further graduate studies, I decided that I'd have to find a better summer job.

I had been working for the English publisher, Thomas Nelson and Sons, as a stockroom boy. The pay was low, and the work remarkably hard. I had only been on the job ten days, but after an afternoon stacking cases of the *Highroads Dictionary* (familiar to every Ontario school child) ninety-six copies to the case, in piles ten cases high, I saw that this state of affairs could not go on. These packing cases were made of heavy cardboard, strongly stapled and bound; they weighed seventy-five pounds each and they had to be piled carefully in a complicated stacking system. You had to fling the top row of cases into the air, much as you'd launch a basketball. I started to look for something less strenuous.

At length an official of the National Employment Service who handled summer placements at Hart House, a Mr. Halse, a man remembered by generations of Varsity types, suggested that I try to get on the city. I took an afternoon off from Thomas Nelson's and went up to the City Hall, to Room 302, a big room on the west side with a pleasant high ceiling. I was received with courtesy and attention, and after filling out some forms I got a job as a labourer in the Works Department, Roadways Division, payday on Wednesdays, hours eight to five, report to Foreman

Brown at Number Two Yard on College Street tomorrow morning, thank you! I stood at the counter a little out of breath at the speed with which I'd got what I came for.

"You're not very big," said the clerk at the counter. "Are you sure you can handle a pick and shovel?" As the wages were twice what I'd been getting, I thought I'd try it and see.

"I can handle it," I said. I've never seen anybody killing himself at the pick-and-shovel dodge. I asked the clerk for the address on College Street and, oddly enough, he didn't know it.

"But you can't miss it," he said. "It's next to the Fire Hall, three blocks west of Spadina. Ask to see Mr. Brown. And you'd better get on the job on time, the first day at least."

I thanked him and strolled back to Thomas Nelson's where I explained that I'd found something that paid better, and would they mind letting me go at the end of the day. They didn't seem surprised.

"You've got three days' money coming," said the stockroom superintendent dolefully. He sighed. "I don't know how it is. We can't keep anybody in that job." I said nothing about the cases of dictionaries.

Although it was the middle of May, the next morning was brisk, a bright sunny day with the promise of warmth in the afternoon. I was glad that I'd worn a couple of sweaters as I came along College Street looking for Number Two Yard. It wasn't hard to find. It stood and still stands just west of the Fire Hall halfway between Spadina and Bathurst, on the south side of College. It's the main downtown service centre for roads and sidewalks, responsible for the area bounded by Bathurst, Jarvis, Bloor, and the waterfront. Any holes or cuts in the roadway, any broken sidewalks, or any new sidewalks not provided by contractors, are tended by workmen from this Yard. It also serves as a reception desk for calls connected with trees, sewers, and drains from all over town. There's always a watchman on duty to attend to such matters, day or night.

I walked into the office and stood next to a washbasin in the corner, feeling a little nervous. Most of the other men on the crew were ten years older than I, although I spotted a couple my own age. None of them looked like students, even the young ones; they were all heavily tanned and they all discussed their mysterious affairs in hilarious shouts. There was a counter in front of me, and behind it some office space with three desks, a space heater, some bundles of engineers' plans of the streets hanging in rolls above the windows. It was the kind of room in which no woman had ever been, but it was very clean.

Outside a green International quarter-ton pickup with the Works Department plate on the door came smartly into the Yard. A one-armed man got out and began to shout abusively at the windows of the Fire Hall. This was the foreman, Charlie Brown, who conducted a running war against the firemen because they persisted in parking their cars, of which they had a great many, in his Yard. He bawled a few more curses at the face of the Fire Captain which was glued to a third-storey window, and came inside, immediately fixing his eyes, which were brown, small, and very sharp, on me.

"Goddamn-college-kids-no-bloody-good," he shouted irritably, running it all together into a single word; it was a stock phrase. He glared at me pityingly. "Where the hell are your boots?" I was wearing a pair of low canvas shoes of the type then known disparagingly as "fruit boots."

"Cut 'em to bits in five minutes!" he exclaimed, quite rightly. I wore them to work one day later on, and the edge of the shovel took the soles off them in under five minutes.

"Go across the street to the Cut-Rate Store. Tell them Charlie sent you. Get them to give you sweat socks and boots. You can pay for them when you draw some money." I tried to say something but he cut me off abruptly and as I went out I could hear him mumbling, "Goddamn-college-kids-no-bloody-good."

I had a good look at him as he banged noisily around the office when I came back wearing my stiff new boots. He was a burly man, about five-eleven, with a weathered face, a short stump of a right arm — the crew called him "One Punch Brown" — a pipe usually in his mouth. He was the kindest boss I ever had on one of those summer jobs; there was no reason for him to care about my shoes. The workmen cursed him behind his back but they knew that he didn't push them too hard. And yet he managed to get the necessary minimum of work out of them. I found out, purely by accident, that the way to make him like you was to say as little as possible. It was fear that made me answer him in monosyllables but it suited him.

Charlie had four men in the office with him and three gangs of labourers out on various jobs, widely separated in the midtown district he was responsible for. In the office were an assistant foreman named George — I can't remember his last name — and a clerk named Eddie Doucette who sometimes chauffeured Charlie around town. Usually Charlie drove himself, and how he could spin that little International, stump and all; he used the stump to help steer, along with the good arm.

Then there were two patrolmen who kept checking the streets and alleys in our district, reporting any damage to the roads and sidewalks, and the condition of any recently accomplished repairs. Johnny Pawlak was one of them, a slope-shouldered rangy guy of thirty-three or thirty-four, a bowler and softball player, the organizer of all the baseball pools. The other was called Bill Tennyson, a lean, wiry, chronically dissatisfied griper, always in trouble over his non-support of his family, and half-disliked and suspected by the rest of the men in the office for vague reasons. Finally there were the three gangs out on the job: Wall's gang, Mitch's gang, and Harris's gang. Wall ran a taut ship, Harris an unhappy ship, and Mitch a happy one. I never worked for Wall, but I did the others, and the difference was wonderful.

When I got back from the Cut-Rate Store it was already half-past eight. "What are we going to do with this kid?" I heard Charlie Brown ask rhetorically as I came into the office.

"Aimé's still off," said George softly. "You could send him out with Bill and Danny." They stared at me together.

"Ever handled a shovel?"

"Yes."

"Go and help with the coal-ass."

"Coal-ass?"

"Do you see those men and that truck?" They pointed out the windows. Across the Yard beside a couple of piles of sand and gravel a stubby old guy and a man my own age were sitting, smoking idly, on the running-board of a city dump-truck.

"Go out with them today. And take it easy with the shovel or you'll hurt your hands."

I left the office and walked over to tell the two men, Bill Eagleson and Danny Foster, that I was coming with them.

"What's your name?"

"Hood."

"All right, Hoody," said the older man, Bill, "grab a shovel." After a moment he and Danny stood off and studied my style.

"Do much shovelling?"

"Not a hell of a lot, no."

"Swing it like this, look!" They taught me how, and there really was an easy way to do it, one of the most useful things I've ever learned, a natural arc through which to swing the weight without straining the muscles. It was the same with a pick or a sledge; the thing was to let the head of the instrument supply the power, just like a smooth golf swing. When we had enough sand and gravel, we yanked two planks out of a pile and made a ramp up to the tailgate.

"We'll put on the coal-ass," said Bill Eagleson.

"What's that?"

"Cold asphalt. It's liquid in the barrel and dries in the air. We use it for temporary patches."

Danny and I rolled an oil-drum of this stuff around to the bottom of the ramp. Then we worked it up to the tailgate and into a wooden cradle so that one end of the drum was flush with the end of the truck. Bill screwed a spigot into the end of the drum and we were all set.

"You're the smallest, you sit in the middle," they said flatly.

Apparently Danny and the absent Aimé fought over this every day. When we had squeezed into the front seat, Bill checked over the list of breaks in the roadway and we set out. It was already nine o'clock.

As we drove slowly along, the barrel bouncing and clanging in the back, they told me that our job was to apply temporary patches where damage had been reported by the patrolmen or a citizen, to save the city money on lawsuits. The idea was to get the patch down as soon as possible. They weren't meant to be permanent but they had to last for a while.

We stopped first behind some railway sidings on the Esplanade, next to the St. Lawrence Market, to fix some shallow potholes. Bill filled a large tin watering-can with coal-ass and spread the black tarry liquid in the hole. Then Danny and I filled it with gravel. Then more coal-ass, then a layer of sand, and finally a third coat of the cold asphalt to top off.

"It dries in the air," said Danny with satisfaction, "and tomorrow you'd need a pick to get it out of there." He was quite right. It was an amazingly good way to make quick repairs that would last indefinitely. From the Esplanade we headed uptown to Gerrard Street between Bay and Yonge where we filled a small cut in the sidewalk. Then Bill parked the truck in the lot behind the old Kresge's store on Yonge.

"Time for coffee," we all said at once. We sat at the lunch counter in Kresge's for half an hour, kidding the waitresses, and I began to realize that we had no boss, that Charlie wasn't checking on us in any way and that Bill had only the nominal authority that went with his years and his drivership. Nobody ever bothered you. Nobody seemed to care how long you spent over a given piece of work, and yet the work all got done, sooner or later, and not badly either. If you go to the corner of St. Joseph and Bay, on the east side, you can see patches that we put in nine years ago, as sound as the day they were laid down. By and large, the taxpayers got their money's worth, although it certainly wasn't done with maximum expedition or efficiency.

When we'd finished our coffee it was obviously much too late to start anything before lunch, so Bill and I waited in the truck while Danny shopped around in Kresge's for a cap. He came back with something that looked like a cross between a railwayman's hat and a housepainter's, a cotton affair that oddly suited him. We drove back to the yard, arriving about eleven forty-five, in comfortable time for lunch. We were allowed an hour for lunch but it always ran to considerably more. The three big gangs didn't come into the Yard except on payday, unless they were working close by. It seemed to be a point of protocol to stay away from the Yard as long as possible. Each gang had a small portable shed on wheels, in which the tools, lamps, and so forth, could be locked overnight, and these sheds are to be seen all over the downtown area.

After lunch we fixed a few more holes. About two-thirty or three we parked the truck in the middle of Fleet Street with cars whizzing past on both sides. Danny handed me a red rag on a stick. "Go back there and wave them around us," he said. "We'll fix the hole."

I stood in the middle of Fleet Street, that heavily travelled artery, and innocently waved my flag, fascinated to see how obediently the cars coming at me divided and passed to either side of the truck. Now and then a driver spotted me late, and one man didn't see the flag at all until the last second. I had to leap out of his way, shouting, and he pulled way out to his left into the face of the oncoming traffic and went around the truck at sixty-five.

Pretty soon Bill and Danny were finished and we got into the truck and drove off. "Payday tomorrow," said Danny thoughtfully. "You won't draw anything this week, Hoody. They pay on Wednesday up till the previous Saturday."

"We'll buy you a beer," said Bill generously. He began to tell me about himself. He was an old ballplayer who had bounced around the lower minors for years, without ever going above Class B. Afterwards he came back to Toronto and played Industrial League ball until the Depression killed it. Then he had come on the city, and had now been with the Roadways Division for fifteen years.

"Just stick with us, Hoody, and keep your mouth shut," he said, repeating it with conviction several times.

"You'll be with us at least until Aimé gets back," said Danny.

I asked what had happened to Aimé. It appeared that he'd been found sitting in a car that didn't belong to him, in a place where the car wasn't supposed to be. He got thirty days and it was taken for granted that he'd be back on the job, same as ever, when he got out. Many of the men had had minor brushes with the law. A few weeks later Danny got caught, with two of his friends and a truck, loading lengths of drainpipe which they planned to sell for scrap, at a City Maintenance Station south of Adelaide Street. They just drove the truck into the station after supper and spent six hours loading pipe. They might have got twenty-five dollars for it, dividing that sum between them. It didn't seem very good pay for six hours' work; when I suggested this to Danny he shrugged it off. He hadn't figured out that his time was worth more than he could possibly have made on that job.

Bill Tennyson, the sulky patrolman, had often been charged with non-support by his wife, and with assault by his father-in-law. He passed his nights alternately at his nominal place of abode, where his wife and children lived, and at a bachelor friend's apartment in the Warwick Hotel. An unsettled life, and an irregular, whose disagreeable circumstances he used to deplore to me in private lunch-hour chat. Charlie disliked him, and used to ride him quite a lot; he was the only man in the whole crew to whom Charlie was consistently unfair. He had that irritating goof-off manner which always infuriates the man who is trying to get the job done. Yet he had no vices, drank little, didn't gamble. No one knew how he spent his money and no one liked him.

He had his eyes on Eddie Doucette's desk job. But Eddie could type after a fashion, and had some sort of connection at the Hall which everybody knew about and never mentioned — he might have been a nephew of the City Clerk or the Assistant Assessment Commissioner — I never found out for sure. But nobody was going to get his job away from him.

Eddie wore a cardigan and a tie, and rode around in the truck with Charlie and George, while Tennyson wore sports shirts and walked his beat. The rest of us wore work-clothes of an astonishing variety. My regular costume, after Aimé came back and I had to get off the coal-ass crew, was an old Fordham sweatshirt which my brother in New York had given me and which by protocol was never laundered, jeans, work-boots, and the same pair of sweatsocks every day, and they too were never laundered; they were full of concrete dust at the end of the day and by September were nearly solid. I could stand them in the corner, and they never bothered my feet at all as long as I washed off the concrete as soon as I came home.

That first day we got back to the Yard about four. We walked into the office, clumping our boots loudly and officiously on the floor. Charlie and George had gone out somewhere in the truck and wouldn't be back that day. Apart from Eddie, the only person in the office was a man who was sitting in Charlie's swivel chair, bandaged to the eyes. He seemed to be suffering from broken ribs, collar-bone and arm, shock, cuts, abrasions, sprains, and perhaps other things. He was having trouble speaking clearly and his hands shook violently. He and Eddie was conspiring over a report to the Workmen's Compensation Board.

This man became a culture-hero in the Works Department because he was on Compensation longer than anyone had ever been before. Everyone felt obscurely that he had it made, that he had a claim against the city and the province for life. He would come back to work now and then, and after a day on the gang would be laid up six weeks more. They spoke of him at the Yard in awed lowered voices.

"How do you feel, Sambo?" asked Bill solicitously.

"Not good, Bill, not good."

"You'll be all right," said Bill.

The injured man turned back to Eddie who was licking the end of his pencil and puzzling over the complicated instructions on the report. "It says 'wife and dependents,'" he said uncertainly. "We'll put them down anyway. If it's wrong we'll hear about it."

"I want to get my money," said Sambo.

"You'll get it soon enough."

I could think where anybody could pick up that many lumps all at once. "What happened to him?" I asked.

"He was Aimé's replacement till yesterday," said Bill unconcernedly, "but some guy on Fleet Street didn't see the red flag. He was our last safety-man before you."

I thought this over most of the night, deciding finally that I would have to be luckier and more agile than Sambo. The next day was a payday, and in the press of events I forgot my fears and decided to stick with the job as long as I could. At lunchtime, the second day, most of the men expressed commiseration at the fact that I would draw no money until next week.

Bill Tennyson came out of the office with his cheque in his hand and an air of relief written all over him.

"Nobody got any of it this time," he said, as nearly happy as he ever was; his salary cheque was almost always diminished by the judgments of his creditors. "How about you, Hood, you draw anything?" I told him that I wouldn't get paid for a week and he stared at me dubiously for a minute, coming as near as he could to a spontaneous generous gesture. Then all at once he recollected himself and turned away.

Charlie Brown told me that if I was short he could let me have five dollars. I could have used it, but it seemed wiser to say "no thanks" and stretch my credit at my rooming house for one more week. He seemed surprised at my refusal, though not annoyed.

"You're on the truck with Bill and Danny, aren't you?"

"Yes."

"Stay out of trouble," he said cryptically and went out and got into the quarter-ton, holding a roll of plans under his stump and stuffing tobacco into his pipe with his good hand. All over the Yard men were standing in clumps, sharing a peculiar air of expectancy. Some went off hastily, after eating their sandwiches, to the nearest bank. Danny Foster let his cheque fly out of his hand and had to climb over the roofs of several low buildings on College Street in order to retrieve it. A quiet hum of talk came from the toolshed behind the office where the gang-bosses ate whenever they came into the Yard. There they sat in isolated state, old Wall, ulcerated Harris, and the cheerful Mitch, the best-liked man at the Yard, sharing their rank, its privileges and its loneliness.

The undertone of expectation sensibly intensified as the lunch-hour passed; payday was different from other days. The whole business of the gang-bosses on paydays was to ensure that their crews should be on a job proximate to a Beverage Room. One of the reasons that Harris was so unpopular was that he was a poor planner of work schedules; his men often had to walk six or even eight blocks from the job to the hotel. Mitch, on the other hand, seemed to have a positive flair for working into position Tuesday night or Wednesday morning, so that one of our favourite places, the Brunswick perhaps or the Babloor, was just up an alley from the job. I don't understand quite how he managed it, but if you worked on Mitch's gang you never had to appear on a public thoroughfare as you oozed off the job and into the hotel; there was always a convenient alley.

Bill and Danny and I left the Yard sharp at one o'clock bound for some pressing minor repairs on Huron Street behind the Borden's plant. When we got there we couldn't find anything that looked at all pressing, except possibly a small crack beside a drain. We filled it with coal-ass, Bill laughing all the while in a kind of sly way. I asked him what was so funny.

"Johnny must have reported this one," he said. "He knows where we go."

"Go?"

"Oh, come on!" he said.

"Should we stick the truck up the alley?" asked Danny.

"Leave it where it is," said Bill. "Nobody's going to bother it." He was perfectly right. The truck sat innocently beside the drain we'd been tinkering with for the rest of the afternoon, with CITY OF TORONTO WORKS DEPARTMENT written all over it in various places. A casual passerby, unless he knew the customs of the Department, would assume that that truck's occupants were somewhere close by, hard at work. Everything looked — I don't quite know how to put this — sort of *official*. Danny leaned a shovel artistically against a rear wheel, giving the impression more force than ever.

We walked up Huron Street towards Willcocks.

"Where are we going?" I asked, although by now I had a pretty good idea. Anybody who knows the neighbourhood will have guessed our destination already. I'm talking about that little island of peace in the hustle and bustle of the great city, the Twentieth Battalion Club, Canadian Legion, at the corner of Huron and Willcocks. This was the first time that I was ever in one of the Legion halls. I had always innocently supposed that you had to have some kind of membership. Nothing could be further from the truth, and the knowledgeable drinkers of my time at the university would never be caught dead in a public place like the King Cole Room or Lundy's Lane.

It was a custom hallowed by years of usage that Charlie Brown, George, and Eddie Doucette should spend Wednesday afternoon in the Forty-Eighth Highlanders Legion Hall over on Church Street. It gave one a feeling of comfort and deep security to know this.

We went into the Twentieth and took a table by a big bay window. The houses on the four corners of Huron and Willcocks were then perhaps eighty-five years old, beautifully proportioned old brick houses with verandas at the front and side, and a lovely grey weathered tone to the walls. Like many of the original university buildings, these houses had originally been yellow brick, which the passage of nearly a century had turned to a soft sheen of grey. It was one of those beautiful days in the third week of May without a trace of a cloud in the sky, the trees on Willcocks Street a deep dusty green, and now that most of the students had left town the whole district seemed to be asleep. That was one of the finest afternoons of my life.

"Are we gonna go back to the Yard?" said Bill to Danny, really putting the question of whether they would take the truck home with them or not. They were deciding how much they meant to drink. And the nicest thing of all from my point of view was that they took completely for granted that they would take turns buying me beers. I was always glad that I had frequent opportunities to reciprocate.

There was an unspoken decision to make an afternoon of it.

Over in the opposite corner, fast asleep with a glass in front of him, sat the inevitable old Sapper who would revive later on to give us a detailed account of his exploits at Passchendaele. Next to him were two Contemptibles with identical drooping wet moustaches engaged in another of their interminable games of cribbage. All afternoon their soft murmur of "fifteen-two, fifteen-four" droned away peacefully in the background. It was a place where a man could stretch out and take his time. In all the time I was in the Twentieth after that, though I saw plenty of men thoroughly drunk, I never saw one really troublesome or nasty.

At a big round table in the middle of the room, all by himself, shifting a pair of small eyes in a head of heroic proportions, drinking mightily, sat a young man whom I vaguely remembered having seen around the university. This was the tenor, Alan

Crofoot, now a favourite of Toronto audiences but in those days dabbling in the graduate department of Psychology a block away. We grew to be good friends later on and I often reminded Al that this was the first place I'd seen him close to, though we didn't speak. Once or twice that afternoon he glanced across at our table, plainly wondering why I had FORDHAM lettered on the front of my sweatshirt. I let him work on it.

There wasn't a waiter; you had to go to the window. In a minute Danny came back with three ice-cold Molson's Blue and glasses on a tin tray. As a matter of fact we had had a fairly busy morning, we were sweaty, we had just had a heavy lunch — nothing ever tasted any better than a cold beer on a beautiful afternoon with nothing to look forward to but more of the same.

In those days I had a small local reputation as a better than fair beer drinker with plenty of early foot, though with nothing like the stamina or capacity of Al Crofoot, say, or any of half a dozen other redoubtable faculty members and graduate assistants of my time. But I couldn't even stay close to Bill and Danny, who drank two to my one, never appearing to feel it and never becoming obstreperous or downright disagreeable as I regularly did myself, and as my usual drinking companions often did. It was a great pleasure to pass the afternoon with them. And when five o'clock came they both pressed money on me, in the unspoken recognition that I would naturally go on to another Beverage Room after dinner. We parted on the best of terms.

Soon this comfortable alliance was dissolved by circumstance, when Aimé arrived back at the Yard after doing his thirty days. He flatly refused to go out with one of the gangs; he had earned his place on the coal-ass crew, he felt, and no goddamn college kid was going to get it away from him. Bill and Danny were indifferent in the matter, as was natural, and at length, about a quarter to nine the first morning Aimé was back, Charlie called me in from where I was sitting smoking to ask me how I felt about it. You see, he respected the prescriptive right that I'd already acquired in the job. There was an unspoken but very strong sentiment at the Yard that once a man got his hands on a soft spot he acquired a kind of generally sanctioned right to it. Charlie peered at me sidewise as I came into the office and leaned casually, as I'd already learned to do, on the counter.

"What about this, Hood?" he asked sharply but, I sensed, half-apologetically. "Aimé wants his job back."

"Fine," I said. He looked at me with relief, palpably surprised that I hadn't made more of a fuss.

"You'll have to go out with Harris," he said warningly.

"Okay."

Aimé looked at me. "No hard feelings, kid, you understand."

"No," I said, smiling. He went outside and picked up a shovel. Soon I could hear him wrangling with Danny over who was to sit in the middle.

"Goddamn French-Canadian bastard!"

"Shut your fat mouth, Foster!"

The three of them got in the truck and drove off.

I sat in the office wondering how things would be on Harris's gang. He had the reputation of being a driver, a tough man to please. He hadn't been a boss long and the responsibility bothered him, mostly in the stomach. He had a lean hatchet face and sunken cheeks, the face of an ulcerated man, with hysterical eyes and a marked Birmingham accent. Like many of the men at the Yard he had a lot of trouble with his wife.

He and his boys had been piddling around with a tiny sidewalk installation on Bloor Street, between the Chez Paree and Palmer's, for several days. They couldn't seem to get the camber shaped right and the rain lay in puddles instead of draining off into the curb. Twice now they had had to come back to the job to rip out recently installed bays of concrete. Bloor Street, you understand, was the street of all streets about which we had to be most careful — Toronto's Fifth Avenue — our display street as far as Charlie's professional reputation was concerned. He hadn't

FLYING A RED KITE

wanted to let Harris handle the job, but Wall's gang was tied up elsewhere and the work had to be done immediately.

As a finisher, Harris lacked confidence in himself and the resulting sureness. A concrete finisher has to be able to coax the water in the concrete to the surface, together with as many air-bubbles as possible, smoothing the surface and shaping the sidewalk — sculpting it — so that it curves almost invisibly from a high point in the centre down to either side. This is all done by the eye and the hand, sometimes with the aid of a level and a piece of two-by-four, but always pretty crudely, and Harris didn't have a good enough eye. Concrete is an interesting medium, plastic enough to allow some correction but quick-drying enough to require a firm decisive trowel-stroke and what a draughtsman would call a good line.

Driving me over to Bloor Street, Charlie said little, but I knew he was embarrassed about taking me off the coal-ass truck. I didn't really mind because I'd expected to get a little light exercise on this job, but you'd have thought he was sending me to Siberia.

"Here's another man for you, Harris," he said when we got out of the quarter-ton in front of the Laing Galleries.

Harris eyed me with a great sourness; like everyone else at the Yard he knew that while I wasn't exactly weak, I was damned clumsy. I knew what he was thinking but he couldn't very well say anything; he'd been after Charlie for an extra man for weeks.

"Can you use a sledge?" he asked me doubtfully.

"Sure."

"Go and help them throw the broken stuff in the truck."

I said nothing and walked along the street to where the rest of the gang were cleaning out some bays.

"Got you working now, Hoody," said Freddy Lismore as I wandered up.

"Don't let Harris throw you, kid!" said Wally Butt, the assistant finisher. I grinned and, bending over, began to pick up pieces of broken sidewalk, the largest weighing not much more than thirty-five or forty pounds. Some of them had sharp edges though, and could cut your fingers badly if you weren't careful. Fortunately I had a pair of cotton work gloves in my hip pocket. I wasn't killing myself, but as I lofted a chunk of concrete into the truck Charlie came over and spoke to me.

"You're out of shape," he said briefly. "Work into it slowly."

"All right," I said, "and thanks." He disappeared in his little truck and Harris came back, giving me a highly critical stare. I took it easy all right, but everybody in the gang took it even easier. And as is always the case with any gang of workmen, there was one guy who pottered around between the toolbox and the job, doing absolutely nothing. On Harris' gang that would be "Gummy" Brown, always called "Gummy" to distinguish him from Charlie "One-Punch" Brown, the foreman. Gummy had a single black tooth on the left side of his upper jaw — all the rest was a great void, justifying the nickname. He had been drunk, it was held universally, since the world began.

If you counted Gummy, Harris had seven men under him, and the use of a truck owned by its driver and rented by the city. This truck-driver went back and forth from the asphalt-plant on the waterfront, bringing loads of ready-mixed concrete — we almost never had to mix by hand — and the art of managing the gang largely consisted in exhausting the last load for the day at about ten to four, leaving plenty of time to clean off the shovels and put up barricades and lights, moving at a sober and godly pace, before quitting time. At ten to five Gummy Brown would get the keys to the tool-box from Harris and we'd stick the shovels, picks, crowbars, and trowels in the box. Gummy would lock it with enormous satisfaction and we'd all walk off the job, meeting there by prearrangement the next day. While we were on that Bloor Street job, I had a two-minute walk around the corner to where I lived and I used to be home washing my feet before five o'clock. And this comfortable situation lasted through the early part of the summer.

★ ★ ★

I stayed with Harris for about six weeks that first summer, all through the ill-fated Bloor Street job, then on Robert Street fixing householders' sidewalks a bay at a time, insignificant jobs, and finally around the Art Gallery and Hashmall's Pharmacy on Dundas Street. I broke out concrete, used the sledge, floated off — the works. The only thing I would never risk was swinging the sledge at a spike. I could never hit the damn thing — poor timing and eyesight, I suppose — and it was dangerous for the man holding the spike.

It might be of interest to the reader to follow a simple job from start to finish. First came the problem of getting the old cement up and out, which could be managed in several ways, depending on its age and hardness. If there happened to be grass or mud at the edge of the sidewalk, we took a long bevelled bar and worked it under the concrete, placing a rock under the bar for leverage. Then a couple of us would rock up and down on the bar to see if we could lift the slab; usually we could. When it was a foot or two off the ground, one of us would hit it in the middle with the sledge, splitting the whole slab into small chunks which could then be thrown into the truck to be disposed of at the waterfront as fill. We would clear out eight or ten bays at a time, shovelling out the rubble underneath and levelling the ground in readiness for the fresh mix.

There could be complications. At a ramp behind the bus terminal on Elizabeth Street we found that the old concrete was over three feet thick, to take the weight of the buses. Worse still, it was criss-crossed by heavy reinforcing wire which resisted pliers and had to be cut, strand by strand, by driving a spike through it with a sledge. This reinforcing wire had to be watched carefully for it was rusted and the broken ends were dangerously sharp; that small job lasted nearly two weeks.

When we had prepared the ground we would send the truck for a load of concrete. This always meant an hour's wait, either around ten-thirty or about two in the afternoon. It made a nice break. We would take things easy, cleaning off the shovels or sneaking a bit of leftover concrete to a homeowner to be used for a patio. The great thing was to melt inconspicuously into the landscape so as not to attract the attention of the ratepayer.

When the truck appeared, we either dumped the concrete into the road and shovelled it into wheelbarrows for delivery to Harris and Wally Butt, on their knees together at the edge of the new installation, or if we were only fixing scattered single bays, two of us would climb into the well of the truck and throw down shovelsful from on high. There was a certain amount of horseplay involved in this; more than once somebody down below caught a great lump of wet concrete in the pit of his stomach.

One morning in late June I was standing in the back of the truck about eleven o'clock, shovelling the stuff into a bay, sweating and feeling pretty loose, when Charlie Brown's head appeared out of nowhere at the side of the truck. The edge of my shovel just missed him and an enormous gout of wet concrete went whizzing past his ear.

"Watch what you're doing!" he said. That's only a rough transcription of what he actually said. In fact he was speaking the dialect that Alastair MacCrimmon and I used to call "cityese," an exotic English, rhythmic, heavily cadenced, comically obscene, with an unmistakable structure. If I were blindfolded in Rangoon and heard two men speaking "cityese," I'd be able to spot them instantly; there's something unique about the scansion.

Charlie got down off the truck and spoke to Harris.

"I need Hood in the Yard," he said.

"Why don't you take 'Gummy'?" asked Harris protestingly. I felt proud.

"I want somebody who's alive," said Charlie disgustedly, motioning to me to join him in the truck. I looked at Harris inquiringly but he shook his head. He didn't know what was up.

On the way back to the Yard Charlie told me about the watchmen. There had to be somebody in the office from around four in the afternoon until eight the next morning, as well as all day and all night on the weekend, which worked out to sixteen eight-hour shifts weekly.

Three old men approaching retirement split fifteen shifts amongst themselves, leaving an extra one to be filled in by one of the workmen. And each of these watchmen was entitled to three weeks' holidays a year for a total of nine weeks to be filled in through the summer. Charlie had decided that my combination of supposititious book-learning and puny physique made me the ideal replacement.

"You can put in the next nine weeks on this job," he said encouragingly. "That'll take you down through August, and then I'll find something else for you to do." I was due to leave towards the end of September.

Now the thing was, I'd been getting used to the work on the gang and enjoying it. On the other hand, every man at the Yard would have given his eye-teeth to acquire this sinecure. I didn't want to turn down what was obviously meant as a kindness, so I said nothing.

Charlie looked at me curiously. "What's the matter? Don't you want to do it?"

"Sure," I said, "It's fine, Charlie." And it turned out to be an interesting job, each shift presenting novel problems. The four to twelve, and the daytime shifts on Saturday and Sunday, brought the most service calls. The twelve to eight was mainly a matter of arranging seat cushions from the swivel chairs on top of the desks, or on the floor, and trying to sleep. Once in a great while you might get a call in the middle of the night, usually from the Traffic Squad, to report that the barricades were down or the lights missing on a hole in the road. Then you had to call out an emergency truck from one of the Yards — there was only one truck available, each Yard providing a stand-by driver in turn — and direct the driver to the danger spot. The time of the call, the trouble, the location, the remedial action, and the precise time that the driver called back to say that the repair was in effect — all these things had to be noted down in a Daily Journal and initialled by the watchman. These books were sometimes produced as evidence in damage suits by City lawyers, and so had to be kept up carefully.

But most of the twelve to eight I spent sleeping, or talking to policemen who came in for a smoke and to warm themselves, or to nap for an hour or to hide from the Sergeant. These men patrolled one of the toughest parts of town and were as eager to stay out of trouble as the rest of us. They hated the corner of Bathurst and Queen, for example, because of the half-dozen enormous taverns located there, which meant that Friday and Saturday nights on that corner were real hellers. I'd often seen eight policemen standing in pairs on the corners of that intersection and wondered why. The answer, I was told, was that they just didn't want to come alone.

Many of these fellows were English immigrants, bewildered by the Toronto attitude to the police. They were always complaining about times when they'd been losing a fight and hoping in vain that a citizen might give them a hand. I remember one Englishman in particular who was leaving the force and taking his family back to England because of this kind of thing. He felt alone and threatened in a country where incivility and disrespect for the law seemed accepted and regular.

None of these constables knew much law; none had a clear idea of his powers, and these were constantly exceeded in some circumstances and allowed to lapse in others. They hated and feared all lawyers, and were easily cowed by them. I know one drunken lawyer, a driver of spectacular incompetence, drunk or sober, who despite his erratic behaviour awheel, and despite the dozens of times he's been stopped by traffic officers, has never been fined nor even summoned to court. He bounces aggressively out of his car, announces that he's a lawyer, and the policeman, unsure of his ground, backs off.

On the other hand, when the officer feels that he has the upper hand he is perfectly ready to exceed the limits of his mandate, and is apt to be quite cynical about it. One young constable admitted to me that he always bulled the College Street crowds around, pushing people and threatening them with arrest to persuade them to move on, when there was no conceivable charge he could bring. Most of the people in the crowds, Jews and DP's, had no notion of their rights and legal safeguards and were easily intimidated.

But most of the younger policemen were decent unassuming men, not too happy with their rates of pay and promotion, considering the nature of the work, but proud of what they were doing and even of the opinion that it was a dignified public service. I asked them about favouritism on the force and they all agreed that there was very little, and that a man would normally be judged on his merits. Their testimony carries some weight too, because they were all in junior positions and there was nothing in my questions to put them on their guard.

Another instructive aspect of the watchman's job was our emergency sewer service. When there is a very heavy rain the Toronto sewers cause trouble; they are not equipped to carry off the excess water, being designed for normal conditions of flow. If there is an extremely heavy rain they back up, and the water begins to rise in cellars all over town, especially on low ground, in hollows and valleys and on the lower slopes of hills. And the only real cure for this abnormal state is the end of the storm.

Understandably enough, few householders are aware of this. When they observe the flood rising in the cellar, with its sometimes dismal and offensive accompaniment, they become alarmed, and the result is a flood of calls at the Yard, none of which distinguish between a genuinely blocked and defective sewer — with a tree root in it, say — and one which is in perfect shape but which is just too small for downpour conditions.

I remember afternoons, almost always on the weekend, when the phone rang as soon as I put it back in its cradle, for hours on end. I'd get panicky elderly ladies, people who raved in exotic foreign tongues, frightened children, Bohemians with basement apartments in which their folksong records floated soggily round and round — every imaginable stripe of complaint. There was simply nothing to be done until the storm was over. I tried telling them so but it did no good and at length I learned simply to note the call, and imply, without actually making a commitment, that a service truck would be along. Of course no such service call was ever made unless there was a clear indication in the complaint of some genuine blockage or break. But I never told anybody that.

I channeled and re-routed calls of this and other kinds until the end of August, when the three elderly watchmen had all enjoyed leisurely vacations. By that time I was pretty much regarded as one of the office staff, and Charlie was visibly reluctant to send me back to Harris — it might create a dangerous precedent. The day after the last of the watchmen came back I ambled into the Yard wondering how he'd work it out. He had, you see, a kind of problem in status, or prestige, to resolve. But he was equal and rather more then equal to it.

It was the Tuesday after Labour Day. The Scotch guy (a man never known by any other name, always "the Scotch guy," with a thick burr and a great genius for killing time) was sitting outside the tool-shed when I meandered in. He said nothing but grinned cheerily. When I went into the office Charlie handed me a small can of black paint, a small can of white, two brushes, a box of cleaning rags, and a set of stencils from zero through nine which could be fitted together to form any number up to 9999. He told us where to find a little ladder and the Scotch guy ran to get it. We threw the things in the back of Charlie's pickup truck and he drove us to the foot of Jarvis Street, where we got out. I was still quite in the dark.

"I want you to re-paint the numbers on the lamp-posts," he said. I'm not joking, that's what he said. "When you get to Bloor Street, come into the Yard and I'll give you a list of other streets." He got into the truck and sped off along Queen's Quay while we looked at each other scarcely able to credit our luck.

We painted our way up Jarvis Street at a snail's pace — boy, did we take it slow! I'd go ahead and slap on a background of black paint. Then I'd walk back — we only had one ladder — and we'd work along, putting on the fresh numbers in a creamy off-white, a kind of eggshell or buff tint. We got up to Bloor Street on Friday afternoon, a matter of four days. When we appeared at the Yard Charlie glared at us in extreme vexation.

"What the hell are you doing here?"

It would not have been possible to go slower.

"We finished Jarvis Street," I said apologetically.

"What, the west side too?"

"I'm afraid so."

He began to root around in his desk and finally drew out a few dog-eared sheets of foolscap with a list of street names on them. He flourished it in the air and then handed it to the Scotch guy.

"Do these!" he said. He looked at us and began to smile and at last to laugh. "There's fifteen hundred dollars in the Estimates to be spent on this job," he growled. "Now get out and don't let me see you around here for at least three weeks."

So I finished out my first summer without any strain.

When I came back to the Yard the next year, I had only two more years' work to do in the Graduate School. I had held a good fellowship which took care of most of my expenses, I'd had a highly remunerative job at the CN Express, where you could log seven or eight hours' overtime if you had the nerve and could evade the foreman, so I wasn't hurting for funds quite as much as before.

I went back because I liked it and I even persuaded a friend of mine, Alastair MacCrimmon, to apply for a similar job. He was then an intermittent student at the University and is now a film technician at CBC. Every night in the Chez Paree from eleven till two, he and I would sit around that summer exchanging our observations of life on the city. He was working at Number Six Yard and apparently things were managed there much as they were under Charlie. We used to amuse ourselves by playing a game which we called "Translate into Cityese." Alastair would feed me a line in ordinary spoken English, or I would feed him one, and the idea was to render it with the peculiar diction, cadence and rhythm of the men on the gangs, getting the feeling as authentic as possible.

"Goodness me," I might say, "we filled that hole in the road yesterday, and there it is again." Alastair would translate this flawlessly.

"The men at the Hall have not sent up our cheques," he would come back straight-faced, "and here it is nearly noon." This would stand a lot of translation.

"Someone has stolen all the lights off the barricades," or possibly, "Itchy-Koo has been drinking and cannot work."

Or most enigmatic, even gnomic, of all: "The truck has stopped and will not go."

It was Alastair who created the legend, on the city, of what Itchy-Koo said when he hit his foot with the sledge, crushing the metatarsal forever. He said: "That hurt!"

It was understood that I would get back my night-watchman's job when the holiday time came; but I put in most of May and June on Mitch's gang. When you remember poor old Harris's anxiety-ridden behaviour, it was a revelation to see the difference in Mitch's methods. He was very relaxed and so was his gang. Everybody had a good time; we were always close to a Beverage Room. And though it was the smallest of the three gangs, we could handle a moderate-sized job much faster than Harris, and nearly as professionally as Wall. The first thing we did that spring, as I remember, was a major installation of double sidewalk on Spadina Avenue just north of College outside the Tip Top Tailors branch store. We were right across from the Waverley Hotel and that branch of the Canadian Bank of Commerce of which my father had been manager fifteen years before.

In those days Dad used to do a lot of loan business in the district with furriers and garment-trade people during the season, and with independent sales agents, small jobbers and importers, smallwares and novelties salesmen with tiny agencies, and the like. One of these freelance salesmen, a man called Earl Darlington, came to Dad one day with a peculiar request for a short-term note. Earl could sell anything — he could charm the monkeys off the trees — but he never handled the same line two weeks in a row and so had no established line of credit. However Dad listened to the story, which was colourful and involved. He had a chance to buy the refrigerator in the Waverley for next to nothing because they meant to replace it. This was not what you and I think of as a refrigerator, but an enormous thing the size of an apartment living-room, with walls in which the cooling devices were intricately cemented. The whole room had to be removed, walls and all. It was like transporting a small house.

Darlington told Dad that he had a buyer for this monstrosity, the old Hunt's Confectionery on Yonge Street, next to Loew's Uptown. All he needed was the money to put a deposit on the refrigerator and to hire a truck with a flatbed trailer, and a gang of men, to move the thing. Dad listened to this beguiling tale and thought it over, talked to the manager of the Waverley, and in short concluded that it was a chance for Earl to make a dollar, so he let him have the money.

After surmounting fantastic obstacles they got the refrigerator out of the hotel in one piece and onto the trailer. They had the necessary permit from the police to move it, after business hours, and they hauled it up to a lane behind Stollery's on the corner of Bloor and Yonge. In went the trailer and down the lane, but before they got to Hunt's rear door the refrigerator got jammed between the walls of two buildings abutting on the lane. They couldn't back up; they couldn't go forward though they tried their damnedest. They were stuck fast. In desperation Darlington told the driver of the trailer and the gang of labourers to go home and get some sleep — he could see his quick profit being eaten up by overtime — and they'd try again next day. Then he went home himself, leaving about four tons of refrigerator immovable in the lane.

When they came back next morning the trailer was parked where they'd left it but the refrigerator was gone, vanished. Stolen, by God! And it was never traced.

Eventually Dad wrote off the loan.

Watching the men on the gang slide across the street and into the Waverley reminded me of this story and I told it to Mitch, who got a big chuckle out of it. He was then, I should say, about thirty-two or thirty-three, which seemed middle-age to me, though it doesn't any more. Everybody liked Mitch, even Bill Tennyson who came out with us for a day once in a while, moody, difficult, but after a couple of hours' joking with Mitch he would loosen up a bit and tell us about his latest scrap with his father-in-law, an ex-bantam-weight who liked to mix it with him now and then.

Then there was Frank Hughes, another nice fellow — Mitch had all the easy-going types out with him — a hockey player who had spent the previous winter in the Eastern League. He was going to the Detroit camp in the fall and was putting in the summer with us to stay in shape. I don't know how much good the work on the gang did him as far as staying in shape went; but at least, like the rest of us, he got a good tan. Frank used to play fastball with Sherrin's down at the beach and he was enjoying a very good year at the plate, which made him even easier to get along with. Like all ballplayers, he loved those base hits. He weighed around one-ninety and had one of the most powerful builds I've ever seen. He wasn't broad-shouldered; he had low sloping shoulders and a cavernous chest and magnificent legs. He was a defenceman and though I never saw him play, they tell me he could really dig. I weighed around a hundred and forty, but the odd thing was, I had about an inch of reach on him. We used to spar around comically for the amusement of the gang and the passing girls who always had an eye on Frank — he was a very handsome man.

"You look like a pretty good light-weight, Hoody," he'd say. This always convulsed Mitch.

"Try and hit me," I'd say, dancing around jabbing, or pretending to tie him up inside. Like most students, I had terrible co-ordination.

"Going to get in shape on the city," we'd sing absurdly, and this was also good for laughs. Then we'd swing our shovels for a minute as though our lives depended on it. A girl would go by and we'd straighten up and inflate our chests, holding ourselves immobile.

"Who's she looking at, Mitch," Frank would say, "me or Hoody?"

The poor girl would blush and we'd gurgle happily and foolishly to ourselves. We never tried to offend or embarrass a passing girl but they never could resist a peek at Frank, and if we caught them at it, why then the joke was legitimate.

But life on Mitch's gang was too good to last, at least for me, though it went on and on for them and still does. When vacation-time came I went back on the night-watch at the Yard, guarding the piles of sand and gravel and the tools in the shed, feuding with the firemen or throwing a football with them, depending on the state of our relations.

Early in June in the summer of 1953 there occurred the most momentous event of my career as a fill-in watchman, the Coronation of Queen Elizabeth II. There were weeks of preparation of one kind or another in case of crowds, but somehow the most weighty arrangements of the whole affair went untouched until seven-thirty on the morning of that eventful day.

It was a fit day for a Coronation, the sky an absolute crystalline blue, the air dry and soft, and College Street slumbrous and deserted at seven o'clock in the morning. I had promised Jimmy Baird, whom I was to relieve, that I would come on early so he could go home and get dressed up with his medals on for the parade. The bagel shops were silent — you could hear birdsong on College Street!

I was whistling "Land of Hope and Glory" softly to myself as I came into the office. The sound woke Jimmy who stared at me with infantine sleepy eyes, hardly recognizing me — the emergency calls never woke Jimmy — as he rolled off the top of the desk where he'd been lying, straightened his collar and tie, and prepared to leave.

"Anything doing?" I asked.

"Not a thing." There was never anything in the book after Jimmy had worked a shift. I suppose the sight of his lifeless body was enough to frighten marauders away, though; he looked quite dead when he slept.

"Tommy Cowdrey's the driver," said Jimmy as he left. "If anything comes in, call him." He slunk out the door. I stood in the gateway to the Yard for a while, looking east and west along College Street, and there wasn't a sound, nothing stirred. Then, a long long way off, perhaps as far away as Sherbourne Street, I could hear a streetcar, the clicking of the points as the trucks passed over them and then the rumble along the street; it was coming fast and I could predict exactly from the sound when it would come in sight away along to the east about St. George Street. A car with an Alabama plate went slowly past with a tired driver slumped over the wheel. They must have driven all night. A single policeman idled in front of the Mars Grill.

Inside the office the phone rang suddenly, urgently. I caught it on the third ring. It was seven-thirty. "Number Two Yard," I carolled into the mouthpiece, and then I got a shock.

"This is the Commissioner," said a tense voice. "Is Foreman Brown there?"

"No, Mr. Chambers."

"Then you'll have to get hold of him. This is an emergency." The hair stood up on my head; there was real urgency, even fright, in the Commissioner's voice. "We've got to erect a temporary Comfort Station in Queen's Park," he said. "The bandstand facilities won't be nearly enough. I've just had the Parade Marshal on the phone and he's furious." He began to give me explicit instructions.

"We'll use the same model we used on VE Day. Twenty-four compartments, twelve of each. Brown has the plans. He'll need workmen, lumber, paint or stain, buckets, chloride of lime, and the appropriate signs. Get him into the Yard and call the crew. Then call me back."

"Yes, sir."

"Very good. Who's speaking?"

"Hood. Fill-in watchman."

"All right, Hood, I'm counting on you. Get busy!"

I called Charlie at once and he was galvanized into action. "You'll find the plans for the model in my desk. Do you know where the key is?"

"Yes."

"Call Eddie and tell him to pick me up. Then get out the plans. Then call Wall and tell him to call six of his best men and have them meet me at the Yard. They'll draw double time, tell him, but they've got to come in. I don't know how we forgot about this." He hung up in great distress of mind and I began to carry out his instructions.

By eight-fifteen Eddie and Wall and six labourers were standing uncertainly in the Yard. Charlie was inside on the phone like some great captain adjusting his tactics after a military disaster. "My right flank is crushed, my centre in full retreat, my left wing collapsing. Very good, I shall attack!"

"Send the partitions to the bandstand," he was shouting, "and some green stain, and don't forget the signs like last time." At eight-thirty he and the men departed for the site of the proposed Comfort Station.

As you remember there was an enormous parade that day which was to assemble on the university front campus, the back campus, and in Queen's Park, and which was to move off at one-thirty. Besides the marchers and police and civil dignitaries, there would be great crowds of spectators, hotdog and ice cream vendors, flag and souvenir salesmen — altogether about seventy-five thousand people. I wondered if twenty-four compartments, even adding on the bandstand facilities, would be enough.

Soon there came an anguished call from a payphone at Hart House. It was Charlie. "No buckets!" he wailed.

"No buckets?" I echoed, thunderstruck.

"They're out of them at the Supply Department. Now look, Hood, we've got to have those buckets. There are ten thousand people here already and they all want to use the facilities. Call the Commissioner and ask him to get them from Eaton's Mail Order. They're sure to have some."

I called the Commissioner and he was aghast. "There won't be anybody there today. Maybe I'd better have it broadcast."

"Don't you know anybody at Eaton's?"

"I know Lady Eaton, of course," he said doubtfully. "I've met her at civic functions. But I can't call her."

"We've got to have them, sir"

"All right," he said "I'll get the buckets. What size?"

"The largest," I said, "galvanized iron." He hung up and in a matter of seconds Charlie was back on the line. "What about those buckets?"

"Chambers is calling Lady Eaton," I said, and he seemed reassured.

At eleven the buckets arrived on the site and instantly the crowds swarmed around the workmen demanding access to them. But the walls and roof weren't complete yet, and Charlie was afraid of offending public decency; he held the besiegers off until the partitions were up and the roof decorously in place while the swarms of bandsmen, hotdog vendors, and children with balloons grew thicker. At length the last nail was driven home, the last plank solidly in place, the buckets in a glittering phalanx.

The Parade Marshal blew his whistle, the drums rolled; it was one-thirty. The parade moved off and the crowds began to disperse, streaming down University Avenue towards the reviewing stand. In fifteen minutes Queen's Park was deserted except for a child chasing a floating balloon. The Comfort Station went unused.

Away off down on Front Street bagpipes skirled.

Muttering curses, Charlie ascended to the roof-tree, and taking a hammer ripped out the first of the planks. For him, for all of us, the holiday had been a magnificent fiasco. "*C'est magnifique, mais ce n'est pas la guerre.*" For weeks a pall of meditative, reflective gloom hung about the Yard.

Nothing in my second summer exceeded the high adventure of that day. There were a few memorable happenings, but the glory seemed dimmed. There was the time that Charlie incautiously named Gummy Brown to fill in the extra watchman's shift. I had been on the job for eight hours prior to his arrival and had spent the evening watching the fights on television, on the third floor of the Fire-hall. After the fight was over I had a couple of cups of tea and a chat with the Fire Captain which was interrupted by a hail from the ground floor, which drifted up through the holes in the floors through which the brass pole descended.

"Gummy's here," shouted one of the hook-and-ladder men.

"Tell him to come on up for tea."

"I don't think him can make it."

The hook-and-ladder man was wrong because in a minute a red and black face hove into view on the stairs. It was Gummy, drunker than usual, if that were possible, and making heavy weather of the ascent.

"Chrissakes, Hoody!" he got out. "Whyncha in the office?"

"The fights," I said.

He began a disconnected tirade to the effect that one should never leave his post, seizing a stalk of celery as he eased along the table towards the teapot and inserting it in his mouth.

"Can't chew it," I heard him say before he slumped over.

"Come on, man," said the Fire Captain, "on your feet!" This Captain was a bit of a puritan who disapproved of the free-and-easy manners which obtained under Charlie's aegis. "On your feet!" he said again.

Gummy lifted his head and squinted at him and then, discerning the voice of authority, he rose and lurched backwards out of the door of the lunchroom.

"Watch it there, Gummy!" I cried, but too late. He disappeared soundlessly, magically, through the hole which circumscribed the brass pole, falling freely three storeys to the cement floor of the garage and breaking both legs. Fortunately he was completely anaesthetized against the pain, which otherwise might have been very great. He lay there, the celery stalk between his lips, quietly gumming it like a cow with a cud, while we eased him onto a stretcher and waited for the ambulance.

"Take my shift, Hoody," he said as they carried him off. "Double time."

I saw the Compensation reports on that one, and you'd have supposed that Brown, Norman, 37, married, was the very model of sobriety and conscientiousness. It was at length established that as Gummy's shift hadn't actually begun he was not entitled to compensation. The case was appealed on the grounds that he had been travelling to work, though how a fall through a hole could be construed as "travel to work" rather eludes me. The last I heard, the appeal was pending.

The damned old snake of a Fire Captain was a troublemaker. One evening when I was doing a four to twelve, a Friday night as I recall, four friends of mine appeared with a case of beer and an old car. One of these was later to become a reverend and dignified professor of law at a hoary academic institution and I won't embarrass him by mentioning any names. It was his idea that we should consume the case of beer during my shift and then hasten to the Chez Paree in the car to get in another couple of hours. There were two men and two girls besides me, and the girls drank perhaps a pint each, giving the rest of us a good start.

There was a good deal of singing and noise, and though I had drawn the blinds, a policeman friend of mine twice entreated us to be more quiet, not for his sake but because some people on Nassau Street, two blocks away, had lodged a complaint. And at that he drank a pint of our beer, carefully rinsing off his mouth and hands afterwards.

Now while we were enjoying ourselves in this innocent and peaceable fashion, that spy of a Fire Captain crept across the Yard, peeked around the drawn blinds, and noted carefully what was going on. Having satisfied himself with what he considered enough evidence to obtain my discharge, he withdrew unnoticed. Next day he went to Charlie and told all, but without realizing it he had played into Charlie's hands. It was perhaps true that I was treated with coolness, even severity, for a day of two. There was even some talk of sending me out with a gang again. But Charlie knew, and I knew, and finally the Captain knew too, that the folk-ways were too strong. The affair was passed over and, in fact, when one of the watchmen suffered a heart attack in September, Charlie kept me on till Armistice Day, a wholesome object lesson to the Fire Captain. I carried on my graduate work during the days.

My last few weeks on the job, the nights were getting pretty chilly, and I had instructions from Charlie to keep the space-heater on all night. "I'm always cold when I come in at eight o'clock," he said, "so keep things good and warm for me, Hood." I promised him that I would. When I went off the job for the last time, on the cold morning of November the 11th, Charlie nodded to me curtly.

"We'll be seeing you, Hood," he said, his sharp little eyes looking all around the office to see that things were in good order. And then, amazingly, "Take care of yourself." I nodded silently and, leaving the Yard behind me, I started for home.

I only ever saw them once more. Four years later I was on Richmond Street on Midsummer's Day, going in to be interviewed by Jack Kent Cooke for the editorship of *Saturday Night*, a job which I had no business applying for and didn't expect to get. As I came abreast of the Consolidated Press Building, my throat constricted and I stopped in my tracks.

For there they all were, Mitch's gang, lounging around a dozen open bays, waiting for the truck. There was Mitch, grinning as cheerfully as ever, Gummy hobbling idly around on a cane, Bill Tennyson, who recognized me and came over to say hello. And there, parked across the street, was a new green International quarter-ton and in it, gripping a pipe between his teeth and puzzling out a roll of plans, sat Charlie. Everything was just the same; they were all the same and would always be the same. I said a word or two, jokingly, to Tennyson, and then he went away.

I glanced at the sky; it was a hard blue and there wasn't a cloud to be seen. I squared my shoulders and went inside to my doomed-to-be-mutually-unsatisfactory interview. And it struck me after it was over, that silly interview on which Jack Cooke wasted half an hour of his time and his indubitable charm, that I'd be wiser not to try for impossibilities but to set down records of things possible, matters like these, tales of the way one man paid for his education in the bad old, good old days before the creation of that warm featherbed for talent, the Canada Council.

THREE HALVES
OF A HOUSE

East of Kingston the islands — more than eleven hundred of them — begin to sprout in and all around the ship channel, choking and diverting the immense river for forty amazing miles, eastwards past Gananoque, almost down to Stoverville. But a third of the continent leans pushing behind the lakes and the river, the pulse, circulation, artery, and heart, all in one flowing geographical fact, of half the North Americans, the flow we live by all that long way from Minnesota to the Gulf.

Saint Lawrence's Gulf, martyr roasted on a gridiron, Breton saint, legend imported by the French to name the life's current of a hundred million industrious shore-dwellers, drinking the water, lighting their houses by it, floating on it in numberless craft. "Seas of Sweet Water," the Indians called the lakes, and to the east the marvellous Saint Lawrence with the weight of the American Northeast inclining to the Gulf.

So the channel must be cut, though the islands press against the current in resistance, cut sometimes through needles' eyes and wearing deep, deep, through solid pressed ancient rock a hundred and fifty feet down, two hundred, icy cold ten feet below the surface. A holidaying swimmer floats up half-frozen in the narrow channel from a shallow dive, swept forty feet downstream in three seconds by the drive of the current, lucky to catch an exposed tree-root at the edge of a corroded island and haul himself ashore, the water sliding and driving beneath him two hundred feet down to the anonymous rock.

Try to swim upstream, brother, at Flowerlea! And feel yourself carried backwards through your best stroke, feel yourself whipped out of yourself as the river pulls at your thighs, hauling you down away eastwards as though you were falling helpless down a chute. Then grab at the skeletal roots, hang on, swing in the water and ride an eddy ashore! Fight the weight of eleven states and half of Canada, something to think about swinging on your sodden shredded branching root while fifty feet away — not an inch more — a ship seven hundred and fifty feet long glides ghostly past, soundless, what a thing to meet on a holiday beach! Not a thing to swim too close to, glistening black walls rising out of the water above you like an apartment building — SCOTT MISENER on the bows and the name of the line reading backwards to the stern in letters twice your height, swimmer, and not a sound from the ship, the current moving the ship as easily as it moves you. A deckhand leans incuriously at the rail, lifting a friendly hand, and is gone, whirled away eastwards while he lowers his arm.

SCOTT MISENER, ERIKA HAMBURG, TOSUI MARU, BRISTOL CITY, MOOREMACGLEN — they hail from everywhere, upper lakers, tankers, the few remaining canallers, ocean-going freighters built by thrifty Danes for the lakes trade, drawing twenty-seven feet precisely, up and down all day and all night with their myriads of sirens sounding the whole range of the tempered scale. The shipmaster confers anxiously with his pilot through the forty perilous miles, threading needle after needle. At Flowerlea the channel is so narrow the summer cottagers can lean over and assess the deck-hands' breakfast bacon. In the fall the last of the cottagers sit around their barbecue pits with a liner in the front yard, the shipmaster pacing about above them, cursing them and their hotdogs, the handiest things to curse. He is afraid of the Flowerlea channel, so narrow, and of the weight of water astern hurrying him along, the navigation season waning and his insurance rate about to jump skyhigh if he doesn't clear the locks by the appointed day.

Late last autumn a shipmaster drove aground off Stoverville at the end of the season; he lost the closing date at the locks and passed the winter iced into the river with a ruined cargo. Each day the sailors walked to Stoverville over the three feet of ice, but the captain, a ruined man, brooded in solitary humiliation all winter in his cabin. He was never seen in Stoverville, although hysterical cables addressed to him arrived daily from Oslo.

He was unlucky, mistrusted his pilot, didn't know the river, hated it, and the river ruined him. He missed all the signs, the waning of the islands, the widening of the channel, the three trees — tamaracks with fifty feet of bare trunk and perky coronas on top — that stand on the promontory west of Stoverville. Making his move to starboard towards the New York shore minutes too late, he felt the current drive his bows so deep into the river bottom he knew he'd never haul her off. He stared at the three tamaracks all winter, counting them and counting them and there were never more than three. This summer, in Oslo, he killed himself.

The tamaracks mark the end of the islands, the beginning of the river's free run from Stoverville to the Atlantic, nothing in the way but the mammoth new locks, then Montreal, Quebec, wider and wider until you can't see across, at last the sleety Gulf. But at Stoverville the river's freedom is a newborn thing, the mass of water has just begun to run, eroding, finding the fastest way down. At Stoverville it's hardly two miles across.

Over there on the New York shore are the old resort towns, fading now, the gingerbread hotels coming down, their gilt furnishings sold off. Now and then a welterweight contender trains here and sometimes a powerboat regatta invites the curious. But the real tourist money goes to Europe or Montego Bay and the old millionaires, who found their way upstate in the seventies from Saratoga, are dead and gone. Between Watertown and Plattsburg, back a few miles from the river, there's nothing. An Army camp, a NIKE site, trees and woods and dunes and the snow belt. And that's it.

On the Canadian side there's Highway Number Two, the worst main highway in the world, with the small river towns dotted along it — Kingston, Gananoque, Stoverville, Prescott — dreaming their dreams dating from the eighteen-thirties of a prosperity which never came. Yet they sleep there along the shore waiting for things to pick up when the hundred and fifty years' slack season shall be over, an occasional coal-boat putting in and water-buses running thrice-daily tours of the islands up to the bridge and back.

Twenty miles north of the riverfront strip the towns begin to shrink in size — Tincap, Newboro, Athens; the farms are scrubbier and smaller and hillier. You still see television aerials but now the rocks begin to stick up through the thin topsoil and you are into the Laurentian Shield with a rocky uninterrupted thousand miles clear to James Bay of round old rock, polished by the last Ice Age. Saint Lawrence again but this time choking off life, not conferring it. And from this hinterland, from the little towns like Athens, people have been moving back down to the shore for sixty years, as soon as they broke their first ploughshares on the intractable rock humping up out of the hillsides. They come back to Stoverville and cherish their disappointments, the growth of their numbers limited by their situation between the river and the rock, the same smooth incredibly ancient rock which beds the river. Life and power flowing beside them and old impregnable rock, out of which nothing can be forced to grow, above them northerly, so they come back one by one into Stoverville from Athens and the other little towns, and here they fashion their lamentations.

"They are painting the house," says Mrs. Boston vengefully, "green and white, so unoriginal. In the thirty years we lived there they never offered to paint it for us. Your father painted every four years, always green and white. He spent thousands on paint, and always the best white lead — money I might have had, or you, that has been absorbed into the walls of that place, with the Hungarians living in the other side."

"Hungarians must live somewhere," offers her daughter mildly.

"But need they live in Stoverville?"

"They make their choices unknowingly, the poor things," says Maura even more mildly, "and I suppose once here they must abide by the original choice. I must say, I think it kind of Grover to let them have the other half of the house."

"Most Stoverville people won't rent to them," says Mrs. Boston, "but Grover does, in preference to me."

"You didn't wish to stay in the smaller half. You had the opportunity."

"Taken a crumb from his table you mean? Accepted the little half, and maintained it as we did the other side for thirty years until they pushed us out? That I should lie awake alone in my bedroom in the smaller half and listen to Grover rattling around on the other side of the wall! I don't know what he proposes to do with all that space, with just the two of them. Ellie, of course, doesn't go out any more, the poor unfortunate. Can you imagine it? Cooped up all day with that man, green and white? The very least he could have done would be to choose new colours. Green and white were your poor father's choice. Heavens, what it cost! It was that dirty grey, you know, but of course you couldn't know. You weren't five years old when we moved in. Your father had to pay for three coats of the finest white lead to cover the grey, the way they'd let it all run down, Ellie's crazy mother!"

"Was she crazy? I remember her."

"Undeniably, and her husband was worse. I tell you, Maura, there's a warped streak in that family somewhere, and it comes out, it comes out. I'm glad they're not my blood relations."

"But they were father's."

"He was a medical doctor, my dear," says Mrs. Boston stiffly, "and he understood these things."

"These things?" asks Maura delicately, lighting a cigarette. She does not wish to pass the entire weekend in these debates.

"Tubercular bone," says her mother, "congenital physical rot. And other things than physical for they've never been right, none of them. Your father at least went from Stoverville to the city, though in the end he came back. But these clumps of Phillipses — they move from the farm to Athens looking for the easy life, and from Athens to Stoverville believing they've found it because they don't have to rise at four in the morning. My dear girl, they infest the countryside, they're a positive plague."

"I'm one-eighth Phillips," says Maura with a faint apprehension.

"But you live in Montreal where medicine and science have penetrated."

"The weak drive out the strong, Mother," says Maura, "like vines driving through rock. You're better off away from either side of that house."

"But to be driven out! And then those Hungarians." She smiles maliciously. "I understand that the ships' sirens terrify the Hungarians, wake them up at night. They think of Russians, I expect." The sirens give everyone dreams, thinks Maura to herself, everyone in Stoverville. *Paaaaarrrrrrpppp.* I am going to starboard. *Mmeeeuuuhhhhhhhh.* I am going to port. They never collide in the channel, even at Flowerlea; they do not astonish us with freakish mishaps, sinkings, or groundings except for a single dead Norwegian, but they are all around us in the night. *Paaarrrrpppp. Mmeeeuuuhhhhh.* They give us dreams in Stoverville, but in Montreal, though they circumnavigate the city, no one notices them. I forget the river in Montreal or in New York while here it rolls through me, head to thighs. I dreamt as a child in my bed at the dark top of the house, their house, probably Grover's room now; he can't sleep with Ellie, she'd never allow it, so virginal at sixty. Poor Grover Haskell, sleeping in my bed in my room listening first to the sirens and then to the cranky breathing of his good wife who has done everything for him, according to Mother, subjugated herself entirely to him, yielded him up her house, for of course it's her house, not his — she's legitimately Phillips. I'm only one-eighth, thank God, so she has the house that was my father's by temporary arrangement because he was only a quarter Phillips and had the house at a nominal rent while Ellie, disguised as Mrs. Grover Haskell, tried to get away to other parts of the world. What is a nominal rent? Daddy never complained of the rent and we knew that one day the Haskells would drift back, allowing Daddy the smaller side while they all four enjoyed a polite Stoverville retirement, except that they didn't. Daddy is dead and Ellie is dying slowly and Grover is not. And my dear mother flourishes.

The year we moved in, the tamarack trees were lonely and beginning to lean over the river, earthfall exposing part of their roots on the promontory's side.

"We'll fix that," Daddy said, and he poured in cement and fill, so the trees are still there. "Those tamaracks look lonely," he said to me, "and they're important. Did you know, Maura," he said, talking as if I were an adult, "that sailors talk about our three trees from here to Duluth?" Then he told me where Duluth was and I remember it still. I think of the sailors at the Lakehead, talking about our three tamaracks, only of course they were never really ours at all but belonged first to her grandfather who was the town saddler and unsuccessful, and then the town magistrate and tubercular. Then they were her mad father's, whom I knew, who moved into the little half of the house to rent us the larger and to resent us — we paid a nominal rent for the privilege of becoming an object of resentment to that frustrated painter.

When I was five he would beckon to me from his side of the porch to show me his new picture, clutching at his brushes with arthritic paws and aiming unsteadily to pat me where he had no business to. "It's a schooner, Maura, do you see?" he said, pulling at the frill on my sleeve. "It's a schooner on the river."

"I like the steamers, Uncle Wallace," I said, and he changed colour, "but I can't help it, I like them."

"This is a schooner, don't you see?"

"But I like the steamers' horns better."

Then Ellie came onto the porch, calming the morning with her still face. She picked up her father's pencils which were rolling hastily away along the porch towards the shrubbery and, handing them to him, kissed him while he stormed at me.

"The child's difficult, Ellie! She abuses my pictures. Everyone always does, everyone but you." She patted him and was silent, listening to his vacuities and smiling secretly at me from her still face around her lashes, drawing her father's sting as he went on rebuking me, not directly — he said nothing to me directly, but he let me hear. "My house, my house. I let them have my house, which I love, and their child must criticize. Let her stay on her side of the porch. Edward Boston is a young fool and his wife is malicious. When I asked him what was the matter with me, he declined to say, the coward — he knows all right but he daren't say. Only he sends his little girl around the corner of my house to make sure that my hands aren't right, that they shake, that my schooners look like steamers because I can't hold my pencil straight, a poor old man; they laugh at me. I'll raise his rent!"

Sitting on the arm of the deep chair in which her father crouches, mouthing his poison, she smiles sweetly along her lashes at me, frightened and trembling, five years old, misunderstanding it all because my father, young and poor as he is, worries about rent, cement and fill and the three trees.

"Look at the new white paint," I wail, starting to cry. "Daddy painted your old house for you." But old Mr. Phillips can't hear as he begins to slide into a soothed nearly senile sleep. Ellie tucks his blanket around him, watches him slide away, and takes me by the hand, walking me back around the corner of the porch to our front door.

"I only said I like the steamers. I didn't mean to make him mad."

"It's all right, darling, he's an old man. It's nothing you've said, he's an old man. He's been disappointed and he's sick."

"But he'll be all right, won't he?"

She stands with me at the door to our half of the house. We look through the screen into the hall, and at the back of the house my mother bustles, moving kitchen furniture with a cheerful scraping noise.

"He'll be all right soon," says Ellie full of comfort, placing her hand on her forehead and drawing me down after her onto the porch swing which rocks gently with a creak of chains as we look into each other's eyes, hers the Phillips eyes, rapt, violet, staringly intense, and her face so sweet and still, mine the brown eyes my mother imported into the family, round and direct, eyes I hated as a child, so agate-like and unblinking, my mother's and mine, not glancing and vivid like Ellie's. All at once she hugs me and whispers secretly: "I wish you were mine."

I am appalled by the notion. "I belong to Daddy."

Ellie kisses me briskly and for a moment we stare together at the tamarack trees on the point. "We love our fathers," she says absently, and turning gives me again her ineffable saint's gaze, visionary, violet, preoccupied. "Find your mother, sweetheart," she tells me, and I trot into the house vaguely disappointed.

"If you were not such an intractable mule," says Mrs. Boston, fixing her agate eyes in a persuasive stare, "you might do well in Stoverville. There are four distinct pieces of house property you might inherit if only you'd be nice to people." She holds up her fingers, beginning to itemize them. "There's our house, to begin with."

Maura emerges from her reverie, balking at this projected death-watch which jerks her suddenly over nearly thirty years to her pallid present prospects. What had been the frill on the arm of a child's frock becomes a table-napkin across which she's thrown a suddenly adult arm, plumper and hairier than a five year old's.

"I've stayed away too much."

"Then come home more often!"

"This is home? Pardon me, mother, but the only thing that brings me to Stoverville is you. And this isn't your home, any more than Montreal is mine. You weren't born here."

"It has grown into my home. The thought makes me weep sometimes now that your father is three years dead."

"You don't go back to your birthplace." Maura hopes to make a point.

"I do not. Nobody there remembers me or my family. We're obliterated. If I have any home, which is dubious, it's here in this crazy town beside these damned ships."

"What's the matter with the ships?"

"They're getting bigger and bigger. I don't know where it'll stop. It was never like this before."

"It's the new locks," says Maura. "The big ships used to stop at Montreal."

"You're past thirty, Maura," says Mrs. Boston. "Do you imagine that Montreal will provide you with a home?"

The faintest enlivening blush dabbles Maura's cheek as she folds and re-folds a table-napkin in her hands. "I meet men of my own age at the studios," she says reluctantly, "and you never can tell."

At this indecency her mother recoils, her life's scheme all at once readjusted. "You do not think of marriage?"

"I think of it all the time," says Maura, crossing her legs irritably, "all the blessed time and I wish somebody would ask me."

"A particular somebody?"

"Since you ask, yes." And then she grows defensive. "You were close to thirty when you married."

"But not past it."

"Thirty is no immutable barrier. Women past thirty have married before this, and will again."

"You mean that you will?"

"Given the chance!"

"Then think," says Mrs. Boston, adapting her tactics, "of the uses of our home as, perhaps, a summer place. Right on the river, a most desirable location."

"I thought that you disapproved of the location."

"I should disapprove less," says Mrs. Boston with regal dignity, "were the house legally mine."

"Ah!"

"There is no need to be ironic, Maura. I am your mother, after all, and I have your best interests at heart."

Maura thinks this over solemnly, seeming from her attitude to fancy a world in which fewer people have her interests more personally at heart. Identification with her interests, not cool appraisal of them, is the desideratum.

"I mean to protect you from Grover and his schemes," her mother pursues. "It is not a Haskell house but a Phillips house, and should come to you. He has no children."

"The poor man," exclaims Maura involuntarily.

"Poor man, bosh!" says her mother with energy. "He never wanted them and Ellie gave in to him everywhere. Poor woman, rather! You know what Grover Haskell is, a monster of selfishness."

"Has he the necessary wit and tenacity?"

"All that he requires. You remember how, three years ago, he brutalized me, wouldn't even let me go on clinging to the littler half, but insisted on what he calls 'a proper rent, considering.' That man had the audacity to ask me to move your father's workbench from one side of the cellar to the other as soon as it was convenient, the tools still warm from your father's palms. I offered him a cord of firewood that your father had stored in the cellar to dry — out of the purest neighbourly feelings — and he told me, as curtly as you please, that he meant to use the fireplaces ornamentally, to fit into their new decor."

"It is their house."

"It is her house, and will be yours, I tell you, if you behave properly. She must know by now what he is, even though she's sick. She has sacrificed everything to him, given in to him, followed him through all his failures like a saint, I tell you, like a saint, and now she's sick. She has never been well since her father died."

"When I was small," says Maura, remembering it with deep pleasure, "I really loved Ellie, she was so good."

"She is a saint. But queer, Maura, queer. She has these visions, you know." And Mrs. Boston begins a rambling account of the phenomenon called "second sight" by means of which events occurring at a distance in space or time may be observed directly by persons with certain particular spiritual equipment. "Your father's great-aunt had it," she concludes, "and I believe Ellie has it, or something like it. When I go to see her I have the feeling that there are other people in the room."

"You go to see her?"

"I do."

"When Grover isn't there?"

"He is always there. He daren't leave her, you know, for fear she'll die while he's out of the house. But I'll grant him one good grace. He usually goes down to the cellar while I'm there. Can't face me, I suppose."

"How does she act?"

"Well, she wanders. She is sorry for what Grover has done to me; she is ashamed for him. She always asks for you, Maura, and you should go to see her, if only out of kindness."

"What's the matter with her?"

"She was always a visionary and religious, and of a self-sacrificing temperament, first her mother and father and now

Grover. She seems to have gone completely religious, speaking in symbols and so on. She has been reading Revelation, I suspect."

"I'll go and see her," concedes Maura, not entirely reluctantly.

Peering through blue spruce and cedar, Grover studies the three tamaracks from the porch, trying to ignore the river below them which he has never loved, and assessing fondly the intervening plantings which have suddenly devolved upon Ellie and himself. When he courted his wife thirty years ago, coming fearfully to the old house because of the uncertainties of her father's temper, pausing on the front walk and studying the movement of dragon-flies in the porch light, he had wished that it were warmer near the house, that someone might fill the space between the house and the tamaracks with sod, flowers, and other trees and vines, to take away something of the starkness of the house's situation, perched icily on the promontory unscreened from the winter reflection off the river's ice. He had been lucky. For most of the subsequent thirty years while he and Ellie tried their luck in Kingston, Belleville, and for a few desperate years in Toronto, they had had a caretaker who paid them for the privilege of keeping the property up and even improving it. A nominal rent but one that paid the taxes — and the house was regularly painted, heated, kept immaculate, ventilated, and the memory of Ellie's terrible father gradually expunged.

Grover had liked Dr. Boston, though he couldn't abide his widow, and had tried to deal fairly with him. He had accepted forty dollars a month from him for nearly thirty years and had never counted it up to see what it came to. Edward had had inexpensive living accommodation and had been free to improve the property for his own comfort if he wished. That the Bostons had come in time to think of his house as immutably their home was certainly natural enough but scarcely his concern. That Dr. Boston had planted and cultivated a perfectly splendid arbor, a lovely jungle of carefully selected trees and shrubs between the house and the tamaracks, that he had installed a darkroom and a new furnace, was his business, done with his eyes wide open. However much the Bostons might have resented their involuntary move into the smaller half of the house, they had been given fair — and more than fair, generous — notice of the event.

Grover knew that the enforced move was not what had killed Dr. Boston, although his death had certainly followed hard upon the move, coming three months after it had been accomplished. He didn't see why he shouldn't do over the house the way he and Ellie wanted it; but Dr. Boston had inconsiderately died and he was to be blamed for it, he supposed. The doctor's widow didn't seem at all interested to see what he was doing with so much unaffected delight to remodel the place according to his own ideas of comfort, his and Ellie's.

But they had gone ahead the way they'd planned during long years of living in inconvenient apartments, dreaming of the wealth of space they'd one day enjoy. They had saved, made sketches, eyed antique stores and scrabbled around in back-concession attics looking for curly maple antiques, planning at length to reclaim the house and furnish their half with their painfully acquired and stored treasures. And when the time had come, despite Edward's inconvenient death, they had gone ahead with their plans. He had done it all for Ellie, had followed her in all things, had done everything for her because he'd cherished her and had hoped to exorcise the crazy memory of her parents.

"Softening of the brain" they'd called it when her mother died, the state of medical science being what it was in the Stoverville of thirty years ago. Like mother, like daughter, and like father too. For Ellie was going the same way — he saw it though he tried not to — and here he was in a house, or half of a house, that wasn't really his, had never been and would never be his, that now, watching her sicken prematurely, he hated and didn't want any more. He couldn't get out of the house, not even to go to the grocery store; there were razor-blades lying loose in the medicine cabinets, mirrors that might be broken and wrists to slash. He didn't know what they might come to and couldn't leave the house for fear.

Light, not sunny light but cold white light, slides through the cedars and spruce, giving them a smoothy suave waxy sheen. Standing on the south corner of the porch, catching sharp gleams off the water through the glancing leaves, he wishes now that they'd kept their last mean apartment in Toronto. It is with a sense of felt physical release that he watches Maura push through a hole in the fence, enter the arbor, and make her way automatically, without pausing to place her feet safely on the springy over-grown turf, along winding paths aslant the promontory, coming to pay her call. Now he sees the oddness of their situation: Maura is a native of the place who's fled and felt no ties; he's an outsider who's gotten stuck fast inside. "Softening of the brain." They have a hospital of a kind these days in Stoverville and he knows what they'll call it.

Then the shrubbery shakes and parts and Maura stands revealed, mounting the sagging porch steps. Behind her the small green and copper leaves whisper together and, all at once, miles away to the east, a steamer hoots once.

"Hello," they say together, almost strangers, and again, with embarrassment, "well, hello!"

"I'm here for the weekend," she says with constraint, "and I wanted to see you both."

"You can see her," he says, forever an inside outsider. How the girl resembles her father! More and more he feels sixty-five and out of place.

"How is she? You know, Grover, she's the one person in Stoverville … well … she was a second mother to me."

"I wish we'd had children."

"You do?"

"Certainly I do. But her health was never up to it."

"Oh! How is she now?"

"Lying down," he says abruptly, with a shiver. "Come along, I'll show you what we've done with the house." He pauses. "You don't mind our doing it over, do you?"

"Of course not. It's yours, after all. But how *is* she?"

She won't be diverted, it seems. "When her mother died, you remember, it was the same thing. But they've a new name for it now, which sounds a little better."

"Most people said that old Mrs. Phillips was out of her mind."

"She wasn't, exactly. They called it 'softening of the brain.' That's the trouble. It runs in the family, don't you see?"

"But there isn't any such thing."

"They don't call it that any more. Now they call it," and he rattles off the foolish phrase, "premature senility induced by an insufficient supply of oxygen to the brain." Her circulation is poor and the artery which feeds the brain is narrowing — like hardening of the arteries — I don't recollect the medical term."

"Sclerosis?"

"That's it. Arteriosclerosis affecting the brain, and hypertension too, of course. She's all right sometimes but she wanders. And then she was always religious, you know."

"Is she still?"

"Worse, if anything. Good heavens, Maura, she sees ghosts. According to her the house is full of people. And I — I can't see anything. I tell you, it's frightening. Come inside, I'll show you around. You see on the floor here in the hall I've installed a parquet, black and white squares. Very cheerful, don't you think?"

He conducts her around the familiar rooms, exhibiting them in their novel guise. Soon they hear a voice calling from upstairs. Ellie's.

"I'm coming down. I've a housecoat here," she warbles with enthusiasm, "and I've had a good sleep, Grover."

She has no footfall. She had been soundless in Maura's memory, never letting the floorboards announce her coming. She had floated around her unfortunate father and mother like a creature from another world, a wraith. Now she floats down the quiet staircase more impalpable than ever, her face bloodless, her hair gone silver, white white white, like someone who lives in the river, Maura thinks, like somebody made of water. She stretches out her arms and floats along, singing that thin melody. What happens in her head, does she hear anything? She doesn't look at you but over your shoulder, seeing things beyond and to one side of you. Poor Grover. No wonder he's afraid that the house is full of people who can't be seen or heard. Her gaze closes around and behind you like water, and you aren't solid.

"My dear child," says Ellie moving soundlessly over the black and white squares while Maura, entranced, feels but doesn't see Grover melt away out of vision bound for his workbench, to feel the cutting edges of his chisels and wonder about them.

The two women embrace and Ellie is so weightless that Maura can hardly feel her hug. She, poor chunky brown-eyed girl, solidly there, whoever else vanishes, feels as if she's tearing an invisible tissue of air as she follows Ellie into the drawing room. So she takes good care to sit facing her across the room, not relishing the idea of that disturbing weightlessness at her side.

"You're always the same girl," says Ellie, plucking at the sleeves of her flowered housecoat with birdlike hands, blue in the veins, crooked fingers locked in an immutable grasp, "and I thank God you've got your mother's eyes and not ours."

Her own eyes can't be still but rove desperately around the room.

"I'm embarrassed for myself and Grover," she says. "I feel as though we've wronged you, although I'm thankful he feels nothing of it, the dear man, I don't believe he knows what's going on." All at once a nervous tic starts up in her left cheek and she straightens her spine, sitting up abruptly on the sofa.

"He showed me the river of the water of life, clear as crystal," she says, blinking.

There is just nothing to be said to this for apparently she has left lucidity behind her, putting Maura in the position of an unwilling witness to a personal collapse. How can she get out, what can she do? There is nothing to do but sit there and make conversation during the rare lucid intervals.

"Seven stars and seven gold crowns, seven tapers, three trees, three thrones," says Ellie, shivering slightly. Then she shakes herself and tries to fix her eyes on Maura. "Grover wouldn't understand, would he?" she begs, and launches into the unforgettable.

"The house is full of gods," she begins, "all around us, gods and the dead. I saw my father yesterday, staring hatefully at the parquetry, and he told me that he didn't understand or like it, finding it bad taste and confusing to the eye. He told me not to marry and I wouldn't listen. I refused to listen though he told me from my cradle upwards. I couldn't bear children though I wanted them so. I mustn't transmit my milky brains to them and yet I tried and tried because Grover wanted them so. They warned me against Grover, both of them. He'll never understand, they said, he'll never guess and you mustn't tell him. And yet our children might have been saved from it, if the doctors knew all they claimed, instead of letting my father go to his grave in the belief that he'd lost his mind."

"Naturally I meant to marry Edward. We were born in the same month to the same family, and outside the forbidden degrees of kindred by a hairsbreadth. He might have helped me and there'd be no question about the house. Because he was a physician, don't you see, and could have stopped me before I came this far. You'd have been my child and you *are* my child though you won't admit it." She glares almost directly at Maura, just missing her eyes.

"*There* he is," she says flatly, "sitting beside you, your father." And Maura vainly resists the motion of her head which assures her that the three-years'-dead man is not there at all.

"I see him. The house is full of him, twenty-eight years of him, poor Edward. He lived his soul into this house and *there* he is."

"He's dead," says Maura, speaking for the first time in minutes.

"Don't stare at me with those hard brown eyes. They don't belong to you. God knows I wanted children and where am I now? A sick old woman being kept a prisoner by a stranger who won't let me alone. I know. He's afraid, afraid." She spreads her palms over her cheeks and smooths the twitches out. "Do you like the way we've changed the house?"

"I think it's all lovely, Ellie," says Maura, crossing the room and taking her by the arm, helping her to her feet. "I've been through it all with Grover. It's all lovely." She leads the other woman into the hallway.

"Are you leaving?"

"I think so. I told mother I'd be home for lunch. Perhaps I can come over Sunday night."

"And then you go back to the city? You'll have children, Maura, I know it. You're going to be married, aren't you?"

At this prescience, Maura shudders. "I hope so," she admits, kissing a dry cheek, "and please take good care of yourself."

As she pushes the yielding shrubbery aside, as it whistles softly around her, she hears Ellie call: "It comes to Grover or to you, and soon, soon." And she resolves to herself that it can't possibly come to her.

"Oho!" says Mrs. Boston with delight of a kind. "Oho, oho! I told you, didn't I?"

"You told me something, but not all that," says Maura, utterly exhausted.

"She must have been having one of her bad days."

"All her days must be like that," reasons Maura tiredly. "She can't have any good days if she's as bad as that."

"It's partly assumed, you know."

"Oh, mother, for goodness' sake! She's dying. She can't reason."

"The poor woman," says Mrs. Boston with real compassion, "and so she said that it would come to you or Grover."

"Yes."

"She must have meant the house."

"Oh, that and everything else."

"There's nothing else to inherit."

"You don't know. You don't know."

"There could be no two people more hard-hearted, Maura, than you and Grover Haskell!"

"Why do you dislike him so much? You should be grateful to him."

"For heaven's sake, why?"

"Oh, I don't know," exclaims Maura, petulantly. "Perhaps because he got her out of the way. He's not a malicious person at all. I like him. I pity him."

"And well you may," says Mrs. Boston, "because he's caught, there's nothing he can do. He hoped for years to get his hands on our house and now he hasn't got it — it's got him. He caught a shark."

"I'll make a prediction," says Maura grimly, "and I want you to remember it. If Ellie dies and leaves the house to him, as I hope to God she does, you, Mother, will be over there three nights a week playing cards with him within six months."

Mrs. Boston springs to her feet and begins to pace up and down the narrow bed-sitting-room which comprises the bulk of her small apartment. She doesn't resemble her daughter, at this strained point in their relationship, nearly as much as usual. She shows in her walk and in the defiant toss of her head how completely she knows that there can be no estrangement between them; she can trust Maura.

"My God, how right you are," she confesses with a full agitation, crushing a hand over her neat straw-coloured hair. "Of course I will be. Out of idle curiosity, you believe, and loneliness." She turns briskly to Maura. "I know mine is not a dignified position. I'm quite aware of what people say."

"People don't say anything, as far as I know."

"You live in Montreal."

"But I hear what goes on."

"Nonsense! You haven't been here in a year." As Maura protests, her mother puts up a grim hand for silence. "I'm not reproaching you. In your place I should do exactly the same. Stay away! Hunt some man down! You can do it!" She smiles at her daughter because they love one another. "I sound like a cheerleader."

"I've nearly done it," grins Maura sourly, "and Ellie knew all about it before I said a word."

"She has radar," says Mrs. Boston, "or second sight."

"You would adore your grandchildren if you had any."

Mrs. Boston winces. "My God, how right you are," she exclaims for the second time in three minutes. "Have some!" she begs. "Start the whole thing off again. I don't want you to be the last. We never meant you to be the only child."

"I've borne it," says Maura.

"So you see me over at Grover's house, playing double solitaire with him, the two of us mourning our barrenness, all alone and exactly like each other. Very well, I've admitted that I don't hate the man. He's not a wicked man, I suppose."

"It's simply that you're both caught."

"He's caught worse than I am, Maura. He's planned and worked to possess himself of that place. He used to come to us on vacations, and when we had him in to dinner he'd look around as if it were already his. You could see his mind at work, estimating the cost of new velour drapes for the dining room. I used to laugh."

"Not tactful, anyway."

"No, he's like an infant. He has no notion of tact. And then he asked us to move while your father was sickening with what killed him, though I will admit in justice that he couldn't have suspected it, and then he moved in and Ellie began to collapse, and now she's gone the way her parents did and at the end they were both suicidal."

"Her mother killed herself."

"So she did, so she did. He knows it and he can't get out; the house owns him." It is complete triumph for her. "When your father and I lived there, we owned the house, we had tenants in the smaller side and we mailed their rent to Ellie. But we had the house, it didn't have us. Now the only people he can find to live in the smaller side are the Hungarians, because everybody in town who can speak English is afraid to go near the place. So the house has him. Oh, I'll go and see him," she concludes.

But Maura is ahead of her, already at the door. "You and he can do the gardening together," she observes. "You can preserve Daddy's arbor. Grover loves the trees."

"You don't have to go down there tonight. You're under no obligation and you've got a train to catch."

"It's been a long weekend," says Maura, "but I told him I'd drop in."

"Well, don't *you* get caught!"

It was a promise fairly made, though one which she repents of as she walks along the shore towards the three tamaracks which guide her into the leafy paths. The river is flat calm, an end-of-autumn calm, with here and there faint smudges on the surface moved by the slight breeze. Maura pauses for a moment before she pushes through the hole in the fence to study the river and wish it altered. What we need here, she decides, are docks and cranes, smoke, drydocks, slipways, a hundred factories; the river has strangled Stoverville. Straining her eyes she looks across to the desolate New York banks behind which, she remembers from the motor trips of childhood, there is nothing. Daddy promised me bears on the New York side but there weren't any, not a bear. Oh God, she allows herself for one second to reflect, oh God, I want children. I want two children.

She pushes through the hole in the fence, remembering the afternoon she caught her party frock on a nail in this same board, sneaking home late from a birthday party by her secret route. She looks for the hole in her frock and the red splash of the rust but there isn't anything there at all, and up she goes along the path to where Grover stands in the twilight on the sagging steps, anxiously looking out for her, with his hands outstretched to help her through the leaves.

"The husband," he begins shakily as soon as he can see all of her, "is not really a blood relation of the wife, is he? That is, he isn't related to her. After all I come from another part of the province and I'm not a Phillips. Am I?" He insists on it. "I'm not a blood relation to my wife, am I? Because this place should be transmitted according to the blood strain and should naturally come to you, all to you. I tell you, Maura, and I'd tell your father too, if I could, that I never wanted this place for myself. We have no children and you're part Phillips. You should get it, and I'm going to see that you do. Because I don't want it. I never did, not for myself. Never. For two whole days Ellie has been going over and over the matter, threatening to leave the place to me, but I told her that I'm not a blood relation. I'm related to her by marriage only."

"That's a closer relation."

"No, it isn't," he shouts, leaping like a trout in a still pool. "This place belongs to you through your father and I've insisted to Ellie for thirty-six hours that she leave it to you. I've torn up her will. I'll make her write another before she gets worse." He shudders. "I'm afraid she's going to die soon." It has gone from twilight to dark through his speech.

"Where is she now?"

"She made me move her bed. She's lying down in your room at the top of the house. She's exhausted. I tell you, Maura, when she isn't herself she says things you wouldn't believe. I don't mean to complain or bear tales but I've never seen her like this and I can't bear it." His throat dries up and closes convulsively and then miraculously opens for his final words as they pace up and down hand in hand on the creaking porch.

"You'll take it, won't you? Look at me, Maura, please! It's so dark I can't see you." He turns to face her and throws his arms stiffly wide apart. "It's yours. It's yours! I don't want it. You will take it, won't you? Take it, take it, please!"

Her little bedroom is dark like a virginal cell in a cloister and Ellie lies on her bed with arms folded on her chest like an effigy on a tomb, her mind whirling with the effort to concentrate and control her thoughts. At regular intervals of maybe thirty seconds her body arches rigidly, projecting her torso and thighs forward and upward into the air, drawing her lower back up off the sheets, the cramped writhings of a woman in childbirth forcing her thighs apart and racking her abdomen, and all to no purpose. But her consciousness doesn't record these convulsions as the stream of her ideas grows fuller and stronger, swollen by many tributaries, sliding faster and faster. *Ppaaaarrrrpp.* I am going to starboard. *Mmeeeeuuuuuhhhh.* I am going to port. SS *Renvoyle* upbound with package freight for Toronto. MV *Prins Willem Oranje* downbound for the locks and the Atlantic, half-laden, looking for a full hull at Quebec City. The horns grow louder and merge with the full downward current of her thoughts. They were never like this before, never so loud, never right in my room like this. The ships are swimming over me and the river through me and the horns are inside my head muddling my ideas all together with the family downstairs in the living-room with the captain from Oslo, seven stars and seven coronets and the three trees on the point for Christ and the two thieves hanging so straight and dark in the twilight on the darkening water I am going to starboard under the stars on the current down the river down east past the Plains of Abraham, farther, to where the river yawns its mouth eleven miles wide, invisibly wide, bearing me away at last to the darkness, the sleety impassible impassable Gulf.

AFTER THE SIRENS

They heard the sirens first about four forty-five in the morning. It was still dark and cold outside and they were sound asleep. They heard the noise first in their dreams and, waking, understood it to be real.

"What is it?" she asked him sleepily, rolling over in their warm bed. "Is there a fire?"

"I don't know," he said. The sirens were very loud. "I've never heard anything like that before."

"It's some kind of siren," she said, "downtown. It woke me up."

"Go back to sleep!" he said. "It can't be anything."

"No," she said, "I'm frightened. I wonder what it is. I wonder if the baby has enough covers." The wailing was still going on. "It couldn't be an air-raid warning, could it?"

"Of course not," he said reassuringly, but she could hear the indecision in his voice.

"Why don't you turn on the radio," she said, "just to see? Just to make sure. I'll go and see if the baby's covered up." They walked down the hall in their pajamas. He went into the kitchen, turned on the radio and waited for it to warm up. There was nothing but static and hum.

"What's that station?" he called to her. "Conrad, or something like that."

"That's 640 on the dial," she said, from the baby's room. He twisted the dial and suddenly the radio screamed at him, frightening him badly.

"*This is not an exercise. This is not an exercise. This is not an exercise*," the radio blared. "*This is an air-raid warning. This is an air-raid warning. We will be attacked in fifteen minutes. We will be attacked in fifteen minutes. This is not an exercise.*" He recognized the voice of a local announcer who did an hour of breakfast music daily. He had never heard the man talk like that before. He ran into the baby's room while the radio shrieked behind him: "*We will be attacked in fifteen minutes. Correction. Correction. In fourteen minutes. In fourteen minutes. We will be attacked in fourteen minutes. This is not an exercise.*"

"Look," he said, "don't ask me any questions, please, just do exactly what I tell you and don't waste any time." She stared at him with her mouth open. "Listen," he said, "and do exactly as I say. They say this is an air-raid and we'd better believe them." She looked frightened nearly out of her wits. "I'll look after you," he said; "just get dressed as fast as you can. Put on as many layers of wool as you can. Got that?"

She nodded speechlessly.

"Put on your woollen topcoat and your fur coat over that. Get as many scarves as you can find. We'll wrap our faces and hands. When you're dressed, dress the baby the same way. We have a chance, if you do as I say without wasting time." She ran off up the hall to the coat closet and he could hear her pulling things about.

"*This will be an attack with nuclear weapons. You have thirteen minutes to take cover,*" screamed the radio. He looked at his watch and hurried to the kitchen and pulled a cardboard carton from under the sink. He threw two can openers into it and all the canned goods he could see. There were three loaves of bread in the breadbox and he crammed them into the carton. He took everything that was wrapped and solid in the refrigerator and crushed it in. When the carton was full he took a bucket which usually held a garbage bag, rinsed it hastily, and filled it with water. There was a plastic bottle in the refrigerator. He poured the tomato juice out of it and rinsed it and filled it with water.

"*This will be a nuclear attack.*" The disc jockey's voice was cracking with hysteria. "*You have nine minutes, nine minutes, to take cover. Nine minutes.*" He ran into the dark hall and bumped into his wife who was swaddled like a bear.

"Go and dress the baby," he said. "We're going to make it, we've just got time. I'll go and get dressed." She was crying, but there was no time for comfort. In the bedroom he forced himself into his trousers, a second pair of trousers, two shirts and two sweaters. He put on the heaviest, loosest jacket he owned, a topcoat, and finally his overcoat. This took him just under five minutes. When he rejoined his wife in the living room, she had the baby swaddled in her arms, still asleep.

"Go to the back room in the cellar, where your steamer trunk is," he said, "and take this." He gave her a flashlight which they kept in their bedroom. When she hesitated he said roughly, "Go on, get going."

"Aren't you coming?"

"Of course I'm coming," he said. He turned the radio up as far as it would go and noted carefully what the man said. "*This will be a nuclear attack. The target will probably be the aircraft company. You have three minutes to take cover.*" He picked up the carton and balanced the bottle of water on it. With the other hand he carried the bucket. Leaving the kitchen door wide open, he went to the cellar, passed through the dark furnace room, and joined his wife.

"Put out the flashlight," he said. "We'll have to save it. We have a minute or two, so listen to me." They could hear the radio upstairs. "*Two minutes,*" it screamed.

"Lie down in the corner of the west and north walls," he said quickly. "The blast should come from the north if they hit the target, and the house will blow down and fall to the south. Lie on top of the baby and I'll lie on top of you!"

She cuddled the sleeping infant in her arms. "We're going to die right now," she said, as she held the baby closer to her.

"No, we aren't," he said, "we have a chance. Wrap the scarves around your face and the baby's, and lie down." She handed him a plaid woollen scarf and he tied it around his face so that only his eyes showed. He placed the water, and food in a corner and then lay down on top of his wife, spreading his arms and legs as much as possible, to cover and protect her.

"*Twenty seconds*," shrieked the radio. "*Eighteen seconds. Fifteen.*" He looked at his watch as he fell. "Ten seconds," he said aloud. "It's five o'clock. They won't waste a megaton bomb on us. They'll save it for New York." They heard the radio crackle into silence and they hung onto each other, keeping their eyes closed tightly.

Instantaneously the cellar room lit up with a kind of glow they had never seen before, the earthen floor began to rock and heave, and the absolutely unearthly sound began. There was no way of telling how far off it was, the explosion. The sound seemed to be inside them, in their bowels; the very air itself was shattered and blown away in the dreadful sound that went on and on and on.

They held their heads down, hers pushed into the dirt, shielding the baby's scalp, his face crushed into her hair, nothing of their skin exposed to the glow, and the sound went on and on, pulsing curiously, louder than anything they had ever imagined, louder than deafening, quaking in their eardrums, louder and louder until it seemed that what had exploded was there in the room on top of them in a blend of smashed, torn air, cries of the instantly dead, fall of steel, timber, and brick, crash of masonry and glass — they couldn't sort any of it out — all were there, all imaginable noises of destruction synthesized. It was like absolutely nothing they had ever heard before and it so filled their skulls, pushing outward from the brainpan, that they could not divide it into its parts. All that they could understand, if they understood anything, was that this was the ultimate catastrophe, and that they were still recording it, expecting any second to be crushed into blackness, but as long as they were recording it they were still living. They felt, but did not think, this. They only understood it instinctively and held on tighter to each other, waiting for the smash, the crush, the black.

But it became lighter and lighter, the glow in the cellar room, waxing and intensifying itself. It had no colour that they recognized through their tightly-shut eyelids. It might have been called green, but it was not green, nor any neighbour of green. Like the noise, it was a dreadful compound of ultimately destructive fire, blast, terrible energy released from a bursting sun, like the birth of the solar system. Incandescence beyond an infinite number of lights swirled around them.

The worst was the nauseous rocking to and fro of the very earth beneath them, worse than an earthquake, which might have seemed reducible to human dimensions, those of some disaster witnessed in the movies or on television But this was no gaping, opening seam in the earth, but a threatened total destruction of the earth itself, right to its core, a pulverization of the world. They tried like animals to scrabble closer and closer in under the north cellar wall even as they expected it to fall on them. They kept their heads down, waiting for death to take them as it had taken their friends, neighbours, fellow workers, policemen, firemen, soldiers; and the dreadful time passed and still they did not die in the catastrophe. And they began to sense obscurely that the longer they were left uncrushed, the better grew their chances of survival. And pitifully slowly their feelings began to resume their customary segmented play amongst themselves, while the event was still unfolding. They could not help doing the characteristic, the human thing, the beginning to think and struggle to live.

Through their shut eyelids the light began to seem less incandescent, more recognizably a colour familiar to human beings and less terrifying because it might be called a hue of green instead of no-colour-at-all. It became green, still glowing and illuminating the cellar like daylight, but anyway green, nameable as such and therefore familiar and less dreadful. The light grew more and more darkly green in an insane harmony with the rocking and the sound.

As the rocking slowed, as they huddled closer and closer in under the north foundation, a split in the cellar wall showed itself almost in front of their hidden faces, and yet the wall stood and did not come in on top of them. It held and, holding, gave them more chance for survival although they didn't know it. The earth's upheaval slowed and sank back and no gaps appeared in the earth under them, no crevasse to swallow them up under the alteration of the earth's crust. And in time the rocking stopped and the floor of their world was still, but they would not move, afraid to move a limb for fear of being caught in the earth's mouth.

The noise continued, but began to distinguish itself in parts, and the worst basic element attenuated itself; that terrible crash apart of the atmosphere under the bomb had stopped by now, the atmosphere had parted to admit the ball of radioactivity, had been blown hundreds of miles in every direction and had rushed back to regain its place, disputing that place with the ball of radioactivity, so that there grew up a thousand-mile vortex of cyclonic winds around the hub of the displacement. The cyclone was almost comforting, sounding, whistling, in whatever stood upright, not trees certainly, but tangled steel beams and odd bits of masonry. The sound of these winds came to them in the cellar. Soon they were able to name sounds, and distinguish them from others which they heard, mainly sounds of fire — no sounds of the dying, no human cries at all, no sounds of life. Only the fires and cyclonic winds.

Now they could feel, and hear enough to shout to each other over the fire and wind.

The man tried to stir, to ease his wife's position. He could move his torso so far as the waist or perhaps the hips. Below that, although he was in no pain and not paralyzed, he was immobilized by a heavy weight. He could feel his legs and feet; they were sound and unhurt, but he could not move them. He waited, lying there trying to sort things out, until some sort of ordered thought and some communication was possible, when the noise should lessen sufficiently. He could hear his wife shouting something into the dirt in front of her face and he tried to make it out.

"She slept through it," he heard, "she slept through it," and he couldn't believe it, although it was true. The baby lived and recollected none of the horror.

"She slept through it," screamed the wife idiotically, "she's still asleep." It couldn't be true, he thought, it was impossible, but there was no way to check her statement until they could move about. The baby must have been three feet below the blast and the glow, shielded by a two-and-a-half-foot wall of flesh, his and his wife's, and the additional thickness of layers of woollen clothing. She should certainly have survived, if they had, but how could she have slept through the noise, the awful light, and the rocking? He listened and waited, keeping his head down and his face covered.

Supposing that they had survived the initial blast, as seemed to be the case; there was still the fallout to consider. The likelihood, he thought (he was beginning to be able to think) was that they were already being eaten up by radiation and would soon die of monstrous cancers, or plain, simple leukemia, or rottenness of the cortex. It was miraculous that they had lived through the first shock; they could hardly hope that their luck would hold through the later dangers. He thought that the baby might not have been infected so far, shielded as she was, as he began to wonder how she might be helped to evade death from radiation in the next few days. Let her live a week, he thought, and she may go on living into the next generation, if there is one.

Nothing would be the same in the next generation; there would be few people and fewer laws, the national boundaries would have perished — there would be a new world to invent. Somehow the child must be preserved for that, even if their own lives were to be forfeited immediately. He felt perfectly healthy so far, untouched by any creeping sickness as he lay there, forcing himself and the lives beneath him deeper into their burrow. He began to make plans; there was nothing else for him to do just then.

The noise of the winds had become regular now and the green glow had subsided; the earth was still and they were still together and in the same place, in their cellar, in their home. He thought of his books, his chequebook, his phonograph records, his wife's household appliances. They were gone, of course, which didn't matter. What mattered was that the way they had lived was gone, the whole texture of their habits. The city would be totally uninhabitable. If they were to survive longer, they must get out of the city at once. They would have to decide immediately when they should try to leave the city, and they must keep themselves alive until that time.

"What time is it?" gasped his wife from below him in a tone pitched in almost her normal voice. He was relieved to hear her speak in the commonplace, familiar tone; he had been afraid that hysteria and shock would destroy their personalities all at once. So far they had held together. Later on, when the loss of their whole world sank in, when they appreciated the full extent of their losses, they would run the risk of insanity or, at least, extreme neurotic disturbance. But right now they could converse, calculate, and wait for the threat of madness to appear days, or years, later.

He looked at his watch. "Eight-thirty," he said. Everything had ended in three-and-a-half hours. "Are you all right?" he asked.

"I think so," she said, "I don't feel any pain and the baby's fine. She's warm and she doesn't seem frightened."

He tried to move his legs and was relieved to see that they answered the nervous impulse. He lifted his head fearfully and twisted it around to see behind him. His legs were buried under a pile of loose brick and rubble which grew smaller toward his thighs; his torso was quite uncovered. "I'm all right," he said, beginning to work his legs free; they were undoubtedly badly bruised, but they didn't seem to be crushed or broken; at the worst he might have torn muscles or a bad sprain. He had to be very careful, he reasoned, as he worked at his legs. He might dislodge something and bring the remnant of the house down around them. Very, very slowly he lifted his torso by doing a push-up with his arms. His wife slid out from underneath, pushing the baby in front of her. When she was free she laid the child gently to one side, whispering to her and promising her food. She crawled around to her husband's side and began to push the bricks off his legs.

"Be careful," he whispered. "Take them as they come. Don't be in too much of a hurry."

She nodded, picking out the bricks gingerly, but as fast as she could. Soon he was able to roll over on his back and sit up. By a quarter to ten he was free and they took time to eat and drink. The three of them sat together in a cramped, narrow space under the cellar beams, perhaps six feet high and six or seven feet square. They were getting air from somewhere although it might be deadly air, and there was no smell of gas. He had been afraid that they might be suffocated in their shelter.

"Do you suppose the food's contaminated?" she asked.

"What if it is?" he said. "So are we, just as much as the food. There's nothing to do but risk it. Only be careful what you give the baby."

"How can I tell?"

"I don't know," he said. "Say a prayer and trust in God." He found the flashlight, which had rolled into a corner, and tried it. It worked very well.

"What are we going to do? We can't stay here."

"I don't even know for sure that we can get out," he said, "but we'll try. There should be a window just above us that leads to a crawl-space under the patio. That's one of the reasons why I told you to come here. In any case we'd be wise to stay here for a few hours until the very worst of the fallout is down."

"What'll we do when we get out?"

"Try to get out of town. Get our outer clothes off, get them all off for that matter, and scrub ourselves with water. Maybe we can get to the river."

"Why don't you try the window right now so we can tell whether we can get out?"

"I will as soon as I've finished eating and had a rest. My legs are very sore."

He could hear her voice soften. "Take your time," she said.

When he felt rested, he stood up. He could almost stand erect and with the flashlight was able to find the window quickly. It was level with his face. He piled loose bricks against the wall below it and climbed up on them until the window was level with his chest. Knocking out the screen with the butt of the flashlight, he put his head through and then flashed the light around; there were no obstructions that he could see, and he couldn't smell anything noxious. The patio, being a flat, level space, had evidently been swept clean by the blast without being flattened. They could crawl out of the cellar under the patio, he realized, and then kick a hole in the lath and stucco which skirted it.

He stepped down from the pile of brick and told his wife that they would be able to get out whenever they wished, that the crawl space was clear.

"What time is it?"

"Half-past twelve."

"Should we try it now?"

"I think so," he said. "At first I thought we ought to stay here for a day or two, but now I think we ought to try and get out from under the fallout. We may have to walk a couple of hundred miles."

"We can do it," she said and he felt glad. She had always been able to look unpleasant issues in the face.

He helped her through the cellar window and handed up the baby, who clucked and chuckled when he spoke to her. He pushed the carton of food and the bucket of water after them. Then he climbed up and they inched forward under the patio.

"I hear a motor," said his wife suddenly.

He listened and heard it too.

"Looking for survivors," he said eagerly. "Probably the Army or Civil Defense. Come on."

He swung himself around on his hips and back and kicked out with both feet at the lath and stucco. Three or four kicks did it. His wife went first, inching the baby through the hole. He crawled after her into the daylight; it looked like any other day except that the city was leveled. The sky and the light were the same; everything else was gone. They sat up, muddy, scratched, nervously exhausted, in a ruined flower bed. Not fifty feet away stood an olive-drab truck, the motor running loudly. Men shouted to them.

"Come on, you!" shouted the men in the truck. "Get going!" They stood and ran raggedly to the cab, she holding the child and he their remaining food and water. In the cab was a canvas-sheeted, goggled driver, peering at them through huge eyes. "Get in the back," he ordered. "We've got to get out right away. Too hot." They climbed into the truck and it began to move instantly.

"Army Survival Unit," said a goggled and hooded man in the back of the truck. "Throw away that food and water; it's dangerous. Get your outer clothing off quick. Throw it out!" They obeyed him without thinking, stripping off their loose outer clothes and dropping them out of the truck.

"You're the only ones we've found in a hundred city blocks," said the soldier. "Did you know the war's over? There's a truce."

"Who won?"

"Over in half an hour," he said, "and nobody won."

"What are you going to do with us?"

"Drop you at a check-out point forty miles from here. Give you the scrub-down treatment, wash off the fallout. Medical check for radiation sickness. Clean clothes. Then we send you on your way to a refugee station."

"How many died?"

"Everybody in the area. Almost no exceptions. You're a statistic, that's what you are. Must have been a fluke of the blast."

"Will we live?"

"Sure you will. You're living now, aren't you?"

"I guess so," he said.

"Sure you'll live! Maybe not too long. But everybody else is dead! And you'll be taken care of." He fell silent.

They looked at each other, determined to live as long as they could. The wife cuddled the child close against her thin silk blouse. For a long time they jolted along over rocks and broken pavement without speaking. When the pavement smoothed out the husband knew that they must be out of the disaster area. In a few more minutes they were out of immediate danger; they had reached the checkout point. It was a quarter to three in the afternoon.

"Out you get," said the soldier. "We've got to go back." They climbed out of the truck and he handed down the baby. "You're all right now," he said. "Good luck."

"Goodbye," they said.

The truck turned about and drove away and they turned silently, hand in hand, and walked toward the medical tents. They were the seventh, eighth, and ninth living persons to be brought there after the sirens.

HE JUST ADORES HER!

Right after that chilling fall of snow the week before Christmas, some young ladies from Miss Harker's School arranged a funny little reunion at The Cow Barn on Route 4 outside Farmington, nothing formally sanctioned by Miss Harker herself, she having been dead these many years, just a small party for a dozen baby graduates in their earliest twenties, who still wanted to see one another. The occasion was casual, even vulgar, a corner of the public dining room with three tables under a dim light, indifferent food and bad cocktails and an insane waiter, but as Betsy Warren remarked they had gotten it up themselves without interference from the older generation — no teachers, no parents, and no husbands or suitors either — and they were happy, perhaps unknowingly, to be thoroughly vulgar in public; they laughed merrily and sang songs and it was a gay evening.

Elizabeth Lovelace led the singing, standing with a corner of the table sticking into her neat and lovely stomach, gently waving her cocktail glass, slopping little waves of gin against the rim and never spilling a drop. She had played that way as a child, with her bowl of oatmeal and a big spoon. In the dark light of the dining room with her eyes fixed intently on the liquid in her glass, her gentle pipe of a singing voice spinning out a Tom Lehrer number, she looked, as children do, so extraordinarily happy and good that staid older diners gazed at her and whispered their pleasure.

At Miss Harker's, Elizabeth had been the object of many friendly small jokes because of her figure, which was exactly a model size, a perfect eight. Sometimes, even after her marriage, the girls referred to her in those terms, laughing as they paid her the sisterly compliment.

"And this is Elizabeth Lovelace, Harry. She's a perfect eight."

And Harry would stare at her rapturously, and jokingly exclaim: "Loveless?"

She always laughed at that. "It's spelled L-o-v-e-l-a-c-e," and the boy would laugh with her, and then she'd say proudly, "Mrs. Lawrence Lovelace. Larry's brother was quarterback of the Harvard freshmen this year, until he broke his arm." And the boy's face would fall slightly as he turned away.

At the little reunion Elizabeth was wearing the latest consequence of her figure, a dark pink wool afternoon dress from Scaasi which her mother had wangled for her. It had been made for the famous (the notorious) Lenny Faber to wear at a private showing, and had never been sold. Because only someone with Liz's figure might wear the dress, her mother had snatched it out of the workroom for her birthday, for a hundred and twenty-five dollars.

She therefore looked, and knew she looked, physically better than anyone else in the room, which was usual, but she also looked better clothed, which was unusual because she and Larry had no money, and neither did her mother who was on a fixed alimony payment from the estate, nor her non-earning bum of a father, nor Larry's parents. Mr. Lovelace was an associate professor of sociology at Wesleyan and earned the appropriate salary.

She and Larry were constantly in an equivocal position; they had probably gotten married two or three years too early. Neither of them had completed a degree. Elizabeth had had one year at Sarah Lawrence and poor Larry had had to go to Syracuse for a variety of interesting reasons, mostly connected with a two-year artistic trip to Mexico, which he had unwisely taken at seventeen. Now they were a year married, with expensive inclinations and small means of gratifying them. It was therefore with a sense of triumph, even joy, that Elizabeth stood up before her friends and led them in song. She knew perfectly well that they sometimes felt sorry for her and discussed her unfortunate circumstances; but nobody at the party looked like her.

It was wonderful how the dress supported her and gave her confidence; it had a lovely smooth-finished weave and fell in a fluid line. She had taken a chance and worn no girdle, and the effect was perfect, one of understated opulence, so she laughed and joked and sang and had a marvellous time. She drank six cocktails made of gin and something else, she wasn't sure what, an action which was very far outside her normal range of behaviour. When it was time to leave she stood beside her car for twenty minutes before she felt confident enough to drive.

Her car was a monstrous old convertible with holes in the top which she kept around because it was essential to her job. She was selling memberships in a home-freezer-and-food plan for a Hartford company and sometimes had to drive a couple of hundred miles in a single day. She earned between three and four thousand a year, most of which she had put into her decor. She had fixed up that old apartment until it was stunning and unrecognizable in its transformation. Now she was composing a portfolio of arty angle-shots which she would send around, perhaps to Lord and Taylor in West Hartford, perhaps to some of the smaller, newer, New York decorators, to see if she could arrange an apprenticeship. She felt that she had ideas of her own which would in time be valuable.

When her head stopped expanding and contracting in the cold night air, she climbed carefully into the car, started the engine and waited for it to warm up; she grew cold and approximately sober sitting there. All at once she shivered violently and she began to think that she might get chilled, sitting in the cold, so she worked her way out of the parking lot, climbed the hill up Route 4, going out of Farmington, and headed home into the darkness. The car's large engine soon began to heat the interior. It grew warm and warmer still, and she felt less chilled and feverish and more comfortable. She stared fixedly along the highway into the darkness, alternately buoyed up and excited, and then cooled and depressed, by the evening. Halfway home, the highway narrowed between the snowbanks and slid into a long avenue of trees, hardly lighted, and she felt herself to be burrowing comfortably into a long serpentine tunnel. She let herself slide and nod and it grew very quiet in the car, and then the road widened shockingly and the lights came back and she was home to Hartford, sitting up with a start. Though she often let herself drowse at the wheel, she had never so far had an accident. She slammed the car's nose into a snowbank that served as her parking space and scuttled into the building. In five minutes she was sound asleep in her slip, in their enormous bed that almost filled the small bedroom. On the back of the closet door, swinging gently to and fro on the hanger, her lovely dress whispered to her. The rustling, and the "ting … ting … ting" of the hanger, were the last sounds she recognized.

The drug house for which Larry travelled handled two major lines, a headache tablet and an ointment for hemorrhoids, and the name of the second item never sullied Elizabeth's lips, she refused to admit its existence, always referring to the company by its imposing name. Fairbanks Laboratories paid Larry seventy-five hundred a year to cover a southern New England sub-territory, providing him with a car and regular sales assistance from the home office. They had told him not to bother making calls during the week before Christmas; by that time druggists were cutting inventory to meet the January slump. He took the week off reluctantly because the enforced vacation would cut sharply into his December earnings. When he got a chance to clerk in a bookstore during the rush, he grabbed it and picked up an unforeseen hundred bucks.

He found that he much preferred the retail book trade to travelling in hemorrhoids, and the owner of the store told him that he was the quickest and most adaptable assistant he'd ever had. At the end of the week he told Larry that he'd be glad to take him on full time, but that he couldn't pay an adequate salary. The best that the bookstore could manage during the regular season was eighty-five a week, with the prospect of small raises if the business flourished.

Naturally Larry couldn't take a job like that; he'd lose his car and about thirty-five hundred a year, and Elizabeth wouldn't hear of it. As things were, she said, they were barely keeping their heads above water on the ten thousand they made between them. How could they possibly manage on that much less? He had to concede that she was perfectly right — there was nothing to be done about it. But he enjoyed the work so much! He could have handled the ordering and billing, and the windows, and freed the owner to cultivate personal contacts in the local market.

If only he had a little capital, say fifteen thousand! The store was due for a big increase in inventory and its owner would have welcomed a congenial partner. But what can you do, if you haven't got it? Anyway Larry was looking around, planning to take some courses in merchandising and market analysis to complete his degree and escape from headaches and hemorrhoids forever. The local schools were no good: New York was the place. If he could only get down to New York, he would have his choice of a bewildering range of courses in any one of a dozen institutions.

He spent the hundred he made at the bookstore on Elizabeth's Christmas present. She wouldn't let him display his books on their shelves because they were mostly dog-eared paperbacks and textbooks. She said she wanted some fine bindings, not very many, to arrange artfully on the few shelves which intruded on her interior. He had checked the second-hand bookstores and had been able to pick up four sets: *Newton on the Prophecies* (1736), *Reid's Essays on the Active Powers of Man* (1781), *Ossian* (1798), and

The Junius Letters (1791). He had them cleaned and oiled, and the gold stampings renewed, and they looked like new.

They had been delivered to the bookstore for him. He sat around for a while, after nine o'clock, talking to the proprietor, thinking regretfully that he would have to hit the road again, Tuesday of next week. They totalled up the day's sales, rearranged the stock for the next day, swept up, locked the safe, and then went around the corner with the mail in four bulky sacks. They had a couple of cups of coffee in a cafeteria next to the Post Office. It was past twelve when Larry got home, carrying his valuable books in a heavy parcel. He was sure that Elizabeth would love the books; they were exactly what she had in mind for the shelves and were obviously expensive. He suspected secretly that they looked like those books in liquor advertisements, all shining blue and red and gold, and forever unread. He didn't want his wife to make a foolish mistake but he trusted her taste and judgment.

He swung his parcel onto the hall table and rubbed his fingers where the twine had galled them. It was very quiet, a single night light shining and no sound of life from their apartment which surprised him because Elizabeth's car was in its proper place and there was a light on in the living room. He could hear an infant's nighttime wailing, far away at the very top of the house. He listened for a minute to the frightened cries and felt sorry for the hungry baby. Then, as he didn't have a key, he knocked quietly at the door.

"Elizabeth," he said sharply, "let me in." He thought that she'd locked the door because of burglars. "Sweetie," he murmured cajolingly, "it's me, Larry, let me in, will you?" But there wasn't an answering sound.

She can't be mad at me, he thought, I haven't done anything. He looked around craftily, giving nothing away, and then called her by their most intimate pet-name, which a burglar wouldn't know.

"Poopsie-pie," he called softly, blushing a little. He hoped nobody else heard him. "Poopsie-pie, open up, it's me, Larry." He knocked harder at the door, beginning to feel tired and a little annoyed. He remembered that she'd gone out with Betsy Warren, and a couple of other girls only slightly less affected and fake.

"Poopsie-pie, let me in please, open up!" It occurred to him all at once that she was probably passed-out-drunk; he imagined Betsy Warren and her pals with genuine detestation.

The narrow hall echoed with his soft solicitations. In the opposite apartment Francis Rosebery and his wife heard the fatuous whispers and the knocking. They usually went to bed just after eleven but had been watching "Mr. Hulot's Holiday" on Channel 3, a special treat. By twelve-thirty, though, they decided that they couldn't sit up any longer. Francis had an enormous pile of legislation on his desk; he had to go through it tomorrow and his eyes would be tired. He was standing in the foyer in his dressing gown when he heard Larry come in and begin to beg for admission. The walls were embarrassingly thin; he didn't care to listen to these entreaties and endearments; he was past all that. That a man might call a woman "Poopsie-pie" and mean it, even a man ten years his junior, made him squirm. He called his wife "Paula" to her face, and referred to her to others as "my wife" or "Mrs. Rosebery." Once in a very long while, when one of them was reminded of the child they'd lost, or of the plain fact that they weren't able to have any more, he might address her as "dear."

He yanked nervously at the tassels on his dressing-gown, not wanting to stay up any later, and hearing unwillingly the appeals in the hall. The knocking grew louder and, as it seemed to him, more desperate. He would never so lower himself, even with a girl like Mrs. Lovelace whom he sedulously ignored when they met in the hall, averting his eyes and darting into his apartment. The bitch, he thought, the bitch, she makes him pay for it twice over. He heard Paula calling from the bedroom.

"Who's that," she asked sleepily, "is it Larry?"

"Who else would it be?" snapped Francis. Then he lowered his voice and added, "She's locked him out."

"Maybe she's asleep," said Paula sensibly, "ask him if he'd like to call her on our phone." It was her suggestion thought Francis, as he drew open the front door and called to Larry. He noticed the dejected slump of the shoulders and the desperation behind the boyish grin.

"Forgotten your key?" he asked kindly. "You can use our phone." He hated to see Larry's eyes but couldn't take his own away. "I guess your wife's dropped off."

"That's right," said Larry, picking up a parcel from the hall table. "Wouldn't want to lose these," he mumbled, setting them down beside the telephone table. "Thanks, Francis, I hope I didn't wake you up."

Paula called from the bedroom. "We were just going, Larry, we hadn't gone."

"Hi, Paula," he said lamely, "I'll get her in a minute." He dialled and they could hear the phone ring loudly in the other apartment. "It's on the night table by the bed," he said, "if she doesn't hear that, she must be stinking." He laughed shortly. "She went to a party with some kids from school. I'll bet she drank gin, the idiot." The phone went on ringing.

"Let it ring," said Francis, deeply embarrassed, "and go and knock again."

Larry went and beat on his front door and finally there were noises and the ringing stopped. Francis grabbed the phone.

"Mrs. Lovelace?" he said, rather curtly, "hold on a second, here's your husband." He handed Larry the receiver.

"Elizabeth? Elizabeth? It's me, Larry. No, it's me, your husband. Oh, damn it, Liz, wake up, it's me." His voice grew shrill. "Come on now, wake up." He turned to Francis and said, "She hung up."

"Call her again!"

"I hate to disturb her. Maybe I could break a window."

"She's awake now. Try again!"

So he did, and he did, and he did, and at the fourth try she revived enough to roll out of bed and come to the door. She wasn't visible but nevertheless Francis felt his senses stir at the idea that she would be undressed.

"Good night, Larry," he said decently, traitorously, and closed the door.

The nosy bugger, thought Larry as his own door swung wide, the nosy bugger with his helpful advice, I've forgotten the books, but they can hide them for me. She wavered in front of him and he put his hands on her small hips, feeling their warmth delightedly through the gauzy slip. He kissed her with rapture, tasting stale gin.

"Imagine that," said Francis, lying chilly in his bed, "can you imagine his letting her push him around like that? I'd kick her bottom, that's what I'd do."

Paula breathed deeply and said nothing.

"I was so embarrassed for him, I couldn't look at him," said Francis reflectively, "why do you suppose he lets her get away with it?"

"He just adores her!" said Paula suddenly. "I think it's lovely, the way he treats her."

"Uxorious," said Francis, peaceful at having given the symptom a name, "uxorious, that's a word I've never used before, and it fits. I think she uses him, nobody has a right to use anybody else." He thought of introducing a discussion of the forms of the categorical imperative but decided that it was too late. The bedroom was cold; his eyes were sore; he was overworked these days.

Francis and Paula were the same age, thirty-four, but had lost their illusions at different rates of speed. He had a good partnership in a distinguished Pearl Street law firm and his greatest responsibility was his position as Chief lobbyist for the building trade in the State Legislature. But he was more than a hireling; he prided himself on his sturdy independence of lifestyle. He was a great amateur of the pre-classical music of the eighteenth century, the compositions of Telemann, Vanhal, Hasse, "English" Bach, Abel, the Mannheim school, and the innumerable partners of Metastasio. He possessed the sole manuscript in this country of Salieri's great work, *Axur, re d'Ormus*, a document which he had laboriously transcribed in a Viennese archive, while Paula roamed restlessly around the city.

That the Roseberys had no children was a circumstance in which they alternately rejoiced and felt dismal. Paula had no work of her own beyond taking care of Francis. She dusted and arranged his music manuscripts, and his thousands of discs, and polished their apartment until it glittered, and at that she had much leisure to observe everything that went on around her. It was she who first noticed in the three or four weeks immediately after Christmas that Elizabeth Lovelace had vanished. Normally the two young women met daily in the hall; they would exchange cautious critical glances and each would reaffirm to herself the superiority of her own notions of chic.

Elizabeth had done her kitchen in a contact paper which simulated bricks with ivy growing out of crannies. She had hung copper pots and pans in a row, in ascending order of size, and there was a clock shaped like an enormous pocket-watch hanging above the pots.

Paula knew that you would find that sort of thing in the decorators' magazines every month, and she carefully avoided it. Instead she bought junk furniture from junk-shops and refinished it, spool cabinets, captain's chairs, commodes. She painted pictures and framed them and now and then bought a drawing or a water-colour, and the Rosebery's apartment resembled no one else's.

When they visited one another, Elizabeth and Paula acted like wild but cautious animals investigating unfamiliar but potentially habitable lairs — the smell of the species reassuring but the burrowing inartistic and misguided.

In two or three weeks Paula grew uneasy at not finding her competitor in the halls and in time her uneasiness communicated itself to Francis. Can he have strangled her, wondered Paula, and in unspoken trailing of his wife's meditations Francis thought to himself, I wouldn't blame him a bit, I'd defend him. They were inclined to be very hard indeed on poor Elizabeth, who was in New York looking for her apprenticeship.

She had gone with Larry's every blessing and encouragement, even his urging. They both felt (she more intensely than he) that if there was anything at all for her in the city, even if it only paid a little bit, that they might risk it without giving their relatives grounds for complaint. She departed for New York in a coarse olive-green wool, cowl-collared, sweater, black pants with a rather baggy seat, and one of those elaborately ragged and messy page boy haircuts, and could be found any day through January and February admiringly and beseechingly sitting in little display rooms, while poor Larry drove hotly up and down the hills of north-western Connecticut, swallowing anew every late afternoon his disappointment at the prospect of returning to their empty apartment.

She called him three or four nights weekly, which helped, usually calling just before he went to bed, sometimes when he was on the point of falling asleep. She would be bunking in with a girlfriend, or reluctantly passing three nights at her aunt's. She said nothing about when she might come back to Hartford; they had agreed that there would have to be hardships endured on both sides.

"I miss you, lover," she would whisper into the receiver. If she were at her aunt's, she would whisper so low that he could scarcely hear her.

"Speak up!" he would say impatiently, and she would giggle.

"You can't speak up when you're saying 'I miss you, lover.'"

Larry's hands shook so, during these chats, that he often flipped his cigarette into the bedclothes and then wasted telephone time searching for the smouldering butt.

"When are you coming up? Does it look like you might find something?"

"Oh, Larry, it's beginning to look promising. You know Ann and Michael Deshler, don't you?"

"God, yes!"

"Sweetie, they're going to open a shop themselves, and they want me to come in as an assistant."

"Will they pay anything?"

"Perhaps not at first."

"We couldn't afford it."

"Well, they might give me thirty-five dollars a week, for my time."

He brightened up at this. "We could swing it on that, if I can get a transfer. That's a hundred and forty a month. We could use it towards the rent."

"If I could make enough to look after the rent, would you come?"

"Oh, sweetheart, I'd come anyway." I shouldn't have said that, he thought. "Come on up, this weekend?"

"I can't possibly get away, honey. You come down!"

"Yes," he said, "I believe I will. Good night," he said, thinking happily about Saturday night.

She chuckled. "Dream about me," she commanded.

Falling asleep, Larry couldn't keep her image out of his mind. He remembered a cold night just after they were married, when he'd awakened to discover his arm hanging outside the covers, icy cold. Purely by reflex, he'd yanked the arm inside and slapped his frozen palm onto Elizabeth's bare belly. Instead of squealing, as he'd expected, she'd stirred slowly, and waking gave the dearest of soft sighs. Ever afterwards, remembering, his nerves had rung with pleasure.

He went down to the city that weekend, and the next, and then for three weeks he was too busy with his territory, and too tired when he came home on Friday to make the trip; the weeks stretched insensibly into months and before he knew it February was almost over. One day late in the winter he woke at his accustomed time to find that there had been a fourteen inch snowfall overnight. It would take him hours to shovel the car out and the parking lot hadn't been plowed. He decided to stay home and have a good rest, maybe stay in bed till noon and then do a little shovelling. But he was so used to getting up at half-past seven that he couldn't go back to sleep. Except for the narrow strip on which he lay, the bed was frigid — when he extended an arm or a leg towards Elizabeth's side he had to withdraw it instantly. Mumbling to himself, he rose and tottered around the apartment aimlessly. As the morning dragged by, the place grew to seem intolerably empty. He looked in the refrigerator for something to eat but found only an old dry piece of cheese, and a shrivelled lemon. He would have to struggle out to the corner for breakfast. At last he pulled on his clothes, washed his face, ran a comb carelessly through his sleep-tangled hair, he didn't bother to shave, and went into the hall to look for his rubbers. Francis Rosebery was standing in the hall, staring out the front door. When he saw Larry he gave a guilty start.

"No mail delivery today," said Francis morosely, "and it makes me laugh. 'Neither wind nor rain nor sleet nor hail nor whatever it is shall stay these couriers from the swift completion of their appointed rounds.' Hah! If one raindrop falls, the Post Office takes two days off."

Larry put his head out the front door to check the mailbox. "You're quite right," he announced, "he hasn't been around and I guess he won't." He sighed involuntarily. "I was expecting a letter." He wished he hadn't said it, for Francis' eyes popped open and shut in a curious way. "Anyway," he went on lamely, "I guess I'll go and get something to eat."

"Come in and have something with us," said Francis quickly.

"Thanks, Francis, but I don't think I'd better. I've got to pick up some things from the drugstore, and I'd better shop for groceries in case Elizabeth is here for supper." There was no prospect whatsoever of her being there but he didn't see why Francis had to know everything.

"We haven't seen much of her lately," said Francis plaintively. "She isn't sick, I hope."

"No," said Larry briefly, "she isn't sick." To himself he whispered other things. There was no need to tell the Roseberys anything. Let them think what they liked.

"Did your wife like the books?"

"What books?"

"Didn't you give her some books for Christmas, the ones we hid for you?"

"Oh those, yes. She liked them fine." In fact she had taken very little notice of them. Larry had put them out on the shelves after she'd gone. "She loved them," he said mendaciously. "I'd better get on my horse."

"Perhaps you could come in for dinner some night?" Francis almost said what he was thinking, that Larry must be desperately lonely, but stopped himself in time. He stood at the door, watching Larry stumble off through the drifts, and then he went dispiritedly inside. He hated winter weather; it made him feel prematurely old.

He sat in an easy chair in his living room, listening to his bones ache — he was certain that he could actually hear them clashing together. Presently Paula came out of the kitchen where she had been contemplating a gourmet cookbook. She threw him a look and decided to say nothing. Francis is in one of his moods, she thought with alarm, I wonder what's wrong? When he had to stay around the apartment for a whole day, he grew

FLYING A RED KITE

bearish and sometimes really disagreeable. But as she knew the
sequence of his moods better than he did himself, she found it
relatively easy to avoid downright quarrelling. She fixed a gay,
cheerful lunch, with a bowl of very hot split-pea and bacon soup
as the *pièce de résistance*; she served it up and waited for Francis to
tell her what was making him cross. He always brought it out if
she kept silence long enough.

He paddled moodily in his soup bowl, putting down his
spoon and taking it up as if reluctant to eat. It was his favourite
soup — he relished all hot soups. As he said, they made him feel
as though he were looking after himself, there was something
healing about hot soup.

"I'll bet anything she's left him," he exclaimed finally, looking
resentful.

Paula didn't have to ask to whom he referred.

"I saw him in the hall this morning," grumbled Francis, "and
he looked terrible. His face was grey, he hadn't shaved; his hair
was all standing up. He's like somebody in Conrad. The poor guy,
the poor little jerk!"

"I certainly haven't seen her around," said Paula. Until now
she had hesitated to draw any inferences however obvious, preferring to let Francis take the lead; he was said to be very good at
sifting evidence and cross-examination. "I used to see her all the
time when she was selling those home freezers. I wonder where
she is?"

"Reno," said Francis glumly, "or in Mexico getting one of
those quickie divorces, the little slut. I had her figured. I knew
she'd do something like this."

Paula thought of asking Francis why he disliked Mrs.
Lovelace so much. But as she knew that he wouldn't give her the
right answer, and as she hated to watch him deceiving himself,
she didn't put the question.

"I don't know why I dislike her so much," he said rather
startling her, "but I wouldn't be their age again for anything, not

172

for anything." He grinned sadly at Paula. "There's a lot to be said for middle age."

"We aren't middle-aged," said Paula hopefully, "and we won't be for another ten years. Thirty-four isn't old."

"It's old enough to be dried out," said Francis. Sometimes he exercised a perverse sense of parody on himself.

"Dried out?"

"Desiccated, *hortus siccus*," he said, with what he seemed to think a pleasing melancholy, "passionless."

Paula felt secretly offended and then was sorry, because he knew at once what she felt.

"I don't mean 'loveless,'" he said defensively, "I mean passionless. Not the same."

"They usually go together."

"Not with us."

"No," she admitted, "I suppose not. I don't know that we're any better off."

"Yes we are," he said positively, "because we're lazy people. To be passionate you've got to get yourself in shape, like a distance runner, and you've got to stay that way. You learn to exhaust yourself just as you break the tape. Larry has to keep himself in shape, otherwise he couldn't take what she hands out. He's rolling with the punches all the time."

"I wonder where she is."

"Reno," he said again, "or Mexico."

"I wonder if he hasn't walled her up in the cellar. She's been gone a long time." They looked sadly at each other. "How long," she put it into words, "how long do the neighbours let things slide before they begin to ask questions? A month, two months, and then an inspector calls."

"He wouldn't dare touch her, you said it yourself, he just adores her."

"That might incite him all the more." She wondered if she really believed it.

"Each man kills the thing he loves? I never did think there was a shred of truth in that, and I don't now. She's alive, all right, she's indestructible."

"I guess so," agreed Paula and the two of them began to eat their cooling soup, conserving its medicinal heat. Cold bones, thought Francis, cold bones.

He wondered and wondered at the complex feelings which their neighbours elicited in him, motives alternately homicidal and forgiving. When he thought of Elizabeth he always thought of the phrase "a punk kid" and then he hastily revised the phrase, trying to fit it to the facts of his feelings. He knew, and he supposed that Paula knew, that a woman like Elizabeth could still make his throat constrict and his pulse race, not because of her smooth buttocks and her always faintly traceable *mons veneris*, but by her fresh idiocy, her perfect unknowingness, her glad irresponsibility, some kind of childlike senselessness that made his head swim with the prospect of self-immolation she offered. You could fall into her and forget everything and that would be that, no more mimeographed bills for the Legislature, no more puttering around with music manuscripts, only slapping and clutching and giggling and quarreling and making up and not speaking for days and aching to speak and goo-goo eyes and babying.

How he hated all that, how he fled it, how he inflicted an Apollonian lucidity on Paula, he understood with every keen modification of clarity. A reputation as a skilled cross-examiner was not perhaps the best equipment to bring to an infatuation. He used to say to his wife, querulously, "Just remember that I have feelings, too."

He couldn't repress his reason, wouldn't apologize for it, was all horror at Larry's supineness, his allowing himself to be swamped by the flood of his wife's senselessness. Before I'd let my wife take off like that, he told himself, I'd chain her up. Thinking this, he couldn't help laughing. Nobody would ever chain Paula up; she didn't invite it. The ideas were inassociable. Paula was, what Elizabeth was not, rational, to an unusual degree in a woman. She had not been quite that rational when he'd married her, but then neither had he. And he didn't think her looks in the least impaired by her concepts. Though never precisely opulent, she was forever trim, the vaunted pride of her corsetiere, living proof of the efficacy of a good foundation garment; she continued, and would long continue, svelte and unimpassioning.

She went to the kitchen for the coffee, rubbing her forehead with the back of her hand — hard thought irritated her sinuses — feeling vaguely troubled and sorry for Francis. Little irregularities disturbed him so. He couldn't possibly know, she knew this with utter certitude, why he felt so drawn to the little Lovelace thing. Paula didn't care, not she, let him for Heaven's sake enjoy a little unappeasable lust somewhere, anywhere, so long as its object were safely in Mexico City. She longed so for Francis to enjoy himself; but he never enjoyed himself, his hobby, his work, his home, his holidays, herself. She couldn't draw him to her anymore, she reasoned him to her, and to do his consistency justice he came, smiling, when she thought the idea up.

No, I don't look as good as she does, at least not in the imaginable nude, thought Paula frankly to herself. I have angles now, where she has arcs and my breasts lapse a little where hers spring up and out, so who cares? In twenty years it will be all the same and then, poor Larry, his sedative will have worn off. Men need women like me for the long pull; these little rubbery things are good in their twenties, and then they're done. She took the trouble to look ahead for Larry and Francis, and made herself feel proud. At fifty, one would have a workable wife and the other a sick doll. In the end, she wondered, facing the problem out, which is better, the short run or the long?

What we had, we have, and we will have, and it's worth the short-term loss. She burnt her fingers picking up the Silex and went back to the living room.

"How do people survive divorces?" asked Francis aggressively, as she sat down. "Even people without any children?" When he heard what he'd said he winced, and looked his apology at her. They had been kindness and tact itself to each other on the question of children, and they were considering an adoption. He flushed perceptibly. "How can there be so many divorces? I only know three or four people who've been divorced. And they all tell me that it was complete hell, that they couldn't live through it again. How could they bear it the first time? Who get all these divorces anyway?"

"There must be a group of frequent repeaters," said Paula, "who bring the average up."

"The divorce-prone?"

"Exactly, people who shouldn't marry at all, like alcoholics."

His face was all dismay. "Do you think Mrs. Lovelace is like that?"

"She may be. She's certainly putting him through hoops."

"It's terrifying," said Francis, "it's a horror."

They contemplated together the consequences to society of the existence of such a group, the ravages, the underminings, the imminent decline and fall.

"How can they be so irresponsible?" said Francis the censor. "They get children and then dismember them psychologically."

"To be fair," said Paula, "the Lovelaces don't have any children."

"They might just as well. I'll bet they don't take any precautions. They wouldn't think twice about bringing a child into the world."

"Most people don't," said Paula, teetering on the brink of fairness.

"We would," said Francis, carried away with his reasonings, "in fact we did." Then he felt a stab of pain. "I'm sorry, dear. I'm honestly sorry."

"It's all right," she said. And they went wretchedly about their business.

★ ★ ★

The final snows of the winter kept them confined when they would sooner have been anywhere else than in the old apartment house. They kept bumping into Larry and thought again of asking him to dinner; but it seemed so condescending and inquisitive that they let the idea go, and he did not encourage the offer. To their eyes, he grew thinner, greyer, more and more anxious, older, more like themselves, less a boy, in short a brand from the burning. They kept hearing the "New World" symphony on Larry's phonograph, turned up very loud.

"I'll bet that was 'their song,'" said Francis. "Wouldn't you know?" And he thought comfortably of his recordings of Hasse and Stamitz.

"I noticed a whole row of whisky bottles on their windowsill this morning," said Paula.

"Can he actually be drinking to forget?"

"I don't know," she said, "but the bottles were there."

They had their romance all worked out, all configured to allow them to hate and despise Elizabeth, to pity and feel contempt for Larry. They allotted all the clichés and fastened on the neighbours every element of bathos that the situation suggested. It made them feel comfortable and hopeful until the Saturday afternoon when they encountered the Lovelaces in the hall. All day the snow had been melting, exposing patches of dirty mud and grass around the building. You could hear trickling water everywhere. At one o'clock the Roseberys decided to drive up to the Centre, not to shop for anything special, just to get out of the house. As they came into the hall, they heard a bumping sound and their neighbours' door flew open. Elizabeth came falling out backwards to land with a thud on the floor at their feet. She was decently covered in an enormous terrycloth bathrobe but plainly had nothing on underneath. Francis caught a momentary glimpse of ivory inner thighs and averted his head. She looked up at them and they looked down at her.

"We were wrestling," she said foolishly. Larry appeared in the doorway clothed, and approximately in his right mind.

"Go and put some clothes on, for God's sake," he said rejoicingly, "hello Francis, hello Paula."

"Hello," they said.

"Did Elizabeth tell you? She has a job in New York, decorating. She's been looking for this job all winter. And I've got a transfer to Westchester." He looked so happy that the Roseberys were a little mollified. "Do you want to buy our broadloom?"

"It wouldn't fit," said Francis absently, staring at Elizabeth as though she were a ghost. He'd never expected to see her again. She got to her feet, pulling the bathrobe around her a bit self-consciously.

"Maybe we can find an apartment we can fit it into," she said, "but I had it cut for this one." She shivered. "I'm cold," she announced.

Larry slipped his arm possessively around her. "Get your clothes on," he said, "we've got to drive to New York this afternoon." The two of them linked arms around each others' waists and wandered blissfully into their apartment. They turned on the threshold and looked at the Roseberys, their cheeks touching. "Goodbye," they cooed. They went inside and shut the door.

Francis almost stamped his foot, he was so upset. Turning on his heel he flounced into his own apartment and didn't come out again all weekend. Paula followed him, thinking various things to herself. When she caught up with her husband, he was deep in his armchair with a fixed glare on his face. "Wrestling!" he said. "God!" She could see that she would have to find something else for him to despise.

"Do you know," she hazarded, trembling, "we made that story up. That was all ours." She wanted to make him laugh if she could, but she didn't know how. "They're beautiful," she said. She wished that Francis trusted her that much. "What is it that you want, Francis?" she begged.

He went on bumping back and forth in the heavy armchair. "I don't know," he said, "I just want to have a good time." *Thump* went the chair. "Do you have to be stupid to be tranquil?" "Serene" and "tranquil" were his magic words, his absolutes, serenity and tranquillity the perverse unattainable objects of his lust.

NOBODY'S GOING
ANYWHERE!

Haggerty stood irresolutely in his workroom trying vainly to ignore the street noises which crowded through the windows, open for the first time this spring, Claudine, Bernard, Marisa, quarreling over tricycles, Brigitte's spaniel barking forlornly, puff of airbrakes from a bus on the corner, the Diesel roar as it hauled away, an alarming screech from a Volkswagen as a ball-chasing child just missed a fatal accident for the second time in three days. The street was overflowing with children free of their winter clothes like freshly-shorn lambs, bounding in the pale sunshine.

This light is no good, thought Haggerty irritably, it doesn't give me any tones, I ought to rent an office in a loft downtown. He put his head out a casement and squinted at the sky, which was a streaked grey, and realized that it was indeed April. The winter had been tediously cold, a genuine old-time Montreal sub-zero mess; but today it felt warm for almost the first time.

As the light was no good, he decided to do some men's-wear roughs. He got out a block of newsprint and began to hunt for a 6-B pencil, there was one around somewhere, he kept his pencils in a stone marmalade jug, and the jug was in plain view on the bookcase underneath his talisman.

His *genius loci*. He tried to ignore the picture (with which he carried on perpetual war) as he examined his pencils one by one. If he acknowledged the picture by the slightest sign, there would be no 6-B in the house. He dumped the jug on the draughting-board and at length found what he was seeking; then he permitted himself a sneer at his talisman.

This god of Peter Haggerty's is an enormous yellowing full page picture from the *New York Times* of the late W.C. Fields, which once illustrated an impassioned plea for NBC TV Programming, an irony of whose inner structure Haggerty was grimly aware. The comedian wore and wears his Micawber hat, a frock coat, peccable gloves unbuttoned at the wrists, and an expression of profoundly mistrustful contempt for his species. He guarded, guards, a poker hand against his chest and is about to place a card on the table, probably the King in a royal flush, and his face, in which the eyes are the arresting feature, moves and slides in a living ecstasy of detesting and detestable calculation, the ultimate caginess.

Haggerty revered this picture, which exactly expressed his own most frequent feelings.

But there was a terrifying doubleness about the picture of Fields. No matter how armed at all points, how guarded aware contemptuous his stance, there was ineradicably in the face the tormenting fearful suspicion that somebody somewhere somehow out there, in the great Beyond, was getting at him in some hidden way, against which he just couldn't cover himself. It was this dawning suspicion in the picture that pleased Haggerty most, this high artistic infirmity of guard.

Still, he had found the pencil he wanted, and switching on the light over the draughting-board, he seated himself and began to execute a series of roughs of a tweed spring topcoat, blocking in the general layout and the copy. As they always did when he was doing this sort of work, the first six sketches emerged as rule parodies of the essence of topcoat, hate-filled gibes at all who might conceivably buy and wear such a garment from such a store. And then as always, having worked off the effects of looking at his talisman, his hand steadied and he settled down to serious production.

On the eighth or ninth try he began to get what was needed and the coat began to seem wearable and even desirable, but at this point the door to the workroom opened noisily and Sally came into the room and stood next to his chair, looking up at him expectantly.

"What is it, Sweetie?" he said absorbedly. He didn't want to stop just at this moment but he was always telling her to run away and play, and didn't like to do it. That was the worst, or almost the worst, of working at home in a small apartment. He was present in the house, and Sally knew it, but he might as well have been downtown from nine to five for all the attention he could give her; it was an imperfect situation; maybe he should take a studio.

"Mummy's doing the drying," she said, "and she asked me to go out and play."

"She didn't tell you to come in here, did she?" he said with some vexation.

"No."

"Then why …" he began and checked himself. Someday soon she wouldn't be so eager to see him, in about fifteen years, and he would be wise to seize the present good. "Can't you find something to do?" he asked gently. She had about four million toys.

"I thought I'd come and talk to you."

"Daddy's working, dear, you know that." Her face fell, and then she gave him a little smile and he felt sad. "Would you like to help me?" he asked, trying unsuccessfully to conceal his impatience.

"Yes, I would."

"I'm doing some drawings," he said, "and you could do some, too, and then we can see which are the best ones. Would that be fun?"

"Oh, yes!" she said, very pleased. More than anything else, she loved to draw and paint. The Haggertys suspected that she might have some talent, though at three-and-a-half there isn't enough to go on.

"Just a minute," he said, going into the bedroom, where he extracted the cardboards from some freshly laundered shirts. He brought them back in and handed them to her. "Here's something to draw on," he said, "now you get your pencils and I'll show you what to draw."

"They're all broken," she said dolefully, and if he began to look for them and sharpen them he might as well knock off work for the morning.

He took a ballpoint out of his hip pocket and gave it to her; he carried it to make notes and was used to having it handy. "That's Daddy's special pencil," he told her, "and it isn't a toy, so you be careful of it, won't you?"

"Yes."

"O.K., now here's what you do." He showed her some of his crumpled-up roughs. "I'm drawing coats today, see? Now you take the cardboards and the pencil and draw some coats, three or four of them, and then we can see which is the best one. O.K.?" He had once or twice used her drawings in children's-wear layouts, with some modifications, and they had been striking and very fresh.

"O.K.," she said happily, and stretching out on the floor began to draw with enormous concentration. As she settled into it he watched the back of her head, her neck and shoulders, very moved as usual by the pathetic delicacy of their line. Then he went back to the draughting-board, sure that he had silenced her for the time being. He hated to think about it that way; like most young parents in similar circumstances he felt a great concern about his relationship with his child — only one so far, thank God — and he worried continually and felt obscurely guilty about putting her off, placating her, trying to find friends for her who would take her off his hands.

Peter and Helen felt especially guilty about the hard time

they had given Sally by moving to Montreal; she knew no French and had been accustomed to English-speaking kids who didn't talk as well as she did. Finding herself unable to hold her own with the other children on this strange new block, who talked to each other in what was to Sally a devilish and bewildering gabble, she had grown extremely dependent on her parents. From a sturdily independent child, eager to get out of the house and run with the gang, she had changed into a home-body, not a whiner or a crybaby, it was simply her policy to avoid trouble.

Peter and Helen hoped that this spring, after a year in the city spent mainly in watching children's shows on the French TV, she might get along better on the street. When the cold weather stopped, she began to get out with her wagon and tricycle, and fewer and fewer were the unhappy occasions when she came in on the point of tears. To the great relief of her parents, she explained that she had found a friend.

They wondered if this friend spoke French, and eagerly quizzed Sally about him.

"His name is George," she said.

"ZZheorzzhe?" asked Haggerty, giving it an approximately French pronunciation.

"No, George," she said positively.

"Well, does he speak English?"

"Yup, and Hungarian."

"Hungarian?"

"Yes, and he's very nice. He keeps Bernard from knocking me down, and when Brigitte took my tricycle he got it back. He's eight." She went out on a strict schedule, having figured out precisely when George was around to look after her.

"It's a polyglot town," Haggerty said to his wife. "The kid must be one of the refugees. A lot of them came here."

"Maybe she'll learn Hungarian instead of French," said Helen with a grin, "maybe both."

"I'd better have a look at George," said Haggerty, "and get the score on him." He kept his eyes open for a couple of weeks, but so far hadn't bumped into the lad.

"George is a Jew," said Sally, one night at supper, "and he plays the violin. He has a black bag with his violin in it, but he won't take it out with kids around. He says it's very precious. It's a Hungarian violin."

Her parents eyed one another silently, waiting for her to go on. She seemed to be pleased by the unaccustomed attention, but said nothing more about Jews, Hungarians, or violinists, changing the subject to mud and toy shovels, and leaving them neatly on the hook. When she'd gone to bed they dug out Spock and the three other child-care manuals which the insurance companies had sent them at Sally's birth; but they found no satisfactory entries on the emergence of the social conscience in the three-and-a-half-year-old. Apparently it didn't emerge unless somebody made it emerge. She likely had no inkling what a Jew or a DP was or was not. Mind you, she always noticed Negro children, especially on buses, usually shouting something like: "Look, Mummy, a *brown* baby," to her liberal mother's discomfiture, and going across the aisle to cuddle and kiss the infant in question. It was the overt difference in pigmentation that she noticed; the social intricacies simply didn't exist.

Peter and Helen wondered if they should try to tell her about them, or whether they should let her find them out for herself, and so far they had found no answer.

As he finished the topcoat sketches and stuck them in a Manila envelope, Haggerty brooded about these matters, as he sometimes did for weeks at a time. He didn't want to inject the poisons, even as inoculation. But the world was such-and-such in structure, and she shouldn't be isolated from it, for her own good. He turned from the draughting-board to look at her and found to his surprise that she was standing beside him with a look of apprehension on her face.

"What is it? What's the matter, Sweetie, have you finished?"

"I broke it," she whispered, holding out the pieces of the ballpoint. She had unscrewed the barrel and the cartridge and spring had fallen out. Involuntarily he let a spasm of annoyance flicker in his face, and she began to look really frightened, which gave him a perverse pleasure.

"It doesn't matter," she said, "we'll buy another one at the store."

"God," he said viciously, "you spoil everything, don't you?" It put her on the verge of tears. She had apparently lost the little spring which operated the propel-repel mechanism. Suddenly he felt a wave of nauseating self-contempt; was he doing that kind of thing all the time? What the hell, should he make his daughter hate him for a lousy half-cent spring from a thirty-nine cent ballpoint? He took her in his arms.

"I'm sorry I said that, dear," he said, as expressively as possible, "you're right, it doesn't matter a bit, not a tiny bit. When we go to the store this afternoon we'll buy two of them, one for you and one for me, and you can have some ice cream too." This was the right thing to say because for some reason she loved going to the store, any store, with him. But it didn't unsay what he'd said, and the gratuitous and unnecessary hurt would persist, and be remembered, another failure of love for him to chalk up on the board. Why do we say these things, he wondered, what does it matter? I want her to love me, and I want to love her. And he thought flashingly: I want my children around my deathbed, I don't want to die alone. Neurotic patterns, neurotic patterns, there was no need to take quite so long a view, he was well under thirty.

They held their arms tightly around each other for quite a while as he repeated. "It doesn't matter a bit, not a bit, it doesn't matter." Then she smiled and he began to tickle her, and peace and contentment were restored.

"Did you finish any coats?"

"I did two," she said, "and then I tried to fix the pencil and I lost the little spring from inside."

"Keep the pieces for your junk box," he told her munificently, "and this afternoon you can pick a new one for yourself in any colour you like."

She wriggled out of his arms and climbed onto the window seat to check the passing scene. For a few moments there was silence in the room as Haggerty busied himself finding the materials for a finished execution of his topcoat sketches, with which he hoped to catch the one-thirty mail.

"There's George," said Sally suddenly.

"Where?" he asked curiously, looking out the window beside her.

"There, there, he's waiting for the bus. I want to go out, please." She trotted to the front door and he held it open behind her; it was nearly lunchtime and in a minute he would have to retrieve her. He went back into his workroom and assembled the materials for this afternoon's work, dropping pencils and pen nibs here and there, and treading on them. Apart from his left hand, Haggerty's body was not especially well co-ordinated.

Now and then he looked out the window to see if he could spot Sally and her friend. He could hear her excited chattering but couldn't quite crane his neck far enough around to bring the bus stop into view. Pulling on his cardigan, he walked out onto the front steps and there he saw his daughter and a considerably larger boy giggling and punching each other harmlessly. The boy was certainly several years older than Sally, but was doubtless glad to have any friend, his own age or not, considering his circumstances. Haggerty came up to them just as the bus pulled up and the little boy moved to get on.

"George has to go downtown to see his Daddy," said Sally. There was no time for introductions, and when the bus had gone they went inside for lunch.

"George is going to New York with his Daddy," said Sally through her peanut-butter sandwich. As she was an uncannily accurate recorder and transmitter of neighbourhood gossip, her parents saw no reason to question the statement.

"When is he going?"

"Saturday, on the train with his father," she said sadly.

"Why?"

"To meet some people on the boat."

She almost always got such details exactly correct, perhaps because she simply repeated what she'd heard, perhaps because she had the historian's conscience — it was hard to tell. When she had finished her sandwich and milk she went out with her tricycle to see if George had come back yet, leaving her parents to mull over her communique.

"Probably going to welcome some more refugees," said Helen, "these people stick together. They rent each other houses and things like that. It isn't as if they were all alone." She had been feeling rather lonely herself, for most of their first year in the city.

"I'd like to know more about these people," said Haggerty, feeling vaguely worried for some unexplainable reason, "they sound sort of interesting. I wonder if George is any good on the violin."

"I think he may be. He told me one day that he'd been playing for four years, since they left Budapest, and he's only eight."

"Maybe he's some kind of prodigy. He's certainly nice to Sally." In Haggerty's eyes this forgave anything.

"I think he's a nice little boy," said Helen, "he's very polite and a little odd, a little grown up for his age. He seems to act responsible for Sally, and he told me he liked to look after her."

"That's a very good thing," said Haggerty with pleasure, "everything's coming along nicely. I told you she'd make friends." He spent a cheerful afternoon finishing up his current assignment but missed the one-thirty mail by giving his sketches an unusually high finish.

★ ★ ★

On the weekend he was kept busy amusing Sally, inside the house and out. He kept the weekends free for his family, and on this Saturday and Sunday much was demanded of him. Sally missed George quite a lot. She kept asking how far it was to New York, how long a trip there and back would take, and when George and his father, and perhaps their friends off the boat, might come back. She kept moping off up the street a hundred feet or so to stand in front of George's apartment house, ignoring the calls of the French children who genuinely seemed anxious to include her in their play. Haggerty didn't want to play nursemaid too overtly, and he encouraged her to mingle with Brigitte and Marisa and the others, whose talk he was beginning to understand. For one thing, they were closer to her own age than George, and might in the long run be better friends for her. But she simply walked past them to wait for the friend of whom she felt sure, and her father couldn't really blame her. Every time he brought out her tricycle or wagon one of the other children appropriated it, in the friendliest way, with no objection from Sally.

He began to grow tired of providing playthings for everybody on the block while his own child made no use of them, a rather petty motive, he supposed, but a genuine one of which he wasn't truly ashamed.

"Come and ride your bike, dear," he urged, but it did no good. Claudine or Brigitte diverted themselves with the gay red and white three-wheeler, playing fireman or ambulance, and Sally went on moping. Haggerty felt aggrieved, though for no good reason. In the evening he had to go looking for the tricycle for nearly an hour before he finally located it up an alley at the end of the block. He didn't expect any consideration from toddlers, but he began to wish that George would hurry back.

"We'll send her to a *maternelle* in the fall," he said with decision. Until now he had been opposed to nursery schools on the grounds that they were faddish and an evasion of parental responsibility. Now he was beginning to see their point.

FLYING A RED KITE

Helen brightened up at this. "Really?" she asked. "Oh, boy!" And it wasn't that they were anxious to be rid of Sally, they were honestly puzzled and they wanted to do what was right.

They were very glad indeed to hear that George was back from New York. Sally was full of details about the trip; but the details as she developed them were dismal, even shameful. Apparently the trip had been nightmarish, utter disaster, whose proportions their daughter was in no position to appreciate, though she was perfectly competent to describe them. One afternoon in the middle of the next week she bounded into her father's workroom and asked, in the sprightliest way: "What's a coronary attack?"

"A what?" said Haggerty, blanching.

"A co-ro-na-ry-a-tack."

There wasn't the least hint of gravity, displeasure, or sorrow in her face; she didn't know what she was talking about. And if there was one thing he did not want at any time to discuss with her, this was it, but how should he evade it? How long and how legitimately could he go on putting her off? She and George were not experimental children in Rousseau's Eden, they were not to be protected indefinitely. But three-and-a-half is too young for some kinds of experience. He chose to direct her attention elsewhere, and began to show her a sample line of pastels which Grumbacher had sent him on approval. She grabbed one and painted her forearms a vivid blue, chuckling happily.

"Blue," she said intently, "what a blue, look!" She held up her wrists and he wondered if the stuff was washable. "George's father has one."

"One what?" said Haggerty, walking innocently back into it.

"A coronary attack. He got it in New York." Something or other, maybe the sound of the words, had fascinated her and she repeated them several times. "Quack, wack, coronary attack." She enjoyed rhyming play and loved the children's poetry books from which her parents read to her, sometimes for hours. "Mack, nack, quack, lack," she went on.

"You got that out of *Make Way for Ducklings*," said her father, "those are the names of the ducklings."

"Nack, lack, coronary attack," she said. "George and his father didn't meet those people. They weren't on the boat."

At the prospect of this abyss of implied misery yawning before him, poor Haggerty quailed and wanted to run. He had the sensibilities, without quite the talent, of a really good artist, and in an instant he saw the whole desperate story, stretching back over a decade, the merciless political oppression, the slowly fomented rebellion and its inhuman defeat, the flight of the refugees. It was certainly all there in the dreadful story lurking three apartment buildings away on the peaceful Montreal street. He didn't want to guess at the rest of it — the Austrian refugee camps, separated families, lost children, hungry, even famished, three-year-olds. The arrival in totally strange Canadian towns and the sometimes silently heroic beginnings of a new, forever haunted, life. He could see it all and he did not want to look. He refused to consider his daughter and his wife, lost, wandering along unfamiliar roads wondering if he had been caught or had managed to escape and was looking for them. Not in Canada, he thought, we've never had that and who's to say that we won't? He suspected that this was the morbidity of fancy of the failed, or at best third-rate, artist.

"Why weren't they on the boat?" he demanded unwillingly. He was certain that she would have the information and of course she did. She would have got it from George who would have got it from his father, and God knows how he got it.

"They were arrested at the border," she said, with a finality that assured him that it was all she knew; she didn't even know what a goddamn border was, but she could tell him all this. "It made George's father sick, and that's when he got his coronary attack, in the station. George sat up all night in the train with his father being sick."

"Have another piece of chalk," Haggerty said mechanically, offering them as he would a box of candy. She selected a pink one and began to colour her legs. "You look like Boadicea," he said smilingly, a little desperately, "She painted herself with woad. All blue. The ancient Britons painted themselves blue." She laughed at him. "Not that it did them any good," he concluded absently.

He felt an intense desire to look at the portrait of the comedian to see if the eyes were moving. What the hell, he thought, you buy annuities, Blue Cross, insurance, furniture, houses, cars, clothing, indulgences, and you can't in the end protect yourself against everything. It can't be done. There's always something else. He looked up at the picture of Fields, bravely meeting the sliding eyes, and the face was more opaque than ever.

A royal flush in spades, thought Haggerty, and it isn't doing him any good.

"The con-duc-tor didn't like Jews, George said. He made them wait in line while his father was sick and he wouldn't help them. I don't think he was very nice to them, do you? I like Jews because George is a Jew."

"You like everybody," Haggerty said.

"I don't like Marisa."

"Well, except Marisa."

"What is a Jew?"

Lord, he thought, this situation is banal, right out of *Partisan Review*, the liberal father and his innocent child. Lionel Trilling would love it; he'd want to put it in a sociology book, Lionel and Wystan and Jacques and all the boys down at *Mid-Century*. She was going to put the question again and he didn't want to listen — there was nothing to be said, he wasn't an anthropometrist but a painter and commercial artist. The Jews were some shadowy men whom he didn't know well, and a bunch of white-skinned girls in their twenties on whom scarlet lipstick would go, lovelies all of them, he liked the black hair, white skin, scarlet lipstick effect. There was a Mrs. Greenwald in his class at the Museum who would never learn to draw worth a damn, but whom he encouraged to continue because he liked to look at her. Boy, was she beautiful and, boy, was she stupid. He meant to keep the Jews that way in his thinking, people to look at, *not* newsreels of charnel houses, *not* the mortal sin of the race, *not* Calvary. He stared at his daughter and knowing that it was an evasion, he put the question by.

"Come and show your mother your legs and arms," he said, "little old Boadicea." She rose obediently and followed him to the kitchen where Helen was stuffing the washer with sheets.

"That's a ten-pound load?" he said incredulously.

"A bit over," she said guiltily, "but I'm not telling the machine about it. Maybe it won't guess."

"Don't torment the poor old thing," he said amusedly, and then he saw that her eyes were full of tears. "What is it, what's wrong?"

"That damned George," she said chokingly, "I don't want to be bothered with stories like that."

"Oh, you heard?"

"I was there when he told Sally. Did you get the whole story?"

"I don't know. What did you hear?" he said.

They shared a particular hatred and horror of the notion of the sufferings of children, always gratuitous and unearned. Haggerty remembered that W.C. Fields is said to have hated and despised children, and he was sure he knew why the comedian had taken that line.

"After they met the boat," she began unwillingly, "his father started to feel sick and apparently he nearly collapsed when he found that his friends hadn't made it, but he got George across town and into Grand Central; they had a meal of sorts and walked around the station for half a day, the father getting whiter and whiter. George says he can't understand why his dad was so white. Finally they got in the lineup at the gate, they were sitting on their suitcases. Just before they opened the gate the father got up and left the lineup to move around. He felt nauseated, as if he were going to vomit, but he couldn't. When he came back they had lost their place in the line and the gateman wouldn't give it back to them. They waited at the end of the line for another hour and he had the attack just after the train pulled out."

"Why didn't he get off and go to a hospital?"

"How should I know? Maybe he didn't know what to do with George, maybe he hoped to get home before it got bad. They didn't know anybody in New York. Anyway they sat up together all night on the train and he went to Montreal General as soon as they got in."

"Is he all right?"

"I don't know, but I wouldn't bet money on it," she said.

"What was that stuff about the conductor hating Jews?"

"George said he wouldn't do anything to help his father, he just pushed them off in a corner or something. I don't want to hear any more about it."

"But we will," said Haggerty.

He was right. Sally kept meeting George at the bus stop or along the street and she kept hearing this or that, that his father was in a funny kind of tent, that his blood clotted too much or wouldn't, after drugs, clot at all. The Haggertys felt acutely annoyed that their daughter, knowing nothing of the implications, so conscientiously transmitted these details. They did not care to be haunted.

On a final afternoon towards the end of April she bounded in with the air of one filled with remarkable, even wonderful news, a sort of gospel.

"George's father died," she said, and the way she delivered the line all unconsciously gave it a weirdly comic tone. "He's dead," she said, briefly and precisely.

Peter and Helen looked at each other. Each realized that the other parent had talked to Sally about these things; but there hadn't been any very close collaboration between them on the question of what to say and what to omit. Neither one wanted to speak first.

"George says his father has gone away for good. He won't see him again," observed Sally, looking from one to the other of her parents. She had the damnedest way of knowing when she'd put them on the spot. Then she seemed to think over what she'd said — and she was certainly capable of some sort of reflection — because she said: "Are you going away?" addressing the question to them jointly.

Haggerty broke first, shamefully. He went to his knees and crooked his finger at her, and she waltzed over happily and stood between his knees.

"Are *you* going away?" she said, putting it directly to her father.

He put his arms around her roughly, feeling the smart in his eyes. "Nobody's going anywhere!" he said.

"Won't you die?"

Ah, there it was at last, she'd heard the word before; she was growing up, three-and-a-half, you can't hide it forever. Is three-and-a-half too young? Shouldn't you hide it till they're ready for it? Who's ready? We're never ready.

"Yes," said Haggerty, "I'll die." He heard Helen's sharp intake of breath and felt a stab of irrational anger. I can't lie, he thought. "All must die," he said.

"When?"

"Not for a long long time, Sally, a very long time, so long that there's nothing to worry about."

"Will I die?"

"Yes." He said it gently.

"Oh, but you'll die first?"

I wish she'd let it drop, he thought. "Yes."

"And Mummy will, too. I'll miss you."

"It won't be for a long time. Forget about it."

"Where do you go when you die?"

Now what do you say? What do you do? Oh sure, they had a crucifix in the house and some pictures of the Infant Jesus and His Mother, and they had all been to Church together, which

Sally loved. Are you filling them up with false hopes, crippling their little psyches, by teaching them a religion and the hope of immortality? If it be an illusion, is it a useful and healthy one?

Of course, if it were true, there'd be no problem, he thought hopefully.

Even if it isn't, shouldn't you inoculate them with hope anyway? Can't it be untrue without being false, like a myth or a fiction? He took a deep breath and spoke bravely, taking the irretrievable step.

"If you're a good man or woman or little girl, like you, then you go to Heaven to be with God forever, and when you're with God nobody ever leaves you again. George's father is with God, and someday George will see him again, and he won't be sick."

He caught his wife's sighing slow exhalation and guessed that he had gotten the story straight. Sally grinned. "In any case," he said, driving the point home, "it won't happen for a long time. Nobody's going anywhere. So forget it." He was sure that she would for maybe as much as a year.

"I'm going to take my bike out and lend it to George," she said.

They helped her down the front steps and then hustled quickly inside so as to evade her friend. He's too big for the tricycle, they thought, and soon it will be broken.

Haggerty sat up late that night finishing off an assignment and afterwards monkeying around with some illustrations for a children's book which he was doing on spec. He liked working with the clear vivid simple primary colours and found the illustrations, a horse, a carousel, red barns and white silos, falling perfectly into place under his hand. It was the first time in days that he had been able to do anything easily, so he sat on and on under the picture of the dead comedian till he'd finished six watercolour sketches. Then he smoked a couple of cigarettes and ate a candy bar before going to bed.

Usually he had trouble falling asleep, when he'd worked late, his train of ideas continuing while his head bobbed from side to side on the unaccommodating pillow. Tonight he fell asleep instantly and at once began to dream — bright dreams in primary colours of overcoats, tricycles, trains, horses, and merry-go-rounds. Then he found himself seated before a card table, playing with somebody whose face he couldn't make out, he was holding ten to King of a royal flush in spades and was trying to fill it. He couldn't see his opponent's face but he guessed who it was, and then he knew that he would draw the Ace, so he extended his hand, his good hand, his pencil hand, the left one, and turned up the emblem he'd wished for through his dreams.

FLYING A RED KITE

The ride home began badly. Still almost a stranger to the city, tired, hot and dirty, and inattentive to his surroundings, Fred stood for ten minutes, shifting his parcels from arm to arm and his weight from one leg to the other, in a sweaty bath of shimmering glare from the sidewalk, next to a grimy yellow-and-black bus stop. To his left a line of murmuring would-be passengers lengthened until there were enough to fill any vehicle that might come for them. Finally an obese brown bus waddled up like an indecent old cow and stopped with an expiring moo at the head of the line. Fred was glad to be first in line, as there didn't seem to be room for more than a few to embus.

But as he stepped up he noticed a sign in the window which said *Côte des Neiges — Boulevard* and he recoiled as though bitten, trampling the toes of the woman behind him and making her squeal. It was a Sixty-six bus, not the Sixty-five that he wanted. The woman pushed furiously past him while the remainder of the line clamoured in the rear. He stared at the number on the bus stop: Sixty-six, not his stop at all. Out of the corner of his eye he saw another coach pulling away from the stop on the northeast corner, the right stop, the Sixty-five, and the one he should have been standing under all this time. Giving his characteristic weary put-upon sigh, which he used before breakfast to annoy Naomi, he adjusted his parcels in both arms, feeling sweat run around his neck and down his collar between his shoulders, and crossed Saint Catherine against the light, drawing a Gallic sneer from a policeman, to stand for several more minutes at the head of a new queue, under the right sign. It was nearly four-thirty and the Saturday shopping crowds wanted to get home, out of the summer dust and heat, out of the jitter of the big July holiday weekend. They would all go home and sit on their balconies. All over the suburbs in duplexes and fourplexes, families would be enjoying cold suppers in the open air on their balconies; but the Calverts' apartment had none. Fred and Naomi had been ignorant of the meaning of the custom when they were apartment hunting. They had thought of Montreal as a city of the Sub-Arctic and in the summers they would have leisure to repent the misjudgment.

He had been shopping along the length of Saint Catherine between Peel and Guy, feeling guilty because he had heard for years that this was where all those pretty Montreal women made their promenade; he had wanted to watch without familial encumbrances. There had been girls enough but nothing outrageously special so he had beguiled the scorching afternoon making a great many small idle purchases, of the kind one does when trapped in a Woolworth's. A ballpoint pen and a notepad for Naomi, who was always stealing his and leaving it in the kitchen with long, wildly-optimistic, grocery lists scribbled in it. Six packages of cigarettes, some legal-size envelopes, two Dinky-toys, a long-playing record, two parcels of second-hand books, and the lightest of his burdens and the unhandiest, the kite he had bought for Deedee, two flimsy wooden sticks rolled up in red plastic film, and a ball of cheap thin string — not enough, by the look of it, if he should ever get the thing into the air.

When he'd gone fishing, as a boy, he'd never caught any fish; when playing hockey he had never been able to put the puck in the net. One by one the wholesome outdoor sports and games had defeated him. But he had gone on believing in them, in their curative moral values, and now he hoped that Deedee, though a girl, might sometime catch a fish; and though she obviously wouldn't play hockey, she might ski, or toboggan on the mountain. He had noticed that people treated kites and kite-flying as somehow holy. They were a natural symbol, thought Fred, and he felt uneasily sure that he would have trouble getting this one to fly.

The inside of the bus was shaped like a boxcar with windows, but the windows were useless. You might have peeled off the bus as you'd peel the paper off a pound of butter, leaving an oblong yellow lump of thick solid heat, with the passengers embedded in it like hopeless breadcrumbs.

He elbowed and wriggled his way along the aisle, feeling a momentary sliver of pleasure as his palm rubbed accidentally along the back of a girl's skirt — once, a philosopher — the sort of thing you couldn't be charged with. But you couldn't get away with it twice, and anyway the girl either didn't feel it or had no idea who had caressed her. There were vacant seats towards the rear, which was odd because the bus was otherwise full, and he struggled towards them, trying not to break the wooden struts which might be persuaded to fly. The bus lurched forward and his feet moved with the floor, causing him to pop suddenly out of the crowd by the exit, into a square well of space next to the heat and stink of the engine. He swayed around and aimed himself at a narrow vacant seat, nearly dropping a parcel of books as he lowered himself precipitately into it.

The bus crossed Sherbrooke Street and began, intolerably slowly, to crawl up Cote des Neiges and around the western spur of the mountain. His ears began to pick up the usual melange of French and English and to sort it out; he was proud of his French and pleased that most of the people on the streets spoke a less correct, though more fluent, version than his own. He had found that he could make his customers understand him perfectly — he was a book salesman — but that people on the street were happier when he addressed them in English.

The chatter in the bus grew clearer and more interesting and he began to listen, grasping all at once why he had found a seat back here. He was sitting next to a couple of drunks who emitted an almost overpowering smell of beer. They were cheerfully exchanging indecencies and obscure jokes and in a minute they would speak to him. They always did, drunks and panhandlers, finding some soft fearfulness in his face which exposed him as a shrinking easy mark. Once in a railroad station he had been approached three times in twenty minutes by the same panhandler on his rounds. Each time he had given the man something, despising himself with each new weakness.

The cheerful pair sitting at right-angles to him grew louder and more blunt and the women within earshot grew glum. There was no harm in it; there never is. But you avoid your neighbour's eye, afraid of smiling awkwardly, or of looking offended and a prude.

"Now this Pearson," said one of the revellers, "he's just a little short-ass. He's just a little fellow without any brains. Why, some of the speeches he makes … I could make them myself. I'm an old Tory myself, an old Tory."

"I'm an old Blue," said the other.

"Is that so, now? That's fine, a fine thing." Fred was sure he didn't know what a Blue was.

"I'm a Balliol man. Whoops!" They began to make monkey-like noises to annoy the passengers and amuse themselves. "Whoops," said the Oxford man again, "hoo, hoo, there's one now, there's one for you." He was talking about a girl on the sidewalk.

"She's a one, now, isn't she? Look at the legs on her, oh, look at them now, isn't that something?" There was a noisy clearing of throats and the same voice said something that sounded like "Shaoil-na-baig."

"Oh, good, good!" said the Balliol man.

"Shaoil-na-baig," said the other loudly, "I've not forgotten my Gaelic, do you see, shaoil-na-baig," he said it loudly, and a woman up the aisle reddened and looked away. It sounded like a dirty phrase to Fred, delivered as though the speaker had forgotten all his Gaelic but the words for sexual intercourse.

"And how is your French, Father?" asked the Balliol man, and the title made Fred start in his seat. He pretended to drop a parcel and craned his head quickly sideways. The older of the two drunks, the one sitting by the window, examining the passing legs and skirts with the same impulse that Fred had felt on Saint Catherine Street, was indeed a priest, and couldn't possibly be an impostor. His clerical suit was too well-worn, egg-stained and blemished with candle-droppings, and fit its wearer too well, for it to be an assumed costume. The face was unmistakably a southern Irishman's. The priest darted a quick peek into Fred's eyes before he could turn them away, giving a monkey-like grimace that might have been a mixture of embarrassment and shame but probably wasn't.

He was a little grey-haired bucko of close to sixty, with a triangular sly mottled crimson face and uneven yellow teeth. His hands moved jerkily and expressively in his lap, in counterpoint to the lively intelligent movements of his face.

The other chap, the Balliol man, was a perfect type of English-speaking Montrealer, perhaps a bond salesman or minor functionary in a brokerage house on Saint James Street. He was about fifty with a round domed head, red hair beginning to go slightly white at the neck and ears, pink porcine skin, very neatly barbered and combed. He wore an expensive white shirt with a fine blue stripe and there was some sort of ring around his tie. He had his hands folded fatly on the knob of a stick, round face with deep laugh-lines in the cheeks, and a pair of cheerfully darting little blue-bloodshot eyes. Where could the pair have run into each other?

"I've forgotten my French years ago," said the priest carelessly. "I was down in New Brunswick for many years and I'd no use for it, the work I was doing. I'm Irish, you know."

"I'm an old Blue."

"That's right," said the priest, "John's the boy. Oh, he's a sharp lad is John. He'll let them all get off, do you see, to Manitoba for the summer, and bang, BANG!" All the bus jumped. "He'll call an election on them and then they'll run." Something caught his eye and he turned to gaze out the window. The bus was moving slowly past the cemetery of Notre Dame des Neiges and the priest stared, half-sober, at the graves stretched up the mountainside in the sun.

"I'm not in there," he said involuntarily.

"Indeed you're not," said his companion, "lot's of life in you yet, eh, Father?"

"Oh," he said, "oh, I don't think I'd know what to do with a girl if I fell over one." He looked out at the cemetery for several moments. "It's all a sham," he said, half under his breath, "they're in there for good." He swung around and looked innocently at Fred. "Are you going fishing, lad?"

"It's a kite that I bought for my little girl," said Fred, more cheerfully than he felt.

"She'll enjoy that, she will," said the priest, "for it's grand sport."

"Go fly a kite!" said the Oxford man hilariously. It amused him and he said it again. "Go fly a kite!" He and the priest began to chant together, "Hoo, hoo, whoops," and they laughed and in a moment, clearly, would begin to sing.

The bus turned lumberingly onto Queen Mary Road. Fred stood up confusedly and began to push his way towards the rear door. As he turned away, the priest grinned impudently at him, stammering a jolly goodbye. Fred was too embarrassed to answer but he smiled uncertainly and fled. He heard them take up their chant anew.

"Hoo, there's a one for you, hoo. Shaoil-na-baig. Whoops!" Their laughter died out as the bus rolled heavily away.

He had heard about such men, naturally, and knew that they existed; but it was the first time in Fred's life that he had ever seen a priest misbehave himself publicly. There are so many priests in the city, he thought, that the number of bum ones must be in proportion. The explanation satisfied him but the incident left a disagreeable impression in his mind.

Safely home he took his shirt off and poured himself a Coke. Then he allowed Deedee, who was dancing around him with her terrible energy, to open the parcels.

"Give your Mummy the pad and pencil, sweetie," he directed. She crossed obediently to Naomi's chair and handed her the cheap plastic case.

"Let me see you make a note in it," he said, "make a list of something, for God's sake, so you'll remember it's yours. And the one on the desk is mine. Got that?" He spoke without rancour or much interest; it was a rather overworked joke between them.

"What's this?" said Deedee, holding up the kite and allowing the ball of string to roll down the hall. He resisted a compulsive wish to get up and re-wind the string.

"It's for you. Don't you know what it is?"

"It's a red kite," she said. She had wanted one for weeks but spoke now as if she weren't interested. Then all at once she grew very excited and eager. "Can you put it together right now?" she begged.

"I think we'll wait till after supper, sweetheart," he said, feeling mean. You raised their hopes and then dashed them; there was no real reason why they shouldn't put it together now, except his fatigue. He looked pleadingly at Naomi.

"Daddy's tired, Deedee," she said obligingly, "he's had a long, hot afternoon."

"But I want to see it," said Deedee, fiddling with the flimsy red film and nearly puncturing it.

Fred was sorry he'd drunk a Coke; it bloated him and upset his stomach and had no true cooling effect.

"We'll have something to eat," he said cajolingly, "and then Mummy can put it together for you." He turned to his wife. "You don't mind, do you? I'd only spoil the thing." Threading a needle or hanging a picture made the normal slight tremor of his hands accentuate itself almost embarrassingly.

"Of course not," she said, smiling wryly. They had long ago worked out their areas of uselessness.

"There's a picture on it, and directions."

"Yes. Well, we'll get it together somehow. Flying it … that's something else again." She got up, holding the notepad, and went into the kitchen to put the supper on.

It was a good hot-weather supper, tossed greens with the correct proportions of vinegar and oil, croissants and butter, and cold sliced ham. As he ate, his spirits began to percolate a bit, and he gave Naomi a graphic sketch of the incident on the bus. "It depressed me," he told her. This came as no surprise to her; almost anything unusual, which he couldn't do anything to alter or relieve, depressed Fred nowadays. "He must have been sixty. Oh, quite sixty, I should think, and you could tell that everything had come to pieces for him."

"It's a standard story," she said, "and aren't you sentimentalizing it?"

"In what way?"

"The 'spoiled priest' business, the empty man, the man without a calling. They all write about that. Graham Greene made his whole career out of that."

"That isn't what the phrase means," said Fred laboriously. "It doesn't refer to a man who actually *is* a priest, though without a vocation."

"No?" She lifted an eyebrow; she was better educated than he.

"No, it doesn't. It means somebody who never became a priest at all. The point is that you *had* a vocation but ignored it. That's what a spoiled priest is. It's an Irish phrase, and usually refers to somebody who is a failure and who drinks too much." He laughed shortly. "I don't qualify, on the second count."

"You're not a failure."

"No, I'm too young. Give me time!" There was no reason for him to talk like this; he was a very productive salesman.

"You certainly never wanted to be a priest," she said positively, looking down at her breasts and laughing, thinking of some secret. "I'll bet you never considered it, not with your habits." She meant his bedroom habits, which were ardent, and in which she ardently acquiesced. She was an adept and enthusiastic partner, her greatest gift as a wife.

"Let's put that kite together," said Deedee, getting up from her little table, with such adult decision that her parents chuckled. "Come on," she said, going to the sofa and bouncing up and down.

Naomi put a tear in the fabric right away, on account of the ambiguity of the directions. There should have been two holes in the kite, through which a lugging-string passed; but the holes hadn't been provided and when she put them there with the point of an icepick they immediately began to grow.

"Scotch tape," she said, like a surgeon asking for sutures.

"There's a picture on the front," said Fred, secretly cross but ostensibly helpful.

"I see it," she said.

"Mummy put holes in the kite," said Deedee with alarm. "Is she going to break it?"

"No," said Fred. The directions were certainly ambiguous.

Naomi tied the struts at right-angles, using so much string that Fred was sure the kite would be too heavy. Then she strung the fabric on the notched ends of the struts and the thing began to take shape.

"It doesn't look quite right," she said, puzzled and irritated.

"The surface has to be curved so there's a difference of air pressure." He remembered this, rather unfairly, from high-school physics classes.

She bent the cross-piece and tied it in a bowed arc, and the red film pulled taut. "There now," she said.

"You've forgotten the lugging-string on the front," said Fred critically, "that's what you made the holes for, remember?"

"Why is Daddy mad?" said Deedee.

"I'M NOT MAD!"

"It had begun to shower, great pear-shaped drops of rain falling with a plop on the sidewalk.

"That's as close as I can come," said Naomi, staring at Fred, "we aren't going to try it tonight, are we?"

"We promised her," he said, "and it's only a light rain."

"Will we all go?"

"I wish you'd take her," he said, "because my stomach feels upset. I should never drink Coca-Cola."

"It always bothers you. You should know that by now."

"I'm not running out on you," he said anxiously, "and if you can't make it work, I'll take her up tomorrow afternoon."

"I know," she said, "come on, Deedee, we're going to take the kite up the hill." They left the house and crossed the street. Fred watched them through the window as they started up the steep path hand in hand. He felt left out, and slightly nauseated.

They were back in half an hour, their spirits not at all dampened, which surprised him.

"No go, eh?"

"Much too wet, and not enough breeze. The rain knocks it flat."

"O.K.!" he exclaimed with fervour. "I'll try tomorrow."

"We'll try again tomorrow," said Deedee with equal determination — her parents mustn't forget their obligations.

Sunday afternoon the weather was nearly perfect, hot, clear, a firm steady breeze but not too much of it, and a cloudless sky. At two o'clock Fred took his daughter by the hand and they started up the mountain together, taking the path through the woods that led up to the University parking lots.

"We won't come down until we make it fly," Fred swore, "that's a promise."

"Good," she said, hanging on to his hand and letting him drag her up the steep path, "there are lots of bugs in here, aren't there?"

"Yes," he said briefly — he was being liberally bitten.

When they came to the end of the path, they saw that the campus was deserted and still, and there was all kinds of running room. Fred gave Deedee careful instructions about where to sit, and what to do if a car should come along, and then he paid out a little string and began to run across the parking lot towards the main building of the University. He felt a tug at the string and throwing a glance over his shoulder he saw the kite bobbing in the air, about twenty feet off the ground. He let out more string, trying to keep it filled with air, but he couldn't run quite fast enough, and in a moment it fell back to the ground.

"Nearly had it!" he shouted to Deedee, whom he'd left fifty yards behind.

"Daddy, Daddy, come back," she hollered apprehensively. Rolling up the string as he went, he retraced his steps and prepared to try again. It was important to catch a gust of wind and run into it. On the second try the kite went higher than before but as he ran past the entrance to the University he felt the air pressure lapse and saw the kite waver and fall. He walked slowly back, realizing that the bulk of the main building was cutting off the air currents.

"We'll go up higher," he told her, and she seized his hand and climbed obediently up the road beside him, around behind the main building, past ash barrels and trash heaps; they climbed a flight of wooden steps, crossed a parking lot next to L'Ecole Polytechnique and a slanting field further up, and at last came to a pebbly dirt road that ran along the top ridge of the mountain beside the cemetery. Fred remembered the priest as he looked across the fence and along the broad stretch of cemetery land rolling away down the slope of the mountain to the west. They were about six hundred feet above the river, he judged. He'd never been up this far before.

"My sturdy little brown legs are tired," Deedee remarked, and he burst out laughing.

"Where did you hear that," he said, "who has sturdy little brown legs?"

She screwed her face up in a grin. "The gingerbread man," she said, beginning to sing, "I can run away from you, I can, 'cause I'm the little gingerbread man."

The air was dry and clear and without a trace of humidity and the sunshine was dazzling. On either side of the dirt road grew great clumps of wild flowers, yellow and blue, buttercups, daisies and goldenrod, and cornflowers and clover. Deedee disappeared into the flowers — picking bouquets was her favourite game. He could see the shrubs and grasses heave and sway as she moved around. The scent of clover and of dry sweet grass was very keen here, and from the east, over the curved top of the mountain, the wind blew in a steady uneddying stream. Five or six miles off to the southwest he spied the wide intensely grey-white stripe of the river. He heard Deedee cry: "Daddy, Daddy, come and look." He pushed through the coarse grasses and found her.

"Berries," she cried rapturously, "look at all the berries! Can I eat them?" She had found a wild raspberry bush, a thing he hadn't seen since he was six years old. He'd never expected to find one growing in the middle of Montreal.

"Wild raspberries," he said wonderingly, "sure you can pick them, dear; but be careful of the prickles." They were all shades and degrees of ripeness from black to vermilion.

"Ouch," said Deedee, pricking her fingers as she pulled off the berries. She put a handful in her mouth and looked wry.

"Are they bitter?"

"Juicy," she mumbled with her mouth full. A trickle of dark juice ran down her chin.

"Eat some more," he said, "while I try the kite again." She bent absorbedly to the task of hunting them out, and he walked down the road for some distance and then turned to run up towards her. This time he gave the kite plenty of string before he began to move; he ran as hard as he could, panting and handing the string out over his shoulders, burning his fingers as it slid through them. All at once he felt the line pull and pulse as if there were a living thing on the other end, and he turned on his heel and watched while the kite danced into the upper air-currents above the treetops and began to soar up and up. He gave it more line, and in an instant it pulled high up away from him across the fence, two hundred feet and more above him up over the cemetery where it steadied and hung, bright red in the sunshine. He thought flashingly of the priest saying "It's all a sham," and he knew all at once that the priest was wrong. Deedee came running down to him, laughing with excitement and pleasure and singing joyfully about the gingerbread man, and he knelt in the dusty roadway and put his arms around her, placing her hands on the line between his. They gazed, squinting in the sun, at the flying red thing, and he turned away and saw in the shadow of her cheek and on her lips and chin the dark rich red of the pulp and juice of the crushed raspberries.

WHERE THE MYTH
TOUCHES US

People still listen to their radios, evading the corpse-like glare of the man who breaks down the fat globules. Joe Jacobson has a radio shaped like the fat point of a late Gothic arch, with a fretwork face in front of a faded red curtain, which shields the speaker cone, and below three knobs of which the third — the one on the right — does nothing, although a tiny decalcomania under it says TONE. The other knobs are for volume and tuning but the condenser is shot in the volume control. Sometimes the old set won't speak above a chaste murmur for days and then, all at once, it booms out with an enormous tinny rattle of the speaker and a great crackling noise. Joe swats it with an open palm, hardly looking up from his typewriter or book, and it subsides.

He doesn't want a new radio; this one was in the family for thirty years. When he was still a baby his father burst excitedly into his bedroom late one night, past nine-thirty, with a pair of earphones in his hand and a long black cord trailing behind.

"Babele," said his father, "it's a miracle, listen!" And he clamped the headset on Joe's ears, startling the child. There was music in the earphones.

"CKOC Hamilton," crooned his father, "like it was in the next room! Amazing!" Hamilton was forty-six miles away.

The next day the "Atwater Kent" appeared in the living room and Joe's mother brought him up next to it, sewing her way through eight daytime serials every afternoon. After his parents were dead, he asked his brothers for the radio as his share of the inheritance, wanting nothing else — somebody has to die before you inherit — placing it on his bureau, over the drawer where he keeps his family pictures.

The plywood veneer is peeling at the back of the set and parts of it have flaked off, exposing the cheap pine frame. Every week or so he takes a butter knife and spreads wood glue into the crack, pressing the veneer down, and for a while it holds. Then in the evening, while he writes, he'll hear a pinging sound and know that it's sprung up again. He means to go along, gluing it together as long as he can.

Toby Frankel came to his room that time and made fun of the radio; she couldn't be blamed, knowing nothing about it.

"Joey, on what you make! An associate professor!"

He looked at her blankly and gave the peeling wood a squeeze with the palm of his hand. He will marry Toby anyway, he thinks, when the book comes out. A first-novelist ought to be a bachelor, but on a second-novelist it looks queer unless he writes about North Africa. Once, visiting her in the Group Dynamics Lab, he offered comically to "take you away from all this" but she didn't get the joke, pushing him away when he patted her. She looked up fearfully at the one-way window, unsure, unsure.

So for the moment he lives alone in his room with his radio and his screened sun-porch, not too eager to round off this course of life. Tonight he turns off his desk-lamp while the radio babbles quietly, sits for a moment in the warm summer darkness rubbing his eyes, then he gazes off at the lake two blocks away down Frontenac Street, gets up from his desk and manipulates the volume control on the radio with some care, hoping that it won't scream. He manages to get the Wednesday Night Talk and, lighting a cigarette, lies down on his couch to listen and think of nothing, perfectly aware that his veins will tingle like this until the morning of August twenty-fifth when he can go down to the University Bookstore and admire the display. He understands that one novel isn't a career, that publication day is the day he'll have to start all over again, but hard covers are hard covers, and the bees will buzz in assorted hives; Evanston, Berkeley, Toronto, Madison, Cambridge.

As the slow dark relaxes him and his eyes lose the image of his lamp, the smell of his cigarette sharp and pleasant in his nostrils, he moves his legs tiredly on the couch and listens to the voice on CBC Wednesday Night, peppery, combative, lucid, engaging, and it is, who else, David Wallace. "Summer in the City," Jesus, he's been doing that in the papers, in magazines, in novels, he ought to hire a plane, skywrite the piece in permanent smoke, and get maximum coverage all at once, "Summer in the City." And at that it is a good talk, and nobody will read informal essays any more. He tunes the set more carefully, to get the shriek out of the speaker, stretches out again, and listens.

"Doing what I do for a living," says the familiar, old friend's voice, "I don't get out onto the streets until the middle of the afternoon. You know, we should have the custom of the siesta, as they do in the Latin countries, and most of all in August in the city. My siesta lasts until two-thirty and by then the sun is beginning to get down the other side of the sky, that summer sky, always light grey, nearly white, not the blue of spring or fall. So … anyway … I take my time getting into my clothes. Maybe someday I'll tell you my secret, how to keep from getting sticky in August. But I don't get sticky and I don't move very fast at all. I walk slowly across the bridge, looking down at the poplars and elms in the ravine, and the children from the Hunt Club on their ponies on the bridle path. Sometimes on the other side I have an ice cream soda. Then I walk to the Subway, taking my time and admiring the girls' blouses, and the lovely way their hair moves in the light air and the heat. It's cool in the Subway going downtown and I don't have to rush because I'm just coming into the studio to record this talk. The studio is air-conditioned and very cool, and about four o'clock I begin to wake up, just as the office workers downtown are going home. That way I have the downtown to myself after dinner."

Lying on the couch in the summer dark, Joe smiles very soberly to himself, remembering the places, the studios, the quiet discussions, the beer, a cold-beef plate in the Morrissey Dining Room, with a mint parfait to follow, and David asking his producer to please do something about echo noises on the tape. He can't yet wish himself back there but all the same he remembers — and wonders what Toby would think.

"I might take the ferry to the island if I'm alone at night," says David to the nation and to Joe remembering, "or go to the ball game and sit in the pavilion, the best seventy-five cents' worth in town, watching the gamblers pass large bills from hand to hand, the light planes at the airport, ships in the Western Gap. But usually I'm in a group that talks for a few hours, a drama critic, a young writer from Kingston, in town for a day to see his publisher," and Joe thinks to himself, I wish he'd stop doing that, but David is a paragraph further on now, "and about twelve, when they close the lounges, I say goodnight to my friends, and by now the city is growing quiet. I wander along Bloor Street as people come out of the lounges, getting into their cars, or deciding to go somewhere else for something to eat and another drink, or just walking up Avenue Road hand in hand, under the trees in the dark. I might buy a morning paper at the corner of Avenue Road and talk for a minute to Sammy, who has the newsstand there. Now there aren't many cars, and you can hear the streetcars blocks away. I stroll along, taking my time, going home to work. Because this, you see, is when my working day begins, hours after midnight. I hop a streetcar and go along to the bridge over the ravine, dark now, and the bridle path a grey strip between the deep black masses of the trees.

"When I get home I turn on the sprinkler and the fountain in the garden and sit for a few minutes in the best part of the night, about one o'clock to one-thirty. Far away across the ravine I can hear the night traffic. But there isn't a sound on my street except the splash of water around the cupid in the fountain. Then I go into my screened porch — just to keep off the mosquitoes, don't you see — turn my desk light on, and go to work." He makes it sound wonderful; there was always a wide streak of romance in him.

"I'm halfway into the manuscript of a new book, to follow the one that comes out later this summer. I'm excited about it, and as it grows quieter around me my ideas seem to get brighter and brighter, because I work best at night, best on an after-midnight summer night. And that's my summer in the city. Goodnight, everybody, and stay cool, won't you."

The announcer, another old acquaintance — the Wednesday Night series is like old home week for Joe — comes on to give David his plug, and is particular about urging his listeners to buy and read the new novel which is to appear late in August. Then he does the station break and is followed by strings playing an allegro from one of the Handel Opus Six Concertos.

"Jesus," says Joe violently, aloud, trying to wrench his thoughts away and remembering in spite of himself, "Jesus!"

Seven undergraduates are arguing in the kitchen, making a hideous racket, while Rabbit Wallace pokes angrily around in a pile of cartons and old newspapers beside the radiator.

"Jesus!" says Rabbit with terrible scorn, "will you look at that?" His face is wrathy and terrible, and the seven boys, Joe among them, break off their wrangle to stare at him.

"What is it?" asks one, and they silently follow his finger. Behind the pile of rubbish are lined up six pints of beer, a little cache concealed by some unsportsmanlike drinker so that when everyone else has drunk his last there will be some left for him.

"That's MY BEER," says Rabbit. "Which of you has done this?"

Nobody in the kitchen will confess to it and there are fifteen other possible culprits in the house.

"That's the trick of an alcoholic," says Rabbit angrily, "and it's damned selfish besides. I'll tell you, one of those stinking brandy-drinkers did this. We'll watch and see who comes for it later on, when everything else is gone. He picks up the six beers with tender loving care and puts them in the refrigerator, already a solid phalanx of green glass.

"These aren't cold," he says considerately, the perfect host, "I'll fish out some cold ones." He begins to yank out the bottles next the freezing unit, handing them back over his shoulder.

"Got enough?"

"I'm drinking gin," says one of the boys.

"And I'm not drinking," says another, who is in residence at Emmanuel.

"We'll hang on to the extra ones," says Rabbit to Joe, throwing his arm over his shoulders affectionately, "come on, I'll show you around."

It is all new to Joe, who has never lived in this part of town, this big old house across the ravine with the cupid in the fountain. The Wallaces have just bought it and are doing it over room by room, painting it and choosing the colours themselves. Rabbit leads him upstairs by winding back passages and downstairs by the graceful main staircase, showing him what they mean to do.

"Dad bought it after he came back from New York for good."

"For good?" Joe finds this incomprehensible. He has always believed that anyone who has the option will live in New York forever.

"Dad doesn't like New York. He thinks it hurts his writing. Paris didn't. He liked Paris and wrote well there. But there are too many writers in New York, all sitting around trying to impress each other. You know, Joey, a writer's career is very fragile; it has to be guarded carefully. Joe knows Rabbit can only be quoting his father, that he doesn't know anything about a writer's career at first hand, but what he says has an air of second-hand authenticity and shouldn't be ignored. Rabbit has already chosen his profession, the law, and can't be suspected of harbouring secret writing inclinations, so he can likely be trusted to report his father accurately.

"It's precious," says Joe.

"What is?"

"A writer's career. It has a certain shape of its own. The early works, the middle period, the periods of stagnation and doubt, the triumphant later years, and the final apotheosis."

They are standing at the foot of the staircase and as he rounds off this summary with proper sonority there comes a muffled shout of laughter from the coat closet and lavatory under the stairs. Joe starts nervously and takes a long drink of beer.

"That's Dad," says Rabbit, "I didn't know he was home. Hey, Dad, come on out. I know you're in there." He rattles the closet door. "What are you doing?"

"Shut up, Rabbit," says a voice, "I'm hiding the whiskey. I just got in." Then the closet door opens and Mr. Wallace emerges wearing a sheepish grin, looking first at Joe and then at his son. "It's like the marriage feast of Cana," he says, "except that I won't serve the good wine at the end; they wouldn't appreciate it. Who's this?"

"Joe Jacobson. Goes to U.C. My year."

Mr. Wallace looks at Joe. "You went to Malvern Collegiate," he says quickly but politely, "you got a scholarship," he takes another look, "and I would guess that your father's dead."

Joe stares at him, aware how easy the trick is, but half-impressed anyway.

"Sure it's a trick," says David Wallace, "a trick of observation. I didn't mean to speak lightly about your father." He is a small, lightly built man of fifty or so, with a suspiciously mild manner that conceals a terrifying alertness; he misses nothing. "I read that story of yours in *The Varsity*," he says now, to Joe's enormous gratification. "Rabbit brought it home and told me to look at it.

That's one of those lucky subjects, isn't it," he gives it professional consideration, "that you just daydream your way through. You didn't have to build that story, did you? It told itself."

"That's right," says Joe peaceably, although it isn't strictly true, "I didn't have to invent anything. It just came along and I put it down."

"I wish they were all like that," says Mr. Wallace, whose best-known book is a collection of stories, a marvellous collection, almost every story an anthology piece. "People read my stories," he says with humorous regret, "and they say: 'How easy. All he had to do was set it down as it came.'" He laughs. "I'll tell you something, Mr. Jacobson, there'll be a dozen or so, maybe twenty, stories that you can daydream your way through, that you don't have to build like you were building a house. Don't sit down and write up all those easy stories right off the bat, do you see? Save them, and build your early stories while you're learning how to write. When you've formed your style, then you can do those stories that come along line for line. Don't shoot them off all at once."

Since he hasn't yet read everything Mr. Wallace has written, Joe is on infirm ground. "The story of yours I like best," he says tentatively, "is 'The Girls in Their Summer Dresses.' That's a terrific story."

Rabbit gives Joe a peculiar look, smothering a grunt of laughter. "Joey," he says, "Joey, finish your beer!"

"'The Girls in Their Summer Dresses,'" says Mr. Wallace slowly and kindly, "I remember it. The young married couple on Fifth Avenue and he's looking over the other girls. You know," he smiles, "that's a story of Irwin Shaw's. When it came out I told him how much I liked it. It's in the first *New Yorker* collection, isn't it?" Seeing that Joe is about to die of mortification, he goes into the library to look for the book.

"I'd have sworn your father wrote it," says Joe to Rabbit helplessly.

But Rabbit has disappeared into the host of beer drinkers leaving him to face the music as Mr. Wallace comes back with a book in his hands.

"You're right, you know," he says comfortingly, "it's a subject I might have done myself, and it's about my length for that kind of piece, but it's Irwin's story. I'd never have done it that way. I remember telling him that and he wasn't very pleased with me." Then he leads Joe by degrees into the living room where there are only one or two slowly settling drinkers and begins to reminisce, as though he were talking to himself, in a way that opens Joe's eyes to a hitherto only half-suspected life.

"When I dropped Scribners and they dropped me — it was mutual but I made the first move — Max said to me: 'I'm sorry David that you've been so much under Ernest's shadow. Like Ruth and Gehrig. We know you're not a second-string Ernest but what can we do?' I suppose he had a point, although I'd been selling pretty well, especially the collection, which was a famous book for years. Maybe it will be again, one day, though of course you can't tell about these things. A lot of people have compared me to Anderson because I write about simple people in small towns quite a lot. But I'm not a primitive. I've had some intellectual training of a kind that Sherwood never had, and it hurt him. He had no judgment."

At this moment Joe could listen forever. Sherwood, Ernest, Max, and it is all real because David Wallace is the authentic thing with the fully formed career, with all the contacts. He really has known all these men and what's more they've known him and still do, except that Max and Sherwood are dead and so are Tom and Scott and Ernest.

"I was trained as a lawyer and was actually called to the bar after I left college," says Mr. Wallace, "and whatever you might think about some lawyers, the law is one of the great humane disciplines which can form the mind and give it a toughness that Sherwood never had. I still practise law now and then, just to keep the forms in my mind." He stares alertly at Joe. "Are you going to have a purely literary education?"

Nobody ever put such a question to him before; nobody from his neighbourhood could have thought of it; so he hasn't thought of it himself. "I don't know," says Joe.

"There's no telling, writers grow up like weeds, every-where, in the most surprising circumstances, and there aren't any laws. I think it helps to have a kind of …" he casts around for the word.

"Urbanity?" says Joe, off the end of his tongue.

"The very word. North American writers are rarely urbane — they're afraid to death of it. That's why we don't have those dozens of pretty good second-rate writers like the English have, writers whose good manners and schooling make up for their defects in imagination and talent."

"Is that so?" says Joe, who can think of nothing else to say.

"I don't know. I just thought of it. It might be true."

They are interrupted by the arrival in the living room of Rabbit, four undergraduates with beer bottles who have just heard that Mr. Wallace is in the house and who want to talk impressively with the celebrity, and a fifth miserable creature whom Rabbit accuses of hiding his beer.

"What a trick," he shouts with disgust, "so the rest of us wouldn't have any."

"Honest, Rabbit," moans his victim, "I brought them with me and there was no room in the icebox."

"Balls you did! Where's the empty carton?"

"I had them in my coat pockets. I'd have shared them with you."

"Oh, you would, would you?" Rabbit is too good-natured to embarrass the culprit any further. "I believe you," he says, though he obviously does not.

The eager undergraduates surround Mr. Wallace and ply him with technical questions of a breathtaking naivety.

"Do you feel that you can divorce art from morality?" asks the lad from Emmanuel, and with a polite smile Mr. Wallace turns to answer him. It astonishes Joe that nothing the thronging admirers can say, no matter how terrible, causes Mr. Wallace to lose his courtesy. He files this in his memory as the real professionalism.

"What do you do about myths?" asks another lad, maybe the most dreadful of all.

"I don't quite understand that," begins Mr. Wallace, just the least bit haltingly, and at this Joe quits the living room in search of his raincoat, finds it, and quietly leaves the house.

Afterwards he went there for years, all the way through that literary education which he decided to undergo in the face of Mr. Wallace's hints. Joe reckoned himself to be in a special situation not covered by the older man's mandate. He and all the other Jacobsons were strangers to every literature but the Rabbinical. There could be nothing discomforting, pedantic, unhealthy academic, in a formal literary training for a man who started from scratch as it were, who had to pack into himself the generations of evolution that the mannerly second-rate talents from Oxford would possess from instinct. Years later, when the going was good, when Joe thought that he had some control over his powers of expression and the English sentence generally, he still sometimes recognized that he was fundamentally an untrained writer, and that you couldn't acquire all the instincts of the mannerly Oxford second-rater in a single lifetime. Never mind, he would say to himself, your grandsons will have it in their marrow.

When he came to have something like a personal signature — for he wouldn't of course call it a "style" — he could still feel in his muscles the ache of holding the rules of expression together, and he understood what David had said about Anderson. The lacks, the gaps, not in one's formal education which grew in time to be mighty formidable, but in the larger, lovelier urbanity of the achieved European, were what hurt the first-generation writer.

When he found out that Proust was thought by the French uniquely the master of the imperfect and the past definite, he marvelled and marvels still at the notion of a society which honours a man for his command of a tense. Suppose there were a North American writer who possessed a great and unique mastery of, let's say, the present progressive. What decorations would he receive from a grateful civil authority, what honours reap from literate society?

Imagine a literary hostess: "I want you to meet Mr. Jones, the master of the present progressive." Imagine the response!

Sometimes Joe's friends would ask him, "Why do you go to see Wallace? There's nothing for you there, the guy's written out and has been since the Spanish Civil War." Cozy Walker said it to him first, and the nasty imputation made Joe stiffen his spine against the padding in the booth.

"That doesn't happen to the good ones."

"Sure it does," said Cozy, who had just magisterially completed a doctoral dissertation on the public life of Matthew Prior, "it happens to everybody on this continent. They all start off very brave and big, and in fifteen years they're done, because they've worked through themselves and they never, but never my hopeful little friend, get on to anything else."

"Not true!" said Joe, muddling his Manhattan vortically.

"David Wallace is no good for you, Joe. You can't learn a thing from him, he's a primitive. He never had the least idea how to write, he's a transcriber."

Joe looked fiercely at Cozy. "I read your thesis, Buster, and if that doesn't shut you up, nothing will."

"I don't profess to be a writer."

"I should hope not."

"But you do."

"Yes," said Joe, "and that's my affair. Why don't you drop it, since you don't know what you're talking about?"

"I've never in my life found that a deterrent," said Cozy cheerfully, signalling for another drink.

"Just remember, nobody's ever written out. That's a term used by the ignorant, like you."

"So, O.K. We're all ignorant about something."

"But we don't all talk about it."

He never used to go to David's house for his "local" literary education, not wanting to talk to him about tenses, or the management of relative clauses, but mostly to learn how the literary life was lived, where the stories came from and how they grew, why it was that peoples' careers took this or that shape, why some guys couldn't do anything after forty and some could do nothing before, though these were rare. And on this last point there was always a certain constraint because David had written nothing so good as his first half-dozen books for ten years and was just then trying to work around the difficulty with every atom of craft, technique, ingenuity, he could command.

When Joe asked him about it, he couldn't tell. "They just came," he said, "and neither Helen nor I knew how lucky we were. I just wrote them up and sent them out and they sold, like that."

"I remember," said Helen from the depths of her armchair, "one time David and I were in Chicago, I don't recall what for. But that day *Scribner's Magazine* published two stories by David. There was a little belt of paper around each copy with his name on it. 'Two new stories by David Wallace.' And we just took it for granted."

"They came so easy," said David, smiling affectionately at Helen, "but they don't anymore. There was one story that I simply transcribed from a magistrate's court record. The whole story was in the re-arrangement of course; the trick was to see the story there."

"Edward O'Brien loved that story," said Helen reminiscently.

"Sure. He sent me a four-page letter about it. How do you see the story in the facts? Where does it come from? I used to see them all the time, clear as crystal, and now I have to jockey around, weigh this fact against that, and try to guess which are the right ones."

"It's a question of maturity," said Helen, with her queerly passive certainty, "because to write the story you have to think it important. When we're young, we think every little perception we have is fundamental. But in middle age we're more critical. You simply don't write so hastily nowadays, because you've seen more of the world, and you know that a lot of the moving little occurrences that you witness are not important. Twenty years ago you'd write them up immediately and therefore some of those early stories are naive. But this new novel — it won't come easily and it won't be naive."

"Well, Joe's a young man. How about it, Joe, do you have second thoughts about your story ideas?"

"No. The editors have to do that for me, and they do. When I've had ten rejections on a story I figure that maybe it wasn't such a good idea at that. I don't know. I still can't tell the authentic ones from the fake or the dull. I wish to God I could."

"But they get winnowed out when you send them around?"

"And how."

"I don't understand that," said David regretfully, "because it's an experience I never had. I sold almost everything I wrote for fifteen years, without any effort. Maybe you're lucky."

"But I've written forty stories," said Joe, a little desperately, "which is pretty good for a man my age, and some of them are not too bad. You've read them and you know. And I've sold exactly two of them. Now how am I different from you?"

"You might be less talented," said David candidly, "but not enough to make that much difference."

"He's lucky, he's lucky. Do you know what I read the other day?" said Helen. "I read an article about some screenwriter. He might not be a real writer at all; few of them are. But he said one very interesting thing. When he was asked how he became a writer he said, 'Five hundred thousand people started out to be writers the same day I did. All the others stopped. I'm the only one left.' I think he's got a point."

"If he said that," said David, "he's probably pretty good." "The trick is simply not to stop?"

"That's it, that's it."

Joe sighed. "I wish there were a surer way."

All at once David crossed the room and turned off the television which had been glowing, pictureless, for two hours. "Could we have some buns and coffee?" he asked Helen.

"Yes," she said, "should we expect Rabbit?"

"If he isn't home now, I don't expect he will be."

"He's at a party," said Joe. "I was supposed to go."

"But you came here instead," said Helen at the door, "that's charming."

Joe laughed. "I wasn't trying to make an impression."

"I know, sweetie," she said, "Buns...." she muttered abstractedly, trailing it out the door. David came and stood beside Joe's chair and lowered his voice.

"It's this damned novel that's upset her," he said, "she's really pulling for me to bring it off. The trouble is, she knows me too well."

"I wish there were something I could do," said Joe, "but …"

"But there isn't, is there? I haven't written a novel since just before the war. I did a full-length juvenile, and a collection of memoirs that ran to novel-length, and a lot of travelling and broadcasting, and maybe twenty stories. But I haven't kept up. Boy," he said fervently, "this one better go"

"It'll go," said Joe loyally, "because it's going to be a great book."

"My agent thinks so but then he's prejudiced and besides he's anxious to make some money out of me. I haven't put a dime on his books in ten years."

"He isn't getting tough about it?"

"Lord, no, he's a personal friend! I was his second client. But he wants a picture sale or maybe a play out of it and I'm not certain they're there. It's a difficult subject."

"It'll go," said Joe again. There wasn't anything else to say. And then Helen came back with cinnamon buns and coffee and they talked for a few minutes about Rabbit, who was beginning to have second thoughts about the legal profession.

"He has that uneasy look," said David, "that presages a sudden flight to Paris. I know it well. And I wish I weren't middle-aged." He grinned. "My middle period, my transitional phase." Then all at once he decided to round off the evening with a benediction. "Maybe I can tell you once and for all how it is, Joe, for me, and perhaps for you too. Some idiot once asked me about the myths, and how I used them. Now I don't know about that. I'm not a man for the technical terms of criticism and I wouldn't recognize a myth, I guess, if I tripped over one. But I *can* tell you this: there's a point where the myth, if you want to call it that, the great story of which you've stumbled into a small part, assumes a kind of possession of you. You don't use it; it uses you. I don't mean that you're inspired. But the myth touches you, gets into you and begins to tell the story for you, through you, making the decisions for you. When that happens, and control of the tale passes out of your hands, you almost begin to be in the story yourself. I don't mean to sound poetic but it's like a laying-on of hands. You're touched, you're possessed, you're all committed, engaged, and if the story doesn't please or beguile of itself, you're lost, because you have to set down what is dictated. You have to live your way into the story. And that's how it is." He set down his coffee cup and stretched, and looked embarrassed.

"Living under the myth," said Joe thoughtfully. It sounded like magic to him.

"In and under it — that's the trouble with this new book."

He heard no more of this curious doctrine from David himself but he saw how it worked when the "middle-period, transitional" novel appeared, was revised with utter incomprehension on every side, was dumped and written-off by its publishers, and early allowed to disappear into the limbo of excellent books that haven't sold. Wrong myth, he thought to himself, as he saw David become more and more a journalist, getting his living in television and radio and from magazine and newspaper articles. Wrong myth!

Just as David had prophetically guessed, the design of the "middle period, transitional" book had baffled everyone who read it. With every inner consistency, with marvellous truth to itself, the myth had made him its scapegoat. For not content with dictating a narrative that wouldn't beguile, the myth, or whatever had composed the book, positively offended people and made them dislike the novel and its writer for affronting them with a narrative that didn't fit their sense of where a story ought to come from and go. Wrong myth, wrong audience! And David left in the middle, still trying in the middle of all his journalism to work through those late nights into the middle of another book, trying to get from "the period of stagnation and doubt" to "the triumphant later years."

When Joe left town, the highest diploma clutched tightly in his hand, David was still trying, still reassuring Helen that he would make it, working on a new book, this one about innocence, crystal clear, no puzzlements, with none of the characters on two sides at the same time, with none of the illogicalities which Joe thought nearly Shakespearian but which the public found idiotic.

The two men had their struggles, and to some extent shared them, although Joe never wrote directly to David, so much his senior, so much still compelling a filial piety. He wrote instead to Rabbit who had by now given up the law, or been given up by it, and who was operating a feature syndicate, the first in the country, for a Toronto daily that had visions of national influence. Rabbit, Joe knew, was nurturing secret writing inclinations and might at any moment commit a novel. So they corresponded and he heard incidentally, in Evanston or Cambridge, how the new book was going, how slowly and silently it was evolving. And this secret submarine evolution of a new book which cost David five years' work, and upon which he was risking everything, began to coincide more and more closely with the gestation of Joe's own novel, not his first, but the first that looked anywhere near publishable.

He had gone on turning out stories year by year and by now one-tenth of them sold, an improvement over his earlier ratio of two in forty. Of his newer stories, one in ten was picked up by a quarterly and he banked the rest in a trunk against the day when everybody would know what he was talking about, instead of an occasional perceptive editor, and in the spring of this year he printed his sixth story and began to call himself a writer. He had always told himself that six stories would justify the name and there were times when the slender figure looked unattainable.

Statistics have nothing to do with composition but it is curious how regular a curve describes the early publications of a new writer. There will be at first the hundred and twenty printed slips which give way in time to printed slips with a word in ink at the bottom. This goes on for a while and Joe studies those inked monosyllables and wonders who wrote them, what the initials stand for, what the reader thought.

And then there are the letters which say "We are holding the story for further consideration." These come very late in the day, labourers of the eleventh hour, and now Joe feels the force of the screenwriter's aphorism. "Five hundred thousand began the same year. All the others stopped. I'm the only one left." But the stories "held for further consideration" march back one by one and he tells himself comfortingly that someday somebody will buy them. It'll be slow coming but it'll come, it'll come. "All the others stopped. I'm the only one left."

But no myth has ever possessed Joe and done the story for him; he builds them up with carpentry, nailing the clumsy pieces together and hoping the nail-holes don't show, apologizing by the things he can do for the things he can't, as every writer must.

"Why don't you write a bestseller under an alias?" asks Toby Frankel, the fourth time he takes her out; they are sitting in the LaSalle Beverage Room in the heart of downtown Kingston, having an economical date, three dollars worth of draught beer which is a fair amount of beer at that. He looks at her upper arms which are lovely, round but not fat, one might call them plump, perhaps. Anyway they will cover a multitude of sins.

"You mean a pseudonym," he says hungrily.

"I mean an alias," she says, "I know perfectly well you'd consider it immoral." She is a practising clinical psychologist, or will be very soon, and her ideas of motivation are not his.

"I couldn't do it anyway," he says, "it requires a special skill that I don't have. I couldn't write for a newspaper either without taking the time to learn the technique. And it's taken me ten years to learn the technique of the short story and I'm not finished yet." He thinks this over for a minute and is rueful. "I haven't even started."

"I wonder if anything that takes that long can be worth it?" she says with womanly pragmatism. "You can become a heart specialist or a psychoanalyst in twelve years, and a Jesuit, I'm told, in thirteen."

She is being subtle, for her. "And a short story writer knows more of the secrets of the heart than all three," says Joe, "isn't that what I'm supposed to say?"

She is engaging. "I set it up for you."

"Well, he probably doesn't — but he knows as much. Thirteen years of study ought to yield something in the way of practised application of one's knowledge."

"If the talent is there."

Joe shudders. "My theory," he says hopefully, "is that the talent is in the application to study. The talent *is* the diligence."

"Then anyone can become an artist of the short story?"

"No. Not everyone can do the thirteen years' work."

"I see. The empiricist view of talent. The talented are those who last thirteen years."

"There's no other way to measure it," he sighs, "and I wish you were not studying psychology. I sold a story this morning."

"Joey, you didn't!"

"I did and that makes five; one more to go."

"To go for what?"

"Never mind," he says, "and I'll get an agent out of this one, because I made some money out of it for a change." He watches with amusement as her eyes widen.

"How much?"

"Seven hundred and fifty."

"How long did you take to write it?"

"Thirteen years."

"I mean the actual writing-time."

"Counting revisions, about a month."

"But on your spare time?"

"Uh-huh."

"If you could do that once a month, over and above your salary, you'd be doing very well, wouldn't you?"

He starts to laugh. "I would, but I don't expect they'll all bring that good a price."

"Oh, but it's something to think about, and why are we going on this cheap date anyway? We ought to celebrate." She is already taking that proprietorial tone.

"And spend the whole seven hundred and fifty?"

"Just the odd fifty."

"It's these odd fifties that kill you." He stirs thoughtfully in his chair. "I'll buy your dinner and we can go someplace after. The important thing is, I may be able to get an agent."

"Does it really help?"

"Not unless you're selling a lot. Stories are bought on their own merits, by and large, but an agent helps you to get a careful reading and he looks after the paper work, mailing and such. They're most useful if you're really in business with both feet.

"You will be," she says, with a very friendly gleam.

"Yeah. An agent might help me place a novel, which is very hard. Come on, I'll buy you something to eat. Maybe even steak."

So small a world is the circle of editors, publishers, writers and agents, that even before his big sale appears in print Joe begins to receive cautious non-committal notes from people who would like, without making any positive declarations, to see what else he can do that may be of use to them. In no other market does word-of-mouth play so important a part. Long long before a new writer's name is known to the general public, sometimes several years before, the little group centred on New York, with trading posts in Boston, Philadelphia, Cleveland, Toronto, knows all about him, what he can do, what his prospects are, whether he is ever likely to be any good. The writers themselves, though not so concentrated geographically, are even more inbred. A youngster who lives in Phoenix, Arizona, who is twenty-six, who has printed three stories, can be certain that fifty of his near contemporaries (who are personally utterly unknown to him) nevertheless know through the channels all that they need to know about him, and how much they need to fear him, perhaps because they have met somebody who was in the same graduate school, or because an editor-acquaintance has read him extensively, or maybe because he once worked for six months in New York and went to the parties. It makes altogether for a good deal of taking in each other's washing and it is sometimes doubtful whether anybody reads new fiction except the two thousand men who write, edit, and try to market it.

Joe begins to get these feelers and they give him the worst six months of his life as each of seven publishing houses reads his three novel-length manuscripts, every editor earnestly searching for something he can "save" — this curious technical term "save" which means "make marketable" — and out of the twenty-one chances, twenty are blanks. But, oh, that glorious twenty-first!

He clicks when the last of the friendly Salvationists takes a chance on the latest of the three manuscripts, writing a letter to Kingston and taking the manuscript to the higher echelons — the editorial conference — where the gist of his defence is "we won't make a nickel on this book but with moderate promotion we shouldn't lose anything, which is nice, and anyway we've got a strong fall list and we can afford the risk, and who knows, who knows?"

"Does he have an agent?"

"Yeah, but he won't make trouble, we're doing him a favour. I tell you, George, in all honesty, this is a real borderline case."

"Give them the standard contract and specify the promotional appropriation. Now, where were we?"

"You wanted to discuss the merger, George."

"Sure. Sure. This is a quality house, gentlemen, and I want you to know that the merger won't affect our trade policy one bit. Not one bit. You may think otherwise and you're going to be surprised."

"Textbooks!" says a disgusted voice in a corner but George ignores the interruption and goes calmly on. Of such is the kingdom of Heaven or so it seems to Joe when he gets word of the acceptance from his agent almost concurrently with the sale of his sixth story, that achieved half-dozen, the magic figure. On his next credit-application he describes himself as "Writer, Teacher."

In late May the city sky is topless, clear and blue, you can see through it, and the still oppressive heat of later summer hasn't yet come on to immobilize everyone in the middle of the day. His examination papers graded, the scholastic year behind him, Joe feels free to take a week to go and see the Canadian publishers who will handle his book as agents for New York, to examine, if he can, the dust-jacket design and the layout of any point-of-sale promotional material that they may have in mind. It really isn't any of his business and he ought to keep his nose out of it; he wouldn't dare go near the New York office for a similar purpose. But he has friends in Toronto and things are conducted more informally, so he is willing to take the chance. Also, he thinks with enormous pleasure, he can see David and Helen and tell them all about it, and maybe he can even tell them about Toby, what there is to tell, which is nothing specific except that it is time he got married and she is a girl he knows. After lunch, his first day in, he makes his phone call, forgetful of David's schedule.

"He isn't up yet," says Helen, "but we both want to see you."

"I'd forgotten. And it's nearly one-thirty."

"You know David! He was working very late last night. I guess he finished up around six, six-thirty."

"I can't do that. I have to get it done by midnight or the day is wasted. What's he working on?"

"Another novel, to follow the one that's coming out in August. But he'll want to tell you about it himself. When are we going to see you?"

"Tonight, if it's all right."

"Of course it's all right. Come any time."

He tarries downtown, repressing his eagerness for the meeting, until seven o'clock, when he goes to the Morrissey Dining Room for the sake of his recollections, hoping that he will see somebody he knows; it is handy to the studios and the publisher's Toronto offices and there, sure enough, is Cozy Walker with a nameless girl, a beauty, whom Cozy hastens to exhibit with an air of proprietorship, though without revealing her name or origins.

"What are you doing in here?" asks Joe. It is a kind of desecration to find Cozy in the place, which is really not for academics.

"I'm in television, didn't you know?" says Cozy defensively. "I'm a producer."

"No!" says Joe flatly. "No, you're not!" He doesn't see how it can be true.

"Oh, but I am and this is my script assistant. We do 'Studio,' the half-hour drama series. And that reminds me, Joe, why don't you submit to us?"

"I'll submit to your script assistant any time, if that's what she wants."

"I mean manuscripts," says Cozy crossly, "don't you write plays?"

"I write fiction. That's all I know about."

"Then you'd better learn something else or you'll never get anywhere. Haven't you heard about the anti-novelists? Fiction is dead. What's wanted now is stuff for the mass media. John Osborne writes for TV."

"Sure, and Kingsley Amis writes for the magazines, and have you read his last book?"

"No."

"Read it! All you guys think that writing is dead but it isn't. I'm doing all right."

"You've got a novel coming out in August, haven't you?" says the beautiful script assistant, with respect and envy in her voice. She looks from one man to the other, patently preferring the man in the outmoded medium. "August 25th?"

"I didn't think anybody knew. I thought the publishers were keeping it our little secret."

"August 25th," says Cozy with malicious pleasure, "an interesting coincidence. I wonder what David Wallace will make of it."

"Why should David make anything out of it?"

"Because his book comes out on the twenty-sixth."

"Oh."

"Yes, oh! And I think I can predict that he won't like it very much, dear boy. He's counting on this book to bring him back."

"He's never been away."

"Oh ho ho ho. Go and ask him! Just you go and ask him, my uptown friend."

"I think I will. Goodbye Cozy, goodbye Miss Script Assistant, I wish I knew your name, but poor old Cozy...." He stalks out of the place, feeling his face grow red. He hasn't for several years wanted to punch anybody quite that much. He can quite see the academician as a producer on the parochial little TV network with its ten half-baked writers competing with each other, but not as the doyen and arbiter of the forms of new art. And the remark about David and himself keeps him a little short of breath all the way across town on the streetcar. He doesn't recover his equanimity until the slow walk across the ravine cools him out. But by the time he knocks on the familiar door he is restored and as eager for the meeting as when he'd planned it.

Behind the door is David, unchanged, a year or two short of sixty now but the same slight mild-mannered friend of almost a decade, his face creased in a welcoming grin.

"Come in, come in, Helen's here and I've decided not to work tonight, so we've got the whole of it to ourselves. Are you in town for long?"

"Three or four more days. I wanted to see Fred Callan."

"About your book, wonderful, sure. Are they treating you decently?"

"You know how it is; they aren't spending a cent over the budget."

"It won't be that way next time," says David, which is exactly what he ought to say, so why does Joe feel uneasy? "They'll spend thousands next time. We haven't heard much about the book, all the same."

"That doesn't matter," says Joe, heading him off, "tell me about the new novel." The three of them seat themselves squarely in the same old trio of easy chairs, settling down for what looks like a long night.

"I've seen the jacket," says David eagerly, "I've got one here." He goes to a writing cabinet in the corner, takes out the brightly-coloured piece of paper and flips it to Joe. "They've featured my name on purpose," he says with naive pride, "and they're playing up my European reputation in the promotion. You know, I went to the Plaza for a drink with Jack MacCartney the afternoon we signed the contracts. He did all the work on the book himself. And after we'd had about three drinks he said to me, 'David, you were a GREAT reputation. What happened?' The drinks had loosened his tongue, don't you see? And then he said, 'I'm going to bring it all back.' I believe he wants to play God and that's all right with me because they're spending a lot of money on the book; they're giving me a cocktail party on publication day — that's August twenty-sixth — and they've sent everybody advance copies. They've got a quote from Bill Faulkner which they're going to use. He always liked my things. I tell you, Joe, I'm very high on this book. I think perhaps this is the one."

"It's really good, Joey," says Helen surely, and maybe her testimony is the best of all, and Joe feels more and more uneasy, "it's *his* book. You'll see that the minute you read it. It's about innocence and it makes Leslie Fiedler look gauche."

"You've put a lot of yourself into it?" asks Joe lamely.

"Boy, as Helen says, it's *my* book, Joe. This one is for me."

"A writer's career has a perilous shape," says Joe with a careful smile.

"That's right. 'The triumphant later years, the final apotheosis.' I had a tough middle period but I think that's all over now. You're going to find out, after you've finished 'the early works.'" and at last he puts the awkward question. "When is your book coming out?"

"Oh, that." There is nothing for it but to tell him. "As a matter of fact it's coming out the day before yours."

"The day before mine?"

Helen sits up abruptly in her deep chair, looking from one man to the other wordlessly.

"August twenty-fifth," whispers Joe.

David stands looking at him in amazement. "What do you think you're up to?"

"David, you know how it is with a first novel. You don't tell them; they tell you. It won't hurt your book."

"What a trick!"

"David, there'll be twenty novels coming out that week. Mine won't make any difference to you. You're famous. Your book will be a publishing event. Nobody's going to notice mine."

"He's right, David," says Helen sharply. "It won't make an atom of difference. You aren't competing with each other."

Without taking his eyes from Joe, he puts her view aside. "We're all competing. What's he trying to do to me? There's only so much review space. Of course we're competing. The same week, the day before. Why it's all been planned, hasn't it? Everybody knows you're supposed to be my friend. Some friend! I need all the help I can get." He is terribly upset.

"When they assigned me that date, I hadn't any idea when your book was coming out, not the least idea."

"And you think they didn't? I've had dealings with George before this. They're simply trying to kill my book, blanket it with yours. What happens if yours is very good, tell me that?"

Joe is now a little stung. "It's pretty good," he says.

"It ought to be, for Christ's sake, you've been at it long enough. And then you have the nerve to walk into my house to tell me about it."

"David, be fair," says Helen.

"Be fair, be fair," he says, "was anybody fair to my last book? Fairness has nothing to do with it," and he stands looking at Joe in bewilderment, "and taking the silver," he quotes, "the chief priests bought with it a potter's field which is called Haceldama, that is, the field of blood, even to this day."

Joe picks it up and the implication that because he's a Jew he won't catch the reference freezes him, absolutely freezes him, rooting him motionless in his chair for a second as Helen stares regretfully from one to the other. Talking about myths, he thinks in a flash, talking about being possessed, the guy's possessed, he's disappeared into the myth; it's swallowed him. What am I sitting here for?

Without a word, waiting until later for reflection and self-doubt to assail him, he walks out of the house, the city spoiled for him, the pleasant life he'd looked forward to rejoining spoiled for him, the name of Judas whispering in his ear as he goes.

The strings are still playing Handel as he stands before his old "Atwater Kent" with his hand on the useless knob which says TONE. All at once, miraculously, the shriek and rattle in the speaker fade out and the orchestra becomes smooth and lovely, displaying the movement of the master's mind. He looks blankly at the curtain of faded velvet behind the fretted scrolls and remembers the childlike enthusiasm his father had for all such wonderful contrivances. "It's a miracle, Babele, listen!" He puts his hand gently on the volume control and turns the sound down, way down, until the strings are only a murmur, and he thinks of the dedication to his book, TO MY FATHER, and thinks to himself, I'm glad it's for him, for my father, for my real father, and he moves his wrist slightly and the music stops.

THE END OF IT

In their eyes I have seen
the pin men of madness in marathon trim
race round the track of the stadium pupil.
                — P.K. Page, "The Stenographers"

"Sixty seconds," said a voice in the dark. "Landy ran the first quarter in a minute flat, he set a killing pace and held it. I never thought he'd hold it."

The four men sat silently in the projection room and watched the film of the famous race, "the mile of the century." They heard the crowd noises on the sound track and began to pulse with them, but the film never showed the crowd, it followed the runners as they circled the track. The rhythm of the crowd noises grew steadily more insistent.

"There's Rich Ferguson in third place. He ran his best mile ever and finished third in 4:01 and change. Watch now, here comes Bannister."

The runners seemed to be racing around the edge of the screen, leaving the centre blank. You followed the runners intensely and were aware of the great blank space, the stadium infield, at some inferior level of consciousness.

"You haven't cut once," said Sanderson, "you've simply kept them in focus, and panned all the way round." He grew excited.

"Watch now, this is the great part!" Bannister picked up a cue from his coach at the end of the third quarter and lengthened his stride.

"I wanted to zoom in on Landy but we couldn't. A news photographer caught him when he wobbled. Here it comes, there, there, see that? He had a bad heel that he didn't tell anyone about." They all saw him wobble, lose his rhythm momentarily and pick it up as Bannister went by. Perfectly involuntarily the four men began to pound on the arms of their seats and chant in the runner's rhythm "GO, GO, GO, GO, GO, GO, GO, GO," and the sound in the small projection room bounced from the walls and rebounded into their chant, reinforcing it, "GO, GO, GO, GO, GO, GO, GO, GO," it was bedlam as Bannister broke the tape and the film ended, the lights came on, they saw where they were, they glanced at each other with embarrassment and amusement. They had been naive; they had let what they did for a living move them.

"That's exactly what happened on the day of the race," said Sanderson, "I was sitting in a beer parlour with a crowd of total strangers, we were glued to the set, and the moment Bannister pulled out to pass, everybody in the room picked up his rhythm. By God, you talk about ritual art, it *was* ritual, I've never seen anything like that in my life." He was shaking with pleasure and excitement. "And it happens every time, that's the important thing." He turned to the CBC man from whom they had borrowed the film. "How did you get that, Wilfrid, that's an important piece of film? You could win prizes with it."

"We did win prizes with it, we got an award for photojournalism that same year. It's a very nice sequence, isn't it?"

"Nice? It's a classic," said Sanderson. He turned to the others. "See what I told you? It runs four minutes and it's a single sequence. He doesn't cut or dissolve at any point, and look what he gets!"

"It was pure accident," said the CBC man, Wilfrid Wallace, who felt terribly pleased to hear Sanderson saying these things, the Dean of the Film Board, the best man on documentary since Grierson and Flaherty. Of course, he told himself in qualification, these guys are all either Socialists or nuts. I don't know why but they have this large bleeding sense of the heart of the folk. Comes of shooting all those closeups of gnarled faces. But he listened carefully to what Sanderson was saying and felt flattered.

"We'll have him run it again," said Philip Sanderson to his editor and cutter, "and I want you to watch and see how the effect builds, it has a starting point, you become aware of the crowd at the same moment every time. I've got a stopwatch here and I'm going to clock it. I think it comes towards the end of the second quarter. Just at that instant the audience gets in there with the runners, that's the first important movement. Then for about a minute we can't keep our eyes off Landy, but we sense that Bannister is there. We don't pay any attention at all to Ferguson because we know he isn't a threat, he's straining and straining. Even at this distance we can see him strain to stay in the running. But Bannister is hanging off there in third place full of power." He broke off, struck with another train of thought.

"You see what it is? The motion casts the film *for* you. It writes your script and makes Landy the villain, and he was a nice fellow, I'm told, and it makes Bannister the hero and for all I know he's just a decent British doctor, which is what he is. But the motion gives you a script and a cast and an action. Oh, I'm going to do something about this film; it can't be allowed to moulder away in a library."

"It had to be a single sequence because we broke the other camera," said Wallace, laughing.

"Is that what happened, truly?"

"You know how these athletic meets are, they have officials milling around all over, more officials than runners. And one of these guys — I never knew his name but he had a badge of some kind — got his foot caught in our cable just as the race started and disconnected Camera Two. Then while he was apologizing, he and the cameraman knocked the damned thing over. I swear to God that's what happened, so I couldn't use it at all. I'd had a shooting schedule, just a little bit of a thing on the back of an envelope, and my zoom lens was on Two. It shouldn't have been. It should have been on One, but I just didn't know how to shoot a footrace."

Sanderson smote his brow. "And you got this great thing by accident? If you'd had the other camera working, you'd have messed it up zooming in and out. Oh, Wilfrid, Wilfrid, you lucky bloody bastard!"

"That's life for you. I had to shoot it on One. There was nothing else to do."

"You see," Sanderson said with real bitterness and without humour, "he gets by accident what I've racked my brain for twenty years to figure out."

"It's a remarkable piece of work," said his cutter obsequiously, "it's purely cinematic."

Sanderson stared at him coldly. "Kitcheff," he said, "I know that you are fresh from the University Film Society and I can make certain allowances, but would you really mind not using phrases like 'purely cinematic,' I mean, really?"

Kitcheff was wounded and showed it; that was one thing about Sanderson, he didn't mind your letting him see what you felt. "How else would you say it?" demanded Kitcheff rebelliously.

"Say it some way that means something. Who knows what 'cinematic' is? Nobody knows. You don't have to talk like that."

"All I mean is what you said yourself," said Kitcheff, "it's the art form of timed movement in space, and it dictates the shape of the given piece of work."

"This is a sterile discussion," said the editor, sanctimoniously.

Sanderson reversed his field, rounding on the editor and defending Kitcheff. "We've got to try to say these things some way, otherwise how will we know what we're doing?"

"Leave it to the critics," said the editor, who hoped one day to be a producer himself in a secure situation where he wouldn't have to listen to Sanderson who, genius though he might be, was feckless, undependable in argument, apt to change his mind at any point, and full of crazy ideas.

"Timed movement in space," he was saying just now, weighing it, "it's a nice phrase, Kitcheff boy, but I don't know what it means."

"Don't you tell him, Kitcheff," said the editor hastily, "don't try to tell him or we'll be here all afternoon. Are we going to run it again?"

"We are," said Sanderson, taking up his lecture where he'd dropped it, "and I want you to notice precisely when we feel like pounding the arms of the chairs, and when we actually begin to do it."

"I can tell you that," said Wilfrid Wallace, "it's just where —"

"Shut up for God's sake," said Sanderson, "I want them to find out for themselves. This proves an important point and it's going to make *A Walk Home from School* great documentary, something we've never done before. Purely cinematic, huh!" He walked back to the booth and told the projectionist to run the film again. As the lights dimmed he drew a stop-watch from his pocket and concentrated on the screen with enormous intensity. Kitcheff and the editor, Vasko, glared at him with mutinous envy. He had really extraordinary powers of concentration and could remember every detail of every shot, cut, sequence, angle, from every one of the thousands of movies he'd seen and made. It caused them trouble all the time.

"They used that in *Une Fille pour L'Eté*," he would say, and then they had to spend hours figuring another way to do it. In the dark they heard him fiddling with the stopwatch, clucking and mumbling to himself.

"It's the empty space they're running around," they heard him say, "that's what gives you the effect, you want to get in there beside the runners." Nobody answered him.

"Of course I'm not a psychologist," he said to nobody in particular, "a psychologist would likely tell you differently." And then they all began to beat on the arms of their seats again and only Kitcheff wondered if this was because Sanderson was willing them to do it, and the race was over, the tape breasted, Bannister home and cooled out, lights on. Vasko and Kitcheff smiled happily at Sanderson, and he pumped Wilfrid Wallace's hand with the disinterested pleasure he always took in really good work, his own or another's.

"I'm so glad you could get down to talk to us," he said, "I had the hell of a job worming the piece out of the CBC Library, and the boys had to see it. They're giving me a very bad time just now." He stared expressionlessly at Vasko and Kitcheff, making them fidget. He wasn't vindictive but he would say anything, absolutely anything, with terrifying candour, and they never knew what to expect. "Can you have dinner with Margery and me?" He was leaving them out of the invitation quite openly, but he had meals with them all the time, meals which they never remembered eating, though the food stains were on their clothes and they didn't feel hungry. They had been arguing over *A Walk Home from School* for three weeks now, and their office was full of coffee containers that nobody would admit ordering.

"I'm catching the five o'clock out of the Windsor Station," said Wallace, "I've got to do a football game tomorrow."

"What can you do with a football game?" said Sanderson interestedly.

"Not a hell of a lot. CBS pretty well established the conventions ten years ago."

"I'd like to do one," said Sanderson, "or fool around with the tape."

The others guffawed. "The audience would love it," said Wallace, "but they wouldn't know the score."

Vasko and Kitcheff were hilarious and Sanderson looked innocent. "I have no idea what you mean," he said and then he laughed and put his arm around Wallace's shoulder, walking him out of the projection room and making pleasant chat.

"Do you mean Margery Endicott?" said Wallace as they went out. "I'm in love with Margery Endicott, always have been, always will be. She played Juliet at Hart House my first year in college. I guess she was in fourth year then, but she really looked fourteen, only Juliet I've ever seen who looked fourteen, *ka-bong, ka-bong.*"

Vasko and Kitcheff sat looking at each other as their chief left the room. "She's thirty-four now," they heard him say, "and it's no secret, she tells everybody. You never saw such a thirty-four year old in your life. Did you know we were married for a while?" His voice passed out of hearing.

"He *is* crazy," said Vasko, "it can't be done, nobody will watch it. It's a waste of the taxpayer's money."

Kitcheff chuckled around his pipe-stem; he was an insecure young man who doubted that he could carry off a pipe *and* tweeds, so he settled for the pipe without the tweeds and even at that was afraid. "Who gives a shit about the taxpayers?" he said.

"I know, it's just an expression. But I tell you, Ted, if he shoots a film that runs to one fifteen-minute sequence — and I don't care about the angles, anybody can figure out impossible angles — for one thing we'll be out of a job, figuratively speaking, I mean, if you don't mean to cut and edit the film, where does that leave us?"

"The Film Board never fires anybody," said Kitcheff equably.

"Oh, I'm not worried about my job. They aren't all like him, thank God, none of the other producers think that way."

"None of them are as good."

"Oh, he's good all right, up to a certain point, I'll grant you that, but lately, I don't know, lately I've been wondering about him, some people are great artists and some are just plain crazy, and it's hard to tell the difference. Maybe he's a fraud."

"That has nothing to do with you — you just follow instructions, you're not a policy-maker. And as for me, I'm just a little guy fresh from the University Film Society. We don't have to worry, we aren't responsible, and anyway the world won't stop revolving just because one fifteen-minute documentary is a flop. What difference does it make?"

Vasko was looking around for his topcoat, not paying much attention. "Maybe it's a question of artistic principle."

Kitcheff said, "That's Film Society talk. Sanderson would vomit if he heard you say that."

"He can have principles, why can't we?"

"We can't afford them. Wait till you're a producer, then you can have all the principles you want."

"Yeah, I guess you're right. Let's go over to the Seven Steps and check the talent." They left the projection room, feeling glad that they didn't have to go back upstairs, they were through for the day.

"How did Sanderson ever get into Margery Endicott? He's twice her age," said Vasko.

"Genius, Vasko boy, pure genius."

"Huh!" said Vasko.

As he waited for the operator to locate Miss Endicott, through a bewildering tintamarre of crossed wires, clicks, half-heard confused voices, Sanderson let his thoughts run peaceably along without conscious control, letting his ear, a hot, sore ear pressed against a sweaty receiver, direct his associations. His life with Margery had been fed through a switchboard with a clumsy operator making a bad connection every time they tried to reach each other. It was an idea for a poem, the poet is trying to reach somebody, probably a girl, but he keeps getting "one moment, please" and at length hangs up. He hadn't written a poem for fifteen years, preferring the visual medium; but you couldn't put that idea on film. It wasn't "purely cinematic," there was nothing to it visually.

How do you express the imperfect tense on film?

I used to try and reach her. We used to go around together. We were going to the movies quite a lot in those days. The imperfect, despite its name, is the tense for the good old days back there. It's a flashback, a montage, a long closeup, and a slow dissolve.

I'm being frivolous, he thought, and anyway that's another man's idea, not mine, but you could figure out the appropriate film technique for every tense, not excluding the *plus-que-parfait* and the *conditionnel antérieure*. The French, he thought, who worries about such notions but the French?

Movies have no tense, he decided, movies are all in the present just as you see them, even flashback gives us a present past. That's my problem, he realized all at once, that's my disease. I'm trying to seize the whole present, but literature keeps sneaking in and giving me history. I don't want history, and I don't want to think about Margery ten years ago.

Then the operator found her and she came on the line sounding irritated as all hell. "What are you trying to do to me, Phil? I've got work to do, I'm a busy girl and I'm menstruating like mad."

She doesn't waste any time, he thought. "Take a two-twenty-two," he said and she laughed. Their medicine cabinet had been full of vials of two-twenty-twos, his and hers. "I just want to check about dinner, same time, same place?"

"Oh, sure, sure, *poulet rôti, farci, garni*, this is 'Festival,' you know, and it's all balled-up. I don't know why I do these things, except by now they know how to shoot me."

"I'm the only one who knows how to shoot you," he said. "because I've got first-hand experience of your best angles." The operator click-click-clicked the line.

She chuckled. "I'm not that angular."

"Margery, are you feeling all right? You're not working too hard? You look so thin."

"You should see me in the flesh," she said, and added sententiously, "the camera adds ten pounds."

"Chez Stien, Mackay Street, quarter to eight."

"I've got to run, lover, they're calling me. I'll see you then."
Click-click-click the switchboard in the middle, he thought, it's
a good idea for a poem but you can't get it on film, they tried it
in *Sorry, Wrong Number* and it stank. He came out of the phone
booth, looked at his watch and decided to go home and put on
a necktie, formal wear, a necktie, and nipping out to the sidewalk
he stole a cab from under an administrator's nose.

In his apartment he was God Almighty, Montreal apartments
for the upper-income brackets are all like that, always on the side
of the mountain with a view of the river. His was way way up
almost at the Lookout and all the kingdoms of the earth were
spread at his feet. I've never offered them to anybody, he thought,
they don't belong to me. What am I doing wrong with *A Walk
Home from School*? Is it built on a fundamentally wrong premise?
He began to meditate seriously on his current assignment; he
had nearly three hours to kill and Margery was notorious for her
tardiness, always had been, always would be. I'll have two drinks
in the bar and then she'll come, and I'll be two drinks ahead all
night, another bad connection.

Now the first angle will determine the whole film, just like
Wilfrid's footrace, the lucky bastard, the man came along and
buggered up his shooting schedule by accident. I can't have
somebody come in and smash my lens when I'm not expecting it. How the hell do you get that gratuitous quality? When
they made *The Lady in the Lake* they made a big stink about the
camera as the eyes of the hero, and some schnook kept punching
the camera. They got it all wrong. If I'm going to try something
the same in *A Walk Home From School* I'd better figure out what
went wrong with that movie. Where can I get a print? Making a
mental note to research *The Lady in the Lake*, he went on to his
own problems.

Vision is binocular. Maybe I should use two cameras and
superimpose the results, would that do it? No. That just gives

me a cheap 3D process effect. I wish I were a psychologist, that's what I need to be at this point, how do we see? What makes the whole field of vision cohere and mean something, alive space, the trouble is I don't know, I don't even know if I can find out. Let me think, let's try to pin the thing down. I remember twenty years ago Grierson used to say that film was the supreme medium for rendering reality because it imitated consciousness so perfectly. Was that a tautology?

Grierson. A cantankerous man, hard to deal with, opinionated, gifted, but I'm better than he was, he was too literal-minded. You can't get life itself by copying it; you have to arrange it.

Consciousness is a single sequence, why can't Kitcheff and Vasko understand that? There's no technique to consciousness, we make our arrangements because of who we are; it's a seventy-year sequence, and yet they claim a fifteen-minute sequence will drive people out of the theatre. I've wanted to do this film all my life, and it's going to be my walk home from school, we'll shoot it in Toronto and we'll end up at 27 Cornish Road.

A softball slamming into a left-handed shortstop's glove for the last out, the game is over, and we see the empty field with the players in the middle distance walking slowly away in all directions. We see a forgotten bat lying in the dust beside home plate, we get the sense of emptiness and then we pan around and dolly towards the steps, we climb the steps....

... how am I going to get that last out, the ball coming into the glove? It was the only decent play I ever made in high-school, I was too young for the guys in my grade, and too small, and they didn't like me because I was too goddamn smart. I couldn't help that, but I'm going to get that sense of desertion into the opening frames....

... a left-handed shortstop, wouldn't you know....

... we'll shoot it from below and get the sense of reaching up for the ball, if we could get the pitcher first, then the batter swinging, the flight of the ball, then the catch, no hand, no arm, just the dark mass of the big glove in the bottom picture, then the ball, then the merge with the ball, then where do we go?

I'm not certain how to get that shot, and in my case why am I trying to recreate my own recollections? The camera is for actuality, but perhaps I can get the actuality of the recollections, to hell with theory, I'm not Dr. Kracauer. I wonder if this idea is built on a false premise? I've been drifting around it for years, and if I don't try it now, I might lose it and it's the best script I ever had. I'll just go to the location and shoot it, coming along Farnham Avenue, the trees, I used to bend my head back and look up into the trees and through the trees at the sky, that would be in May and I could see the clouds parading through the dark green, and behind them the blue, dark green on white on blue, heraldic, and all moving as I moved with my head back, except the background of blue, it never moved, it was the field of reference.

The sky is the condition of movement; that's where the light comes from, white through blue.

And on past the stuccoed apartment houses to Yonge Street, to the left past the Packard showroom, now it's a Volkswagen showroom. I wonder if I ought to ask them to put some Packards in the window? Where could we find Packards as of this date? We'd better stick to Volkswagens but in that case I falsify my recollection, and then the Dodge dealership, Mills and Hadwin, across the street. I never walked along the east side, I stayed on the west, past the Esso station, the two candy stores, the Rosehill Barber Shop, God, it's all there in my head, I can see it as if I were there.

Am I by any chance making this picture out of pure regressiveness? I might be. Is that bad?

Maybe all movies are made that way. Grierson used to say "never let your memory get into the picture, stick to actualities, otherwise you've got both feet in literature" and how he hated literature. It was the Scotch in him, or that puritanical reformer's streak, he was an original-sin man if ever there was one. I'm not an original-sin man, I'm an Eden man, we never really left home. *A Walk Home from School.*

When we get to the corner of St. Clair and Yonge, we'll have a big brilliant ball, we'll peek inside the bank and wonder what they do in there, we'll look behind the stagings where they're putting a new Vitrolite storefront on the Osgoode Grill, we'll stand on the corner waiting for the light to change watching the maze of streetcars. There are no streetcars on Yonge anymore but they still run along St. Clair. We'll look up the street to see what's playing at the Kent and the Hollywood, then we cross, east then north, I always walked on the north side of St. Clair, and in a minute we're out of the shopping district past Loblaws and halfway home.

In the distance we see the red dome of Our Lady of Perpetual Help away down the street across the St. Clair bridge. Now here's where the motion has to write the script for us. Kitcheff was quite right, we can't tell the audience in so many words that it's the church of our mother of perpetual help. Is there any way to communicate the feeling visually? In any case I never walked that far, unless I was going to see Philly Daniels, I turned away before I got that far, what I'm heading for now is the bridge, ah, divine bridge, this is where we open out the picture, we come to the bridge and we show them the length and span of it, the few afternoon cars wheeling idly across, we get that sense of open space and sunny air and distance. Then.

We don't cross the bridge. We climb over the rail at the near end as the ground slopes away down underneath the ravine, and we give them the luxuriance of the ravine, foliage, the brook at the bottom, the sound of streetcars rumbling overhead, mud on my shoes, stepping stones in the brook, a boy's whole world, we pan up the bridge-supports, massive concrete grey inhuman ghostly, then we follow the brook north by winding paths through shady groves and we climb back up to Heath Street on the other side.

I want that sunny space and air and then the dark ravine, the foliage, the brook, and to hell with psychoanalysis, I just want it for the picture. I hope. We have a little coda as we climb out of the ravine, walk up Heath Street past kids on their bikes, turn onto Cornish Road, we'll shoot the house, the veranda, the screen door, and that'll be the end of it. I wonder who lives there now, and whether they'll let me inside, or even onto the veranda. It's supper time when we get home. Supper time!

He looked at his watch, seven-ten, my God, where did it go? Time for Margery and dinner. As he rose and went into the bathroom to wash his face and hands and straighten his tie, he thought suddenly, *maybe I can't get it, maybe I'll never get it, maybe John was right and nobody can get it.* I can't put streetcars on a street where they've torn up the tracks. I can't put vanished Packards into Volkswagen showrooms.

He began to whistle softly, a thing he always did when badly worried; then he left the bathroom, put on his jacket, checked to be sure that he had some money, and went to keep his date.

She was not there, naturally, but she had phoned to say that she would be delayed. That they didn't give him the message when he first appeared in the foyer puzzled and at last faintly annoyed him. He had to poke around into all the little rooms, nooks, niches, in which the famous old house abounded, a tiny place, a hole in the wall on Mackay Street and the *fons et origo* of the higher cuisine of Montreal; there were diners who held that Cafe Martin surpassed the little place in the excellence of its wine list, and particularly in the virtuoso treatment of veal. Anyone could make a great dish of beefsteak, but the test of cookery was the cook's approach to the problem of veal.

Sanderson thought Cafe Martin overrated, the magnificence of its *sommelier*, the glow of its chandeliers, its Aubusson, false reinforcements for a middling-to-good table. He wasn't a gourmet, thinking the pastime trivial and even pagan, but he was by trade a *metteur-en-scène* and a shrewd critic of other peoples' decors. He had always preferred Chez Stien for its sly and understated humility, its air of astonishment at its own perfection, its continual ability to surprise its clientele. Since the Film Board had moved to Montreal, Sanderson had become a devotee of the little place. He had always come here, of course, from his first callow times in Montreal when he was young and hopeful, fresh out of college, and afterwards when he'd settled into film production and begun to make a great name, and later still when he was married to Margery and his pictures were winning at Cannes and Venice, and these days, with his marriage six or seven years behind him and his work growing progressively more sure and obscure. Why didn't they simply hand him his messages as he came in, instead of requiring him to pursue his quest through all the purlieus of the labyrinthine old house? He put his head into the owner's rooms, walked past the kitchens, idled in the foyer and finally demanded of the *maître d'hôtel* whether anything had been heard from Margery.

"A message from Miss Endicott for Mister Sanderson?" he asked diffidently. He wasn't a name dropper, least of all of his own name.

"I will see, sir," said the grand personage, courteously enough. His name was Gilles. He had been here for years and certainly must know Sanderson by sight if not by name; but he gave no sign, perhaps pursuing a policy of the house and tactfully ignoring the celebrity of the celebrities who came here. It was a place where you could be inconspicuous, if that's what you wanted. In a moment he came back with a slip of paper in his hand.

"Yes, sir," he said, handing it to Sanderson, "this came an hour ago."

Sanderson examined the note; she would come at eight-fifteen. "Will you keep my table free, please? For two, Mr. Sanderson, and we'll go in about eight-thirty."

Gilles scanned his reservations anxiously. "That will be arranged, Mr. Sanderson. We are rather busy tonight, as you see, but there will be a table."

Sanderson gave him money; he was awkward at such things, having an oppressive sense of the other man as a fellow human being, not caring to treat him as anything less than free. But Gilles put the bill away with a fine ease, turning from him to greet a Toronto writer and his wife who came in on the crest of an expense-account weekend. Some magazine will pay for that, thought Sanderson critically as he eyed the writer, whom he knew slightly and didn't like, as the couple were bowed to a table. My table, he guessed, and they'd damned well better be finished by eight-thirty. He wandered off disconsolately to the downstairs bar to kill forty-five minutes.

He wasn't a heavy drinker, but he liked to drink and decided that there would be time for two slow-to-slowish nibbles before she came. He ordered his first and stationed himself in a corner on an uncomfortable stool. When his drink came he drank half of it on the instant, a Manhattan because he loved cherries, surprising himself with his unaccustomed haste. He let the second half stand for a moment.

She'll have some joke to make about that, he thought, she'll say "you're way ahead of me" or "I'll have to catch up" or something like that. It was not drink that had led to their divorce but work, an innocent enough pastime, they had supposed, although nowadays one was beginning to see in the papers and magazines pieces about "workoholics" who did with their jobs what others accomplish through drugs or drink. He was no workoholic and neither was she, though they had traded accusations to that effect before the term had been invented. He could hear her now.

"I'm so damned tired, Phil, I just can't respond," and he would stand there, desiring her and knowing that he mightn't in charity insist on his rights. When she got finedrawn like that from overwork she was so fatally provocative, at least to him. Some like them plump, but he had adored her fragile shoulder-blades, the huge eyes in the perfect cheekbones, that Picasso line to her jaw. And her other parts were so sweetly harmonious. Her buttocks, he remembered with his dazzling visual imagination, had been those of a child, no bigger than the outspread palm of his hand, and though she was mainly a composition in angles, in that place she was wonderfully curved in a curve without grossness.

"Damn you," she used to say towards the end of it, "you love only my composition, you're always photographing me with your eyes. It's just that you work too hard and I'm not an abstraction."

"If you lose any more weight you will be," he said. "Who works too hard? Who is it that's too tired all the time?" She began to weep quietly.

"We're both too nervous; other men don't make me feel like this, but I love you, Phil, believe me, I love you."

"And I love you," he had murmured sadly, "but perhaps you're right. I don't mean to drive you to exhaustion."

She sat up angrily on their bed. "Do you want to be rid of me?"

"I only want what's right for both of us."

"No, you just want to love everybody by way of the movies. I warn you, Phil, you can't do it. One real woman is better than a strip of celluloid, even if it plays every house in the world, and what you want, you can't get on film. Don't be a power-lover, darling, you're not Nehru."

He laid his cheek against her buttocks and held it there. Whose skin was feverish, his or hers? You could not put this on film; there were lots of things that wouldn't go. He closed his eyes for a second, then opened them and swallowed the other half of his drink, signalling for the second as he swallowed.

He had timed her perfectly, so well had he remembered her inclinations — they might almost have been his own, they were at least mysteriously inside him, dictating the shape and tone of his conduct towards her. As he finished the second glass, he probed the crystal cup to the bottom with his toothpick, pricking and fixing the cherry and finally swallowing it with pleasure, and after that he rose, paid the bar check and went upstairs to find her standing at the door, her coat melting mysteriously from her shoulders — she never took things off, they simply melted invisibly away, and one didn't notice the attendants who cared for them.

"Yes," she said, "well, I said I'd be late."

"It's worth the wait. I'm very glad to see you. I've been wanting to talk to you. I think … no, let's go in." They were ushered to their table and Sanderson was relieved to note that the Toronto writer was still sitting on the other side of the room. At least they were not following that crabbed act. After some low comedy in French they succeeded in making their wishes known and first drinks, and then a series of dishes, began to arrive in a broadening and deepening flow. There were side-tables everywhere, and four attendants, and in an instant, plainly, the chef would epiphanize from the kitchen. They had identified Margery which was odd because she appeared very rarely on the French network.

"What is all this?" he said crossly.

"I did a commercial for Comet Cleanser and Huguette Lamarche dubbed the voice, they've been using it for years on CBFT."

He had internationally fifty times his wife's — he checked himself because she was no longer his wife — fifty times Margery Endicott's reputation. He had been coming here for twenty years and they had not caught his name. In the Montreal Film Festival last summer his *Sonata da Chiesa* had been ecstatically received, and even lauded.

Who gives a damn about it, who cares? But it was a part of his gripe, he was aware, the want of overt recognition. He couldn't have been an actor, and wouldn't if he could. She was laughing at him.

"What's the matter, Phil, do you want my autograph? Don't be afraid to speak up."

He had to laugh with her. "The CBC has a 'no star-system' policy. You'd better be careful with your autographs."

"They've changed all that since they've been losing everybody to the States. I've got a billing clause now, and if they don't meet it, I don't do the show. People seem to want to see Margery Endicott."

"It's unfair," he said, knowing that he sounded like a small boy; she had always been able to force him into this corner.

"Oh, stop horsing around, you know you don't care."

He was glad to see that she was eating, and sorry to see how thin and overtired she seemed, and of course she was seeing him after some lapse of time, and would be thinking about his looks.

"I haven't gained an ounce," he said.

"No, I've shrunk." She put her hand across the table, palm upwards, and he took it gently and pressed it. "Dear Phil," she smiled with her lovely kindness, "my good man."

He was gruff. "I'm in a mess as you'd expect."

"Socialism, or theory of film?"

"I haven't been a Socialist since before we were married, I've dropped all that stuff, ideology is no good for me."

"Would you mind very much not using words like 'ideology'?"

He remembered young Kitcheff and blushed. "I'm just an old comedian," he said, kidding himself, "just an old clown who's been around and who knows all the tricks, just faking my way through."

"And I'm a clean young girl from Swift Current in a starched gingham check."

"Once you were," he said seriously.

"Yes, I was. God, that was awful." Then they both had another drink. "What's the matter?"

"You act," he said, "and you're a good actress, for what it's worth, and when you're older you'll be better because you're going to hang on to your looks, the bones are there...."

"Never mind about my bones."

"… they're what you live on. Listen, what I want to know is, can you tell how you're getting better. I watch your shows, and I see you do things you wouldn't have dreamed of trying when we were married, and yet, you don't really *think* about it at all, do you?"

"No. My head is for hats to go into. I can't think at all."

"But you get better. How do you do it?"

"Practice. It was always there, now I know how to use it." She was suddenly grave. "I started to know after we broke up."

"Yes, I suppose so."

"We love each other, we're a mutual admiration society. You know, dear, I see your things, I've never missed one, and you are so good. *You are getting so good.*" Her eyes were wet.

"Don't do that, Margery," he said.

"You fool," she said, "you're a great man." That hurt him very much. "You're a great man and I'm a cute girl on a regional television network."

Of course he was not a great man and would never be a great man.

"What it is," he said, "is that I can't do it, I don't believe. I can't get it. I cannot get what I want."

"Why you've been getting it right along. I wish you'd use me."

"Can't use actors in documentary."

"Actors are people."

"You can only use them when they aren't looking, in documentaries about actors."

"So make a picture about my *métier*! Show me rinsing out a sweaty bra and pants in the ladies' room at the studio, all my hard life and times. Artists have lives."

"I'm sick of making paradoxes about art and life. It all falls into place." And he quoted:

> *Till that which suits a part infects the whole,*
> *And now is almost grown the habit of my soul.*

"What is it, Phil, what's wrong?"

"I'm fifty," he said soberly, "and I've been on the wrong track. What I've wanted to do can't be done on film."

She was resisting the understandable temptation to say "I told you so." Instead she said, "Let's get married again," and it was the nicest gift anybody had ever offered him; but life is not composed of gifts, though it is itself gratuitous, and though it hurt him to smile he did so, saying, "I really do love you, you know, and I wouldn't put you through that again for the world." They both knew that there was nothing to it and taking their time over a bottle of wine they smiled at each other and in the end decided to catch the late showing of *L'Année Dernière à Marienbad* at the Elysée.

"Resnais is very good," said Sanderson magisterially.

"Not as good as you are."

"It's true."

They found the film pellucid, crystalline, because they knew how it had been put together, and on what good grounds.

In the middle of the following afternoon, having risen very late, having gotten to bed very very late indeed, Sanderson came slinking into the Film Board building like a cat who has breakfasted on goldfish. He was determined to avoid Kitcheff and Vasko if at all possible, he didn't want to face their cross-questionings today, and he had arranged another showing of "the mile of the century" without telling them.

He glanced into the coffee shop to see if they were there, but they weren't, not they, and they certainly wouldn't be in the office, so he figured he was home free and he went directly to the projection room where the projectionist was waiting for him, glancing at his watch. Sanderson was not normally a hard man to deal with but today he harassed the poor technician continually. He made him show fifty feet, stop, run it again, another fifty feet, stop, re-wind, run it again, stop there please, until the poor man was ready to tell him to go to hell. He had never seen Sanderson act like that.

"All right," said Sanderson after some time, with an odd air of triumph, "now I want to see the end of it, the last minute, keep running it over and over, please." He trotted back and forth between the seats and the booth like a distracted man. "Just show me the end of it, that's all I want to see." The projectionist felt an obscure fright, but as he began to run the footage he saw Sanderson settle into a seat and begin to smoke idly, alone in the dark.

This time he didn't cheer aloud, feeling no sense of community; it had been better in the beer parlour, when he'd seen it first. But he sat on, ostensibly quietly, nursing his cigarette, and in his head, in sympathy with the soundtrack, in sympathy with the pulse in his temple, his disembodied interior voice was screaming: "GO, GO, GO, GO, GO, GO, GO, GO." It would go on screaming until the race was over.

Also Available from Voyageur Classics

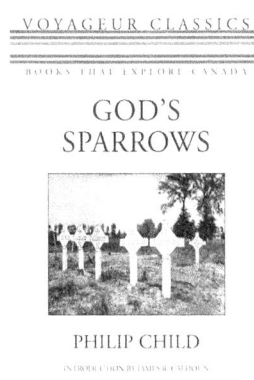

VOYAGEUR CLASSICS

BOOKS THAT EXPLORE CANADA

GOD'S
SPARROWS

PHILIP CHILD

INTRODUCTION BY JAMES R. CALHOUN

God's Sparrows
Philip Child
Introduction by James R. Calhoun

A horrifying description of war, specifically embodied in the vain and inglorious futility of the First World War, *God's Sparrows* is a novel rich in compassion and firm in its faith in the human spirit. Philip Child created a Canadian family saga, a modern pilgrim's progress in which individuals surmount the corrosive effects of brutality, maintaining their ability to love and endure under the most agonizing circumstances. His book, first published in 1937, remains as a stirring testimony to that ability. It offers profound insight into the experience of the First World War, not just as a catastrophe affecting his characters but as a crucible in which the whole of this nation found itself tried.

www.ingramcontent.com/pod-product-compliance
Lightning Source LLC
Chambersburg PA
CBHW070221030726

47505CB00006B/1753